WHEN AUGUST ENDS

PENELOPE WARD

First Edition
Copyright © 2018
By Penelope Ward
ISBN-10: 1792889119
ISBN-13: 978-1792889110

This book is a work of fiction. All names, characters, locations, and incidents are products of the author's imagination. Any resemblance to actual persons, things living or dead, locales, or events is entirely coincidental.

Edited by: Jessica Royer Ocken
Proofreading and Formatting by: Elaine York
Cover Model: Joseph Cannata
Cover Photographer: Adam Zivo
Cover Design: Letitia Hasser, RBA Designs

To
Linda,

WHEN
AUGUST
ENDS

Dance like
Noah's watching.

xo

Penelope
Ward

...

For Kandace Milostan

Thank you for shining your light on the book world

and for teaching us what really matters.

CHAPTER
ONE

Heather

"**H**ave you met the guy who moved into the boathouse yet?"

I'd just returned home to our lakehouse after accompanying my mother to a doctor's appointment this morning. My friend Chrissy had done me the favor of meeting our new tenant to give him the keys while I was out.

I shook my head. "No."

Chrissy was grinning from ear to ear.

"What's that look for?" I asked.

"He's...interesting."

I lifted my brow. "In what way?"

She snickered. "I think you should discover it for yourself."

That could only mean one of two things: either he was extremely good-looking, or maybe we had a psycho living among us.

For the past several years, my family had rented out our converted boathouse on Lake Winnipesaukee—New Hampshire's largest body of water. Located at the foothills

1

of the White Mountains, it's a popular destination for tourists looking to escape the city. As the locals say, "When you're here, you're on 'lake time'."

It was just my mother and me at home now, and Mom didn't work, so the income from the boathouse was a necessity to keep up with our bills. While it sometimes remained vacant in the winter, it was booked pretty consistently in the warmer months and even into the early fall. Sometimes people would rent it for a week and other times longer. It wasn't really that big, so it was usually single people who stayed there, rather than families. This latest guy had booked it for nearly three months, until the end of August—the entire summer. That had never happened before.

"So everything is all set with him?" I asked.

"Yup. Seems like a decent guy overall. Didn't say much, but he was polite. He was wearing sunglasses, so I couldn't get a feel for his eyes. They usually tell a lot about a person, you know?"

I knew his name was Noah, since I'd taken down his credit card information and run a quick background check. But otherwise, I didn't know much about him— Noah Cavallari from Pennsylvania with a Visa card and a clear record.

I never really mingled with our guests. When I was younger, my mother had strictly forbidden me from interacting with anyone staying in the boathouse—you know, just in case they weren't good people. So even as an adult, I tended to keep my distance out of habit.

As part of the deal in renting the boathouse, tenants got housekeeping services—courtesy of me. I'd go in, usually in the afternoons, make the bed and provide fresh towels, much like in a hotel. Guests also got access to the washing machine and dryer in the basement of the main house, which they could access with a key to the laundry room's external door. So they never had to come inside our place at all.

The inside of the boathouse featured a small kitchenette, allowing tenants to cook their own meals. The space was one room, plus the bathroom. There were several windows on all sides, though, which let in lots of light and a view of the surrounding lake.

"How's Alice doing today?" Chrissy asked.

"The doctor is going to adjust her meds again. Overall, not her best, not her worst day."

That was as good as could be expected when it came to my mother, who'd been in and out of mental hospitals for years, depending on the severity of her episodes.

Mom suffered from clinical depression. She'd struggled with it throughout her life, but it had been particularly bad since my older sister's death more than five years ago. Opal had been a decade older than me. She was mentally unstable and had run away from home. During the years we'd been out of touch with her, she'd gotten deeper into her own mind and eventually took her own life.

Losing my sister was by far the hardest thing I had ever experienced. Mom was never the same after that. Until Opal's death, my mother had been able to keep her depression in check enough to be functional. Not anymore.

Chrissy left for her nursing shift, leaving me alone in my bedroom. I looked out the window over at the

3

boathouse. While the structure was on our property, it was set back from the main residence, closer to the lake. You had to walk down a gravel driveway to get there.

Aside from his shiny, black truck parked outside in the distance, I hadn't seen evidence of our new guest at all. And that was fine by me. I would wait until tomorrow afternoon to venture over there for housekeeping. Usually occupants left in the afternoons.

During the day, I took care of everything around here. Then, five nights a week, I waitressed at a local pub called Jack Foley's. That was the extent of my mundane life as it had existed since my mother's depression got really bad. Someone had to run things, and I was the winner of that responsibility by default.

The lakehouse—our main residence—and the smaller boathouse had been in my mother's family for years. After my grandfather died, he'd left everything to Mom, his only child. Since everything was paid off, there was no mortgage. That was a good thing, given the fact that I was the only one with a job. As it was, I could just manage to keep the house running, and there were a lot of things waiting to be fixed.

I don't mean to be a downer when it comes to my life. I have a lot to be grateful for. Living on the lake is one of those things. Even though some days I feel like Cinderella, minus the evil stepsisters, the serene beauty of this place often makes up for it.

The following day, it looked like the coast was clear. The tenant's truck was gone, making it the perfect time to grab some fresh towels and visit the boathouse to clean.

My Saint Bernard, Teddy, thought I was taking him for a walk, so he followed me out the door. I figured I would let him come with me.

The afternoon air was sticky. Hazy sunlight partially blinded me as I made my way over with three towels of varying sizes tucked under my arm and a bucket of chemical supplies hung over my wrist.

Upon entering the house, I immediately smelled his cologne. Masculinity hung in the air. A black men's jacket was draped over the desk chair, and a large, unpacked suitcase was open on the floor. An expensive-looking watch lay on top of a laptop.

His bed was already made. Perhaps he hadn't seen the part of my confirmation email that explained our courtesy housekeeping service, or maybe he was just a neat person and couldn't wait.

The dog jumped up on the bed.

"Get down, Teddy!"

The next thing I knew, the door to the bathroom burst open. Everything after happened so fast. My bucket fell to the floor as I took in the Herculean man standing there wrapped in nothing but a small white towel. My jaw dropped.

Teddy started barking.

Noah's deep voice sliced through me. "What the hell is going on here?"

His hair was wet. I swallowed as my eyes trailed down the length of his body, then up again. I'm not quite sure why I lost my ability to think. I was just completely shocked to see him, let alone like this: mostly bare with water dripping down his sculpted torso.

He isn't supposed to be home.

He broke me out of my trance. "Is there a reason you're staring at me instead of leaving?"

Um...because you're hot as fuck?

I abruptly turned around to face the door. "I just came to clean. I'm so sorry. I'll come back later."

Stumbling, I ran out so fast I left the cleaning supplies behind that I'd dropped all over his floor. I thought I'd left Teddy behind, too, but thankfully he'd followed me out the door.

I'd seen the man for only a matter of seconds, but I now knew why Chrissy had been snickering yesterday. He was drop-dead gorgeous with classic, chiseled features and perfect facial hair. He was really tall, too, and probably the most *manly* man I'd come across in a long time.

He's also rude. That was very clear. *But hot.* Dark hair, ripped body...he looked like he was maybe in his early thirties.

My mother was in the kitchen making herself a sandwich when I returned to the house.

"What's going on?" she asked. "You seem flustered."

I was panting a little. "I just made an ass of myself in front of the new tenant. His truck wasn't there, so I thought it was safe to clean." Closing my eyes, I took a deep breath to calm down. "He came out of the bathroom half-naked. I scared the shit out of him. And instead of leaving, I froze, stood there staring at him. He wasn't happy."

Teddy's tongue hung out as if he, too, was reeling from this experience.

My mother stopped buttering her bread and started laughing—the first time I'd heard her laugh in a long time. Even if it was at my expense, that made me smile. It almost made what had happened worth it. *Almost.*

Later that night, I opened my front door to walk Teddy, only to find the bucket I'd left behind in the boathouse on the steps outside. All of the cleaning supplies were back inside. Noah was a bit of an asshole—but apparently he was a courteous one.

I had no further run-ins with Noah for the next few days. I knocked loudly on his door each afternoon to confirm he wasn't home before entering the house to clean.

On my nights off from work, one of my favorite things was a dip in the lake at sundown. I probably loved that most about having waterfront property. There was no better place to clear my head than in the water.

The lake was also where I exercised. I could never get into things like running or fitness classes. But in the water, it felt like I was weightless, like I could do anything. So, I'd developed my own little water aerobics regimen. Exercises included things like jumping up and down into squats under the water or dancing like a maniac while waving my arms around. There was no rhyme or reason. I just did what I wanted. Anything to get my endorphins going.

This evening I was off, so I was in the lake. I had my headphones on, rocking out to old-school hip-hop while bouncing around doing my thing, when I noticed something charging toward me. Before I knew it, his hands were on my shoulders.

My heart raced.

It took me a few seconds to realize it was Noah.

CHAPTER
TWO

Heather

"What are you doing?" I shouted, my heart beating out of my chest.

He let go of me abruptly. His breaths were heavy as he said, "You're not drowning..."

I took out my earbuds. "No! Why would you think that?"

"You were flailing your arms around like a lunatic. From my damn porch, I thought you needed help."

My pulse was racing. "I wasn't drowning. I was *dancing*."

He gritted his teeth. "Dancing..."

"Yes."

"For fuck's sake..." he muttered.

He then turned around and trudged back through the water, headed to land.

I stood in shock, gazing at his large frame as he slogged away. I'd encountered this guy twice and managed to piss him off within seconds each time.

Then it dawned on me: he'd thought I was drowning and ran in to *save me*. He'd jumped in with his clothes on.

Oh my God. I hadn't been in any real danger, but I still needed to thank him.

"Wait up!" I yelled.

Noah didn't stop for one second as he continued toward the boathouse.

He's really mad.

Things were bad between us *before* this. *I've really done it now.* How was I supposed to know this was going to happen? I'd been doing my water aerobics for months, and no one had ever come around thinking I needed help. In fact, no one had ever come around at all.

When I finally caught up to Noah, he was sitting on the boathouse's wooden porch. I stopped just short of the front steps.

Brooding and pissed, he'd leaned his back against the house. His broad shoulders rose and fell. His black T-shirt was plastered against his chest. His jeans were also wet, and his feet were bare. He was painfully hot—more so than any guy who'd come around these parts in a very long time. Likely ever. He might have been a little old for me, but that didn't stop my entire body from buzzing as I took him in. His age—his maturity—was a major turn-on. My reaction to this man was both exhilarating and terrifying all at once.

He acted as if I wasn't standing there. I watched as he turned around and reached through the open window to grab something inside the house—a cigar. He rolled it between his fingers before lighting up. I'd never liked cigar smoke, but there was something sexy about the way he held it in his hands. Speaking of his hands, they were big and veiny, powerful—hands that could harm just as easily as they could protect.

He wrapped his lips around the cigar, and the tip glowed as he inhaled.

I continued staring at his hands. Calloused and rough, they had seen their share of work. I sighed. Noah Cavallari was a *man* in every sense of the word.

He continued to ignore me, and for some reason that made me even more determined to talk to him—probably opposite of the effect he'd intended to have.

Nice try but "no cigar," Noah.

I cleared my throat. "I'm really sorry about that misunderstanding."

He took a long puff of the stogie and blew the smoke out. He then whipped his head in my direction so fast it startled me. "Who dances by herself in a lake?"

"It was water aerobics," I said.

He closed his eyes, then surprised me with a long, hearty laugh; it vibrated throughout my body.

Well, at least he has a sense of humor in there somewhere.

"What were you listening to when I interrupted your little routine?"

"I don't know," I lied.

"I think you do."

"Alright, I do. But I don't want to tell you."

"Why not? I'm curious as to what kind of music makes someone flail around like that. Can I listen?"

This day probably couldn't get any worse. Figuring I owed it to him, I handed him my headphones, bracing for his reaction.

He bent his head back and started to laugh even harder than before.

11

I'd been listening to "Jump" by Kris Kross.

I snatched the headphones off of his ears. "Happy now?"

"I needed that. Thank you. I haven't heard that song since I was like...seven. Certainly well before your time." He chuckled.

"Yeah, well, it's a good song. It makes me want to—"

"Jump?" He snickered.

I bit my lip, then couldn't help but laugh along with him.

He held his hands up and offered a snide grin. "No judgment. I swear."

"I'm glad I could add some humor to your life," I said. "Clearly, based on your unreasonable reaction to my being in your room the other day, it's much needed."

His light expression faded as he looked at me with daggers in his eyes. "I came out of the shower half-naked to find a teenage girl standing there. What other reaction would have been appropriate?"

Teenage girl?

Oh, hell no.

"I'm not a *teenager*, so you're wrong there. And the answer is *any other* reaction besides the one you gave me. It was a misunderstanding, and your snapping at me was unwarranted." Still miffed, I let out a breath, looking over at the lake and then back at him. "I'm Heather, by the way. We never formally met."

After a pause, he offered, "Noah."

Even the way his name rolled off his tongue sounded sexy.

"I know your name...from your reservation. In fact, I ran an entire background check on you, but that didn't cover personality problems, unfortunately. It's nice to meet you."

"Right. Not a murderer, just a prick who overreacts, apparently. They don't have filters for that."

I took a few steps forward. "I'm truly sorry about what happened just now. Thank you for coming to save me. If I had really been drowning, that would have been heroic."

"What choice did I have? From where I was standing, you looked like you were waving your arms for help. I'd have to be a real dick not to do anything." He turned away from me.

"Speaking of you being a dick..."

That got his attention back.

"I thought you were gone the other day. That was the only reason I went into your space to clean. Your truck wasn't there."

Noah blew out some smoke. "My truck needed a new tire. Didn't feel like waiting the hour at the shop, so I walked a mile back here and decided to take a relaxing shower. We all know how that went."

Our eyes locked for a moment before his mouth curved into a slight smile. I breathed a sigh of relief.

"I'm sorry for snapping at you," he finally said. "I actually regretted it after. I was just taken aback."

"It's okay." I fidgeted, not knowing what to do with my body. Being around him made me very antsy. "I'm twenty, by the way. So, again, *not* a teenager. How old are you?"

"Too old to be hanging out with a twenty-year-old whose tits are falling out."

I looked down at myself. *Shit.* He was right. My tits *were* practically out of my bikini. I was so into him I hadn't even noticed. I covered my breasts with my arms. It wasn't like I'd planned this whole thing, but nevertheless, that was indecent. Instead of feeling shy, though, the fact that he'd pointed it out filled me with heat. On some level he was noticing me in a sexual way. And I liked it—too much, maybe. An excitement I hadn't felt in forever ran through me.

"Why do you do all the work around here? It seems to be just you manning everything. Why?"

No one had ever asked me that before.

"It's my responsibility. Why is that so strange?"

"At your age, shouldn't you be in college or something? Why are you cleaning and shit?"

His question offended me a little, but it made me happy that someone had taken notice.

"It's not exactly my preference. My mother isn't doing well...mentally. So, I've taken on most of the duties around the house and with the rental. I work over at Jack Foley's Pub when I'm not tending to things here."

"You don't need to clean my room anymore."

"But I have to. It's part of the—"

"No more cleaning the boathouse while I'm here," he barked. "I don't like people invading my space anyway. And I'm sure you have better things to do than clean up a grown man's mess."

"Well, if you don't want me to, I won't."

"I don't."

God, he's so grumpy.

And sexy.

"Okay." I shivered.

It was getting cool out, but I wasn't ready to leave. This porch was probably the last place I belonged, but it was where I wanted to be. This was the most invigorated I had felt in a long time.

My teeth chattered. "What brought you to Lake Winnipesaukee for the summer?"

Rather than answer me, Noah got up and walked into the house. The door slammed behind him.

No, he didn't.

Did he really just do that?

I guess I can't ask him personal questions.

Just as I was about to turn around and head home, the creak of the door startled me. He returned to the porch holding a buffalo plaid flannel shirt.

He threw it at me, not so gently. "Put that on. Cover yourself."

"Thanks." I slid my sleeves through the shirt and buttoned it up. It smelled like him, all manly and woodsy—as if someone had bottled the scent of testosterone and sold it. I was already planning to sleep in this shirt.

To my surprise, he returned to my earlier question. "I needed to get away for a while. Picked this place randomly. Didn't run a background check to make sure it didn't come with a prying little innkeeper who doubles as a Fly Girl." He winked.

"What's a Fly Girl?"

"Shit." He sighed and looked down at his feet. "That was before you were born."

"Well, what is it? A Fly Girl? Some kind of superhero comic strip?"

He laughed that hearty laugh I felt between my legs. "There was this comedy show in the nineties...*In Living Color*. Jamie Foxx and Jim Carrey used to be on it. These dancers called Fly Girls would perform in between the comedy sketches before the commercials. Anyway, I was just making fun of your little hip-hop routine."

"I'll have to look it up online. I'm kind of disappointed in myself for not knowing. Normally, I'm pretty well-versed in nineties' pop culture."

I could feel myself blushing, and I didn't even know why.

Clearing my throat, I asked, "Do you work?"

He puffed on the cigar and smoke billowed out of his mouth as he said, "I'm taking a break at the moment."

"What do you do?"

He didn't answer right away. It seemed like he wasn't sure if he wanted to answer my questions.

"I'm a photographer."

"Really? That's so cool. I've always wanted to learn photography. What kind of photos do you take?"

"Everything from nature to portraits. You name it, I've probably shot it. I used to work freelance for newspapers some years back. A wide variety."

"So you work for yourself now? That's why you have the freedom to take time off?"

"Yeah."

I kept prodding. "There are some really pretty shots you could get on the lake, particularly when the sun sets. Is that why you chose to come here? Photographic inspiration?"

"No. I'm not here to shoot anything. I'm taking a break from that. Like I said, I chose this place randomly. It was far enough away but not too far from home. The main requirement was that it was quiet and peaceful, some place I could think."

"So, I guess I'm interrupting your peace, then."

"Nah...botched water rescues are extremely relaxing."

He smiled, and I returned it.

God. I noticed his eyelashes. It seemed unfair for a man to have lashes that long.

There was a bit of silence before I asked, "You think I'm a dork, don't you?"

"Yes."

I laughed at how quickly he answered. He didn't even have to think about it.

He cracked another smile. Every time he smiled at me, I felt my insides stir. I felt like a damn fool, actually. I needed to slap my face to rid myself of this giddy feeling.

I looked out into the distance to try to clear my head. "I've never seen the lake at night from this angle."

"Why not? You live here, right?"

"I don't spend much time at the boathouse. Since childhood, I've been conditioned to avoid the people renting it. My mother always made me stay away. Things are different now, of course, since the responsibility of this place has changed hands, but I'm only ever here to take care of business. I don't spend quality time on this side of the property."

"That's actually a good thing," he said.

"Because I won't be around to bother you?"

"Well, that, too. But I was referring to the fact that growing up your mother made you stay away from the guests. There are a lot of bad people in this world. Having a business where strange people are coming and going can't be easy when you have kids."

That reminded me of a time when it *hadn't* been just me. Whenever anything made me think of Opal, I felt

17

incredibly sad. No way I was going to subject him to that right now, so I kept my thoughts to myself.

He interrupted my rumination. "It'll be getting dark out soon. You'd better go back to your house so your mother doesn't think something happened to you."

"She didn't even see me leave, probably doesn't realize I'm gone. My mother stays in her room most of the time… because of her depression."

He seemed to process what I'd just divulged. "I'm sorry to hear that."

"It's okay."

Things were silent for a while.

He looked around. "You think you'll keep this place forever? It's got to be expensive to keep up. That's not counting all of the work you have to handle."

"It *is* a lot. And I really want to sell the whole property."

"Why can't you?"

"It makes me sad to think about it, for one. The lakehouse and boathouse have been in my family for years, and I love living here. But I think selling is inevitable. The main house is too big for just my mother and me, and it's too much land to maintain. My mother is open to the idea of selling. But there's a lot we'd need to fix up before putting it on the market. That's really the holdup."

He held the cigar between his teeth and looked at me before inhaling. "You have a lot on your plate. It's no wonder you dance around like a goon in the water. Whatever gets it out, you know?"

"That's right. Dancing is a stress-reliever."

Noah stood up and walked off the porch to put his cigar out on the cement. When he returned, he remained standing across from me. I was reminded of just how tall he was as he towered over me. A breeze blew his scent—a mix of cigar and cologne—in my direction. The same smell saturated the shirt I was wearing. I could've breathed it in all night. His nearness was doing things to my body I hadn't ever felt.

Noah looked around. "You mentioned some stuff around here needs to be repaired. What specifically?"

I blew out a breath. Even thinking about it was exhausting. "So much. I'd have to make a list."

"Why don't you do that? Make a list. I'm pretty good with my hands. I'll see if there's anything I can help with while I'm here."

He'd lost me at *pretty good with my hands*. My imagination was running wild. *Shit.* I imagined those hands doing a lot of things—mostly to me.

"I can't let you do that."

"You'd be stupid not to take me up on it. I came for a change of pace, but the truth is, too much quiet isn't good. I like to keep busy."

Biting my bottom lip, I shook my head. "I don't know..."

"Make the list," he insisted.

Noah was right. It would be dumb not to take him up on his offer. It wasn't like there was anyone else knocking down our door to help.

I tilted my head. "What would be in it for you?"

His expression turned dark. "People don't always have to have ulterior motives."

Suddenly feeling bold, I said, "I thought maybe you would want me to go out with you in exchange."

Did you hear that? It was a record screeching.

I admit, that was ballsy, but being around him brought out my flirtatious side. Maybe his cologne and cigar smoke were going to my head.

"You're joking, right?"

Okay. I shouldn't have asked.

"Actually, I—"

"I'm practically old enough to be your father."

Really? That's how he saw me? I knew he was older than me...but he didn't seem *that* old. *No way.* I'd pegged him as early thirties, though I truly had no idea how old he was.

I shook my head. "No, you're not. That's a lie. An older brother, maybe. How old are you?"

Instead of answering, he took two steps forward. "Let me make something clear."

"Okay..."

"I was not insinuating anything by offering to help. And I will not be asking you out, propositioning you, or going anywhere near you, for that matter. We clear on that?"

Okay, then.

I swallowed. Disappointment washed over me as I cleared my throat. "Yes."

"Good." He made his way toward the door, turning around one last time. "You'd better go. It was nice chatting. Get me the list tomorrow."

He disappeared into the house, leaving me on the porch to wallow in his lingering smell and feeling like a complete and utter idiot.

Back in my room that night, I replayed his words.

"I will not be asking you out, propositioning you, or going anywhere near you, for that matter. We clear on that?"

God.

His firm stance only made me more drawn to him. It's funny how that works.

He treated me as if I were twelve. At twenty, I'm old enough to date anyone I want. I don't care if they're forty or eighty. A hundred years ago, the average lifespan of a woman was something like fifty. I'd be almost halfway done with life by now. Once you hit eighteen, age is just a number.

But apparently, that wasn't how Noah felt. Or maybe he was just using the age thing as an excuse. But here's the real issue: I was kidding around! (Sort of.) And he had to go and make it into a serious thing, make it known there was no way in hell anything would be happening between us. What was it about rejection that made me want him even more?

My need to know more about him was pretty intense. I opened my laptop and typed into Google: *Noah Cavallari photographer Pennsylvania.*

His website popped right up. It was the very first search result.

Noah Cavallari Photography. Yup. That had to be him.

I clicked on it. With a sleek black background, the main page of the site featured a slideshow of breathtaking images. From photos taken on African safaris to a presidential inauguration, Noah's career had run the gamut. According to his bio, he was born outside of Philadelphia and began taking photos at a young age. After majoring in photojournalism in college, he'd spent most of his twenties working in construction for his father while taking photos on the side. He'd eventually been able to turn photography into a flourishing, full-time business.

His career had taken him all over the world, but in more recent years, he'd opened a studio and focused on private event photography and headshots. There were no photos of him on the site aside from the bio picture, where his face was covered by a gigantic camera lens. It showed just enough, though, to confirm that this was the Noah Cavallari living in my boathouse.

Well, color me intrigued. He seemed to have a fabulous career—seemed to have it all.

So that begged the question: Why is he here?

I began to theorize.

Oh my God. Is he dying?

No. He seems too healthy, too virile.

Running from the law?

Nope. I did that background check. Came out clean.

Why would he want to come here for three whole months? I didn't get it.

A week or two, maybe. But why so long?

What are you escaping from, Noah Cavallari?

I was determined to find out.

CHAPTER
THREE

Heather

Two days later, a text came in from an unknown number.

At Home Depot. What color exterior paint for the boathouse?

Based on the question, I knew exactly who it was. I'd forgotten Noah had my number. But I gave my number to all tenants in my welcome email in case they needed anything.

The day after our talk at the lake, he'd reminded me to make him the list and prioritize what needed to be done. Since the exterior of the boathouse was in shambles with the paint flaking off, I'd listed that job as the top priority. I still couldn't believe he wanted to help. He certainly wasn't wasting any time getting started.

Heather: How about a gray?

The little dots danced as he typed.

Noah: There are several shades of gray.

I decided to be a wiseass.

Heather: Fifty? ;-)

Noah: Very funny.

Heather: Thank you.

Noah then sent a photo of a paint card with five gray options.

Noah: Do you like any of these?

Heather: So you're familiar with that book?

Noah: Cut the shit, Heather.

Heather: LOL. The second gray is perfect.

There were no more texts after that.

An hour later, I spotted Noah outside the boathouse, getting straight to work. I squinted at his shirtless physique as he rolled primer onto the wood. He was way too far away for my liking. If he was going to be working outside like this all summer, I'd need to invest in a set of binoculars.

My mother snuck up behind me. "What are you looking at?"

"Huh?" I jumped, closing the curtain. "Nothing."

"You were struggling to see something. What's so interesting?"

I sighed. "I was watching Noah paint the boathouse."

I'd told my mother about his offer to help. She was extremely skeptical, to say the least.

"I don't understand why he's doing that. What's in it for him?"

"He seems to want to help. He says he likes to keep busy."

My mother's eyes narrowed. "You'd better be careful. He might want something in return."

I laughed. "Believe me, I *wish* he did. But he's made it very clear he doesn't. Unfortunately, I believe him."

She seemed concerned. It was strange to get any real emotion out of her lately. But the idea of something happening between the new tenant and me hit all the right buttons.

"You say that like you've *offered* something to him."

"I teased him about having an ulterior motive for helping, and he didn't take it very well. He snapped at me. He can't take a joke. He's all business. He thinks I'm jailbait and wants nothing to do with me. He thought I was a teenager when we first met. He treats me like one, too."

"You seem disappointed."

Laughing under my breath, I said, "I sort of am."

"That's crazy, Heather. The last person you should get involved with is someone just passing through town. You don't know anything about this guy. He's also too old for you."

"I don't know. He won't tell me his age." I chuckled.

"Well, I don't care what he claims, no man does what he's doing right now without an ulterior motive. You can't expect me to believe my beautiful, blond daughter has nothing to do with it."

She was getting on my nerves now. I could see why she might think that. But she hadn't experienced what I had with Noah. I truly believed he wanted nothing to do with me, nor did I believe his intentions were anything but good.

"I know you're conditioned to think all men are bad. Based on your personal experience of Dad abandoning us, I can't even blame you. But that's not the case all the time."

Her expression darkened. "I've already lost one daughter. I can't stand to lose another."

She couldn't be serious.

"How is Noah painting the boathouse going to put my life in jeopardy? Think about what you're saying."

"I didn't mean he'd harm you physically. But I can't afford to have you take off with some man."

"Don't be ridiculous. You're taking this too far. He came here to get away from the daily grind for a while. He likes to keep busy and knows we could use the help. There's nothing more to it than that."

She wouldn't drop it. "I'm afraid there is. I might not be thinking clearly half of the time, but I'm not blind. You're my daughter. I know you. I can see that look in your eyes. You're smitten. Women do crazy things for men they're smitten with. And men? They may tell you one thing, but they're weak. If you keep throwing yourself at him, he *will* give in."

I shrugged. "One can only hope."

She rolled her eyes, none too pleased with my humor. "Just be careful."

That evening, I was just about dressed and ready to leave for my shift at the restaurant when I noticed someone over at the boathouse talking to Noah while he worked.

My heart dropped.

It was Kira Shaw, our closest neighbor. Kira was in her early thirties and divorced. With long red hair and killer curves, she was very attractive. She also always seemed to be dating a different guy. In fact, I used to babysit her boys while she went out on some of her escapades. She was perpetually on the prowl and had no issue with bringing different men into her bedroom while her sons were home.

I knew right away she was making a play for Noah. And I didn't like it one bit.

My pulse began to race. Sure, this jealousy was unfounded. I had no business getting involved, but I couldn't help myself. I didn't know much about Noah, but I knew he was intelligent, respectful, and seemed to be a decent human being. That was enough for me to know he deserved more than that washed-up skank in her ridiculously short shorts. She knew how to turn on the charm and could easily trick him. He wouldn't know to stay away from her unless I warned him. Like my mother said, men are weak. I knew Kira was going to act fast, so I needed to do the same.

Under the guise of bringing him a cold drink—something I probably should have done hours ago—I filled a glass with ice water and marched over to the boathouse.

Perspiring, I interrupted them. "Thought you might be thirsty."

Noah looked down at me from the ladder and wiped some sweat off his forehead before stepping down.

He took the glass. "Well, I'm perfectly capable of walking into the house to get a drink, so you didn't have to do that, but thanks."

I shrugged. "You're welcome. It's the least I can do."

I turned to stare at Kira, trying to give her a hint that her presence wasn't welcome.

She couldn't have cared less about me. Her eyes were fixed on Noah's ass as he climbed back up the ladder.

"You've hit the tenant jackpot with Noah here, Heather."

I shot daggers at her. "I know, right?"

"Are you heading to work?" she asked.

"Yeah. But I'm not in a rush. Don't have to be there for another hour." I crossed my arms.

I was totally *late* for work, but no way was I leaving until skankface was gone. She suddenly seemed to pick up on my vibe.

She turned to Noah. "Well, think about dinner, Noah. I'd love to *have* you, and I know the boys would love to meet you, too. Any night that's good for you works for me. You know where to find me for a hot meal and a cold beer."

Sure. That's all she's offering.

Noah barely looked over at her as he continued to paint. "Thanks."

I was happy that he seemed noncommittal and uninterested about the whole thing. But the summer was long, and like my mother said...if a woman throws herself at a man enough, he'll eventually give in. It wasn't like there were a ton of options around here.

The mere thought of them together made my stomach sick.

She nodded once. "Good seeing you, Heather."

"You, too."

After she was out of earshot, I said, "She's making a play for you with that dinner invitation."

Noah continued painting and didn't look at me. "You don't say..."

"She's trouble. You don't want to get involved with her."

"How is it any of your business?"

"It's not. But consider it a friendly warning. I *know* her. She's with a different guy every week. She's only out for one thing."

He stopped for a moment, looked down, and smirked. "Perfect, then."

A rush of adrenaline coursed through my veins. "You don't mean that."

Waving the roller at me, he said, "Is that why you came over here pretending to care about my thirst? Because you saw her talking to me?"

"No," I lied.

"Come on, Heather. I've been out here all day. If you were concerned about my hydration, you would've come a lot sooner. You came out here to stick your nose where it doesn't belong."

"I'm just looking out for you."

"Why? You don't even know me."

I attempted to answer. "Because…"

I had no good reason to give. There was no way I could admit the truth—that I was jealous because she might have a chance with him because she was older and less emotionally high maintenance than me.

"I'd better go. I'm…I'm late for work."

I'd started to walk away when he called out from behind me.

"Thought you said you didn't have to work for another hour."

I turned around and glared at him.

He shook his head, laughing.

He's laughing at me.

Again.

Great. It seemed Noah was either scolding me or laughing at me. There was no middle ground.

The only way to handle this and keep my pride in check was to continue walking away, which was exactly what I did.

Jack Foley's Pub is known for its burgers, local beer selections, and pool tables. While not the fanciest of places, it's a popular joint around the lake. Especially in the summer, Jack Foley's is a happening place any night of the week.

Despite its brisk pace, my shift this evening had been uneventful until about 9PM when I looked toward the corner of the room and spotted him.

What's Noah doing here?

Looking all broody and mad, he stared right at me. Still ticked off that he'd called me out on my behavior earlier, I refused to acknowledge him.

No way was I going to serve him.

"Can you handle table nine in the corner?" I asked my friend and co-waitress Marlene.

"Why?"

"That guy is my tenant, and I don't want to talk to him right now."

She turned around to look at him. "Jesus."

"I know."

"Why the heck are you avoiding *him*?"

"I made a fool of myself earlier. It's a long story."

"He's hot as hell, Heather." She bit her lip. "I'd be glad to service him."

"I asked if you would *serve* him, not service him."

I watched as she waltzed over to Noah and said a few words, only to return a minute later.

"He asked if you could take his order."

Shit.

When I glanced over, he was looking straight at me.

With a sigh, I walked over and made sure to match his cold demeanor. "What can I get you?"

"Shouldn't you be a little more cordial to your customers?"

"Not when I know the customer is here to chastise me."

His expression softened. "I'm not here to chastise you."

"No? Then why did you come *here* of all places? You know this is where I work."

"I came here intentionally, yes...but not to make trouble. I came to apologize."

I inhaled and calmed down a bit. "Really..."

"Yes. I was hard on you earlier. You were looking out for me. I snapped at you for no good reason. I'm sorry. I can be an insensitive asshole sometimes. It's who I am. I don't hide it very well."

"Well, I'm glad you see that. Not that you're an asshole—which, yes, you *can* be sometimes—but that I was only trying to look out for you."

We stared at each other in silence before he spoke.

"Look, not that I owe you an explanation, but I didn't come to Lake Winnipesaukee to fuck around with women or complicate my life. I came to get away from stuff like that. So you don't need to worry about me and what's her name. I don't even remember what her name was, to be fair. All I want is to be left alone—some peace. That's the truth."

"I seriously feel like you think I'm this crazy buttinski."

"A what?"

"Buttinski. You've never heard that term?"

"No. Is that a New Hampshire thing?"

"No." I laughed. "It means someone who meddles in other people's business."

"Oh. Well, then, you're definitely that."

He smiled. I felt goosebumps all over my body. This guy had the strangest effect on me. One minute I was dreading talking to him, and the next all I wanted to do was get lost in his big brown eyes.

I cleared my throat and grabbed the pad of paper out of my apron. "What can I get you?"

"I'll take whatever you recommend. I didn't even look at the menu. I just came to say sorry, actually. But since I'm here, I might as well eat."

"I'll hook you up."

He cocked a brow. "Should I be concerned?"

"No. I'm not gonna spike your food or anything, although maybe I should after the way you spoke to me today." I winked so he didn't think I was still hung up on that whole thing.

I ended up asking the chef to make Noah one of his specialty burgers with mushrooms, Swiss, and fried onions.

I handed Noah the plate with a heaping portion of garlic parmesan fries and watched as he devoured his meal. It gave me a strange pleasure to be feeding him, which was not something I could say I'd ever felt before. *Look at the way he's inhaling that food.* Poor guy must have been starving after slaving away all day.

I imagined what other things he might do with such vigor. I shook my head and forced myself back to work.

Later, when he tried to give me his credit card, I held up my hand. "It's on me."

"I can't let you do that."

"Seriously...it's on the house. Told the chef you were a friend. He insists."

I paid for his meal with my own money. It was the least I could do after everything he was doing around the property.

"Well, thank you. It was really good." He put his card back in his wallet before throwing down a twenty, which defeated the purpose of my treating him.

"You okay getting home later?" he asked.

"Yeah. I have my car."

"That clunker I see parked in front of your house?"

"Yeah. It runs well enough, at least to get me here and back."

"Well, be careful driving home." He stood. "I'll see you around."

He wasn't even gone yet, and immediately my brain began plotting my next opportunity to see him. Without knowing exactly what I was going to say, I called after him.

"Noah…"

He turned. "Yeah?"

What now?

I had nothing to say. I just didn't want him to leave.

After a pause, I fabricated a story.

"My mother wants to meet you…to thank you for your help with the house painting. She asked me to invite you over for dinner this week—on Thursday, my night off. I'll do the cooking, of course, because she isn't capable of making more than a sandwich lately. I told her you would probably say no, but I promised her I'd ask."

Noah chewed his bottom lip and seemed hesitant. He finally shrugged. "Okay."

"Really? You'll come?"

"It's just dinner, right? Why not? Thank you for the offer."

I smiled wide. "Great. Say seven?"

"Yeah. Okay." He nodded. "Goodnight."

"'Night." I watched as he walked away and disappeared out the door.

I was still in a haze when Marlene crept up behind me.

"Spill. Are you fucking that guy or something?"

I shook my head, eyes still on the door. "No."

"Then why are you grinning like a fool right now?"

"I am?"

"Yes. So why *aren't* you fucking him?"

"Because he won't go near me with a ten-foot pole for starters. He treats me like a kid." I sighed. "God, he's...I don't know...different. I can't figure him out... Well, except for the fact that he doesn't seem interested. That part is pretty clear to me."

"You should figure out how to change that. He's hot!"

"I know. He's really amazing looking, isn't he? But you know, Marlene, it's not just that. There's so much to him. He's a talented photographer, like *really* creative. And he's handy as all hell. He's been painting the boathouse to help us. No one asked him to. He's doing it because he knows we need the help. Not to mention, he also tried to save my life."

"*Tried* to save your life?"

"Long story. But things have definitely been more exciting since he moved in. The admiration is one-sided, though."

"Well, heck, anything to spice up your life. I think you need a change of pace with all the shit you have to go through with your mother. You deserve a little excitement."

If only I could contain this giddiness. I had a feeling it was going to be a very long summer in that regard. I already felt myself spiraling out of control.

CHAPTER
FOUR

Noah

I don't know why I agreed to dinner at Heather's. Something told me I was going to regret it.

I guess I was curious as to what the deal was with her mother. I hadn't seen the woman once since moving in. She never came out of the damn house. It was fucked-up.

Yeah. That's the reason you agreed to dinner.

Evidently, I was pretty good at bullshitting myself if I believed meeting Heather's mother was the reason I'd said yes.

Heather had batted her lashes at me at the restaurant, and I forgot my age for a minute when I stupidly agreed. It was hard to not feel like a goddamn horny college student around her. And that was dangerous. *She* was dangerous—particularly because she made no secret of her attraction to me.

From the moment I saw her standing in my bedroom, I'd noticed the way she gawked at me. She had no business looking at me like that, and I didn't like it one bit.

Or maybe I didn't *like* that I *liked* it.

As I strolled through the market, I stopped abruptly and looked down at what I was holding in my hand.

You dumbass.

I'd selected a bottle of red wine to take to dinner tonight, completely forgetting that my gracious hostess was under the drinking age.

I walked back over and returned the bottle to the shelf. What the hell else could I bring?

The smell of fresh bread lured me to the bakery. With little time left, I grabbed a loaf of warm garlic bread before heading to the cash register.

That would have to do. Hopefully she wasn't gluten-free or some shit.

I took my time walking over to the main house. Still unsure whether I'd made the right decision in agreeing to this dinner, I told myself I could always change my mind and cancel. Yet despite having the freedom to do that, I found myself in front of her door, knocking with that gigantic loaf of bread in my other hand.

Someone I didn't expect opened the door. It wasn't Heather or her mother, but rather a guy who looked around Heather's age.

"Who are you?" I asked, looking him up and down.

"Eric. Who are *you*?"

Before I had a chance to answer, Heather's dog came running toward me and rubbed his gigantic head all over my legs. He had the biggest freaking head I'd ever seen on a dog.

The guy repeated his question. "So, who *are* you?"

I finally gave in and scratched the dog's head. "I'm renting the boathouse. Where's Heather?"

"What do you need from Heather?" he asked, seeming defensive.

Who the hell is this guy?

I ignored his question. "Where is she?"

"Her mom isn't feeling well. She's in the bedroom with her."

I should probably just get the fuck out of here.

"Tell her I stopped b—"

"Wait!" Heather suddenly appeared. "Noah, don't go."

The dog barked as if to echo her request.

"What's going on?" I asked.

Heather seemed flustered. "My mother doesn't want to come out of her room. This is typical of her." She looked over at the guy. "I see you've met Eric. He was just leaving."

He stared at her for a few seconds. "Think about what I said, okay?"

"Yeah, sure." She answered dismissively, without even looking at him.

"I mean it, Heather," he insisted.

"Goodbye, Eric."

After he slammed the door, there was a bit of awkward silence. The dog walked over to the corner and planted himself on the floor now that the drama was over.

Looking down at my shoes, I noticed they were pretty dirty. It had rained earlier, and I'd stepped in some mud. I couldn't walk through the house like that.

"You mind if I kick these off?" I asked. "They're all muddy. I don't want to dirty your floor."

"Go for it." Heather said. She watched me remove my shoes. "Your feet are huge."

"Thanks for the notification."

"In case you didn't know." She laughed.

I changed the subject. "So, who was that guy?" I asked, taking a few steps into the living room, still overly conscious of my damn feet.

"It's a long story."

"Well, we don't have anything else to talk about at the moment."

She let out a deep breath. "He's my ex. I wasn't expecting him to show up tonight. I didn't even know he was in town for the summer."

"He doesn't live here?"

"No. He moved to Boston. We broke up shortly after he left for Boston University a couple of years ago. We were supposed to go to BU together, actually. And then things got really bad with my mother, so I never went. He went without me. We thought we could make it work long-distance, but he decided he didn't want to be tied down."

Shit.

"You were supposed to go away to school?"

"Yeah. I was enrolled in their nursing program."

I shook my head. This girl had given up the most important time in her life to be a full-time caretaker at twenty years old. I thought about where I'd been at her age: away at college with all of the freedom in the world. I'd taken it all for granted.

"I'm sorry to hear that—that you couldn't go."

"It's okay. I've gotten used to the idea. Anyway, I really wasn't prepared for him to show up here tonight."

"Listen, I know you're too polite to suggest this, but we can do this another time if your mom isn't feeling well. I can jus—"

"No! I invited you over. This is my night off. I don't want to waste it. Besides..." She looked down at my hands. "You brought...bread."

I'd practically forgotten. "Yeah. Ugh...I didn't have much time to decide what to bring. I had a bottle of wine but then remembered you can't drink."

"Well, legally I can't, but I can certainly drink if I—"

"No, you can't. Not with me giving you the alcohol."

She looked up at the ceiling. "Okay, then." Waving her hand, she said, "Please, come into my kitchen, grumpy." She took the bread. "Can I get you something to drink?"

I stuck my thumbs in the loops of my jeans, feeling uneasy about this so-called dinner for two. "Sure. Anything is fine."

"Seltzer okay?"

"Yeah. Thanks."

She popped open a can of cranberry-lime sparkling water from the fridge and handed it to me.

She stood across from me and watched me take my first sip. "Thank you for the bread." Her face looked flushed. "God, you make me nervous, Noah," she added. "And the fact that this night has turned into a clusterfuck is really not helping. On top of that, you won't even let me have a drink to calm down."

No one could ever accuse this girl of not saying what was on her mind. She was honest to a fault.

"I didn't say you couldn't have a drink. I said I wasn't going to be the one to give it to you."

"Okay." She smiled. "I was half-joking anyway. But I *could* use one right about now."

Ironic that she claimed I made her nervous, because she made me downright uncomfortable. She stood across from me in a tight black shirt with her tits squeezed together. Her long, blond hair, which she typically wore up, was loose and cascading down her back, and her legs were on full display in a tiny denim skirt. I most definitely wasn't supposed to be noticing those things—thus, the discomfort.

"Why do I make you nervous?" I asked. "You shouldn't let anyone have power over you like that. There's no reason I should be making you nervous. I'm just standing here."

"It's not what you're doing. It's who you *are*. From the moment we met, you've intimidated me. This dinner was supposed to be an attempt to get over that, but so far no luck."

I didn't know what to say. I didn't like that I made her nervous, but maybe it was better this way. The alternative—me being overly nice to her and leading her on—wouldn't be good, either.

"You know...." I said. "You shouldn't let people see you sweat. It doesn't matter what I think about you. My opinion is meaningless in the scope of your life."

"Oh, I know that. But I want to get to know you, and it would be nice to do that without constantly fucking things up." She looked back toward the bedroom. "I'm gonna go in and ask my mother to come out one more time, okay?"

"You don't need to do that. Let her be."

She wouldn't listen to me. "Hang on. I'll be right back."

After Heather disappeared upstairs, I wandered around the living room, expecting to find some photos to look at. There weren't any, not a single one. Fathead—that was the name I'd made up for the dog—stared at me.

There was a large collection of figurines on a shelf, mostly children.

Her voice startled me. "I see you've found my Hummels."

"Is that what they're called?"

"Yes. I collect them."

"I was wrong about you," I teased. "You're not a teenager. You're eighty."

She chuckled. "Don't make fun of my Hummels."

"I'm joking."

She moved closer to me. "There's a cool story behind them, actually."

"Yeah?"

"There was this nun...Sister Maria Innocentia Hummel. That's where they get their name. Anyway, she studied the arts before she gave up her life to join the convent. But even amidst that sacrifice, she never lost her identity. She continued her art, and she'd draw these little people. Someone discovered her and made an agreement with her to make them into figurines. After World War Two, US soldiers stationed in Germany sent these to their families. I loved hearing that. To me, they represent nostalgia and innocence—hope. They make me happy. Or, at least, at one time they did."

Interesting. But not anymore? "How long have you been collecting them?"

"Since I was about eight. I'd ask for them for birthdays and stuff. I stopped collecting them some years back, though."

"Why?"

"It's a long story." She didn't elaborate. "Anyway...I'm really sorry, but my mother doesn't want to join us. She's having a bad day. This is very embarrassing."

"There's no reason to be embarrassed about things that aren't your fault." It hit me that this entire invitation was likely bullshit. "She didn't really want to meet me, did she? You said that was the reason you invited me over."

Once again, it didn't take much to get her to tell the truth.

"No," she admitted. "I just wanted to have dinner with you."

I sighed. I couldn't even be mad at her. "So, let's have dinner, then."

A look of panic flashed over her face. "Dinner...shit!"

She raced to the kitchen and opened the oven to remove a burned lasagna.

"I meant to take this out before Eric came by. He totally screwed me up, and until you said the word *dinner*, I didn't even remember I was baking it." She threw the potholder down in frustration. "I don't do the cooking thing all that often, but I normally know how to make lasagna." She muttered, "Shit."

"It's okay. It's just lasagna."

"No. It was supposed be a nice dinner. And I messed it up. Eric showing up really fucked with me."

She almost looked ready to cry. Suddenly, all I cared about was making it better.

"Hey...fuck the lasagna, okay? It's a beautiful night. And we have bread. We can eat it outside."

She managed a smile. "And salad. At least I couldn't burn the salad."

Stepping into action, I headed for her cabinets.

Heather followed. "What are you doing?"

43

"I'm seeing what else you have that we can make real quick." I turned to her. "Do you have canned tomatoes and pasta?"

"Um…yeah…in the pantry."

"Perfect. I'll make pasta and a quick sauce to go with the bread."

"You don't have to do that."

"It's fine. I actually like to cook. It's therapeutic after a long day."

"You should do it more often then, because you're kind of wound up half the time."

As nervous as she claimed I made her, that didn't stop her from being a little ball buster.

"Well, that's why I came to the lake, isn't it? To unwind? I can't help it if a certain someone keeps intercepting."

She fetched me a large can of tomatoes. "Do you really think I'm a pain in the ass?"

I looked back at her as I filled a pot with water. "You want to know the truth?"

She nodded. "Yes."

I shut off the water and placed the pot on the stove. She leaned against the wall, smiling and waiting for my answer.

"I'm tough on you, but I don't think you're a pain in the ass. I actually admire you."

Her eyes widened. "Really?"

"You've made some pretty big sacrifices for your mother. Not just that—I see how hard you work, even saw you getting groceries for the old lady down the road, too. You're a good person, and you find time for others even though you have a lot on your plate."

"You've been stalking me?" she teased.

"No. I was driving by when you were unloading your car and helping Mrs. Benson bring the stuff in. You didn't notice me."

"I still think you were stalking me." She winked and popped open a can of seltzer for herself. "Hey, how did you know her name? You've met Mrs. Benson?"

"Oh, I've *met* Mrs. Benson."

"Uh-oh. What did she do?"

"I was driving by her house one day and noticed some wind had taken her mailbox down. I knocked on her door to give her the mail that had fallen out and let her know I'd fixed it."

"And?"

"Before I had the chance to tell her why I'd knocked, she informed me that I was much better looking than the guys they normally sent her."

Heather laughed out some of her seltzer. "Oh no."

"You know where I'm going with this, then."

"Yes. I accidentally found out one day when I went to check on her. Definitely not something I'll ever forget—learning first hand that Mrs. B spends her Social Security check on male escorts."

"How old is she?" I asked.

"Ninety."

"Damn. Well, she knows what she wants, I guess."

"She must have been pissed when she realized you weren't on the menu."

As I stirred the pasta into the pot, I changed the subject. "So, what did Eric want? He told you to think about what he said..."

Heather crossed her arms and blew a breath up into her hair. "He wants me to agree to go out with him one night while he's home. He says he wants to talk about what happened between us. I don't know if that's a good idea. Hurt me once, shame on you. Hurt me twice...you know that saying."

"He hurt you pretty badly, huh?"

"Well, we were together for a long time, throughout high school. I always knew there was a risk in him going away to college without me. I just didn't think he'd call me drunk and in tears, confessing that he'd messed up and slept with some girl at a campus party."

"Shit. I'm sorry."

She shook her head as if to dismiss my sympathy. "You know what, though? He did me a favor. At least I didn't waste more time with him."

"You should never settle for someone like that. I don't care what he has to say to convince you otherwise."

She continued to watch me cook until I plated two dishes of angel hair pasta and poured the red sauce over them.

"You okay with eating outside?" I asked.

"Yeah, it's a nice night."

We took the food out to the back patio. The sun was halfway down.

Scooting her chair in, she said, "This is a real treat. I should be ashamed at the way this dinner turned out, but I have to say, it's kind of nice being served by you. It might even be worth burning the lasagna."

She grinned, and it took everything in me not to smile back.

46

I pointed to her plate. "Stop smiling and eat."

Heather twirled her noodles around her fork. "Can't stop smiling, but okay."

I needed a lock for my jaw, because I was smiling now, too. It was contagious.

We ate in silence for a while.

Wiping my mouth with a napkin, I said, "What would you want to be doing if this situation weren't holding you back?"

Heather put her fork down and pondered my question. "Well, I would be in college, probably halfway through. I think later I'd want to get my masters to become a psychiatric nurse. But then I'd also want to find some other things I'm passionate about—like you have with your photography. Your photos are amazing, Noah. Truly. I've been meaning to tell you that."

I'd never shown her my work. "You Googled me, I take it."

"Yeah. Hope you don't mind. Your photos from Havana were breathtaking. I've visited that page on your site several times. How did those pictures come about? What made you choose Cuba?"

It impressed me that out of everything on the site, she'd taken notice of that piece. The photos weren't easy to look at, but they were real with a powerful message. Those particular shots were all in black and white.

"It was an assignment for a newspaper five years ago. You could say it chose me. I was working freelance at the time and traveled there with a reporter for a feature on the current state of Cuba and its people. It was one of my longest times away from home, actually. Only the photos are on my site, not the accompanying story."

"Well, that's the beauty of it. The photos tell the story even without the full explanation, which proves your talent. I'm not just saying that. Believe me, I'm a terrible liar. Your work is really amazing."

I was never good at accepting compliments, especially about my work. But I tried.

"Thank you."

"Will you tell me more about it?"

"The Cuba trip specifically?"

She leaned in, her eyes full of wonder. "Yeah."

For some reason, I felt like obliging.

"I don't know if you noticed the shots of the teenagers with tattoos. There's this underground punk culture of young people there. Many of them were high on amphetamines when we were taking those photos."

"Have you ever heard of *Los Frikis*?" she asked.

I nodded, surprised. "Yeah. Actually, I learned about them when I was there."

"Those kids reminded me of a modern-day version of that. Hopefully things are better for the people you photographed than they were for their predecessors. I remember reading about *Los Frikis* and being totally blown away that some of them intentionally injected themselves with HIV to escape their own government. Imagine being forced to do manual labor or imprisoned just because you look different? So you make yourself sick to escape danger by being put in a quarantined sanitarium? That tells you how bad things had to be. It breaks my heart."

I knew my eyes were wide. "Where did you learn about that?"

"I read an article about it some time ago. Some things you just never forget."

"You're right."

"What about the photos of the little kids?"

"That was an orphanage."

"Oh, that's sad."

I stared down into my plate, thinking back to one kid in particular who still had a little piece of my heart.

"There was this one little boy. His name was Daniel. He was only five. He had mitochondrial disease."

"I've heard of that. What is it exactly?"

"It's an inherited condition that affects various parts of the body, like the cells of the brain, nerves, muscles, kidneys, heart. His speech was impaired, and he was confined to a wheelchair. For some reason, he really took to me, kept reaching for me during the week we were there. The first time I met him, I was snacking on a clementine. He grabbed it from me and started eating it. The woman at the orphanage said he never did stuff like that, never interacted so easily with someone. My connection to him was strange but profound. I ended up bringing him clementines every day. I really wished I could have done something more for him."

"Like taken him home?"

"It crossed my mind, believe it or not. I never stopped thinking about him—to the point that I contacted the orphanage a year later."

"What happened?"

It was hard to talk about. "They had closed down. I have no idea where any of those kids are now. It haunts me to this day."

"Oh no. What were you planning to do...when you called them?"

"I don't know. I honestly can't tell you. I just wanted to make sure he was okay—maybe find out how I could help him financially. I made some calls, but no one could tell me what happened to the kids who were there."

"That's scary, but you know, the fact that you were still thinking about him after you left and wanted to help speaks to your character."

It had been a long time since anyone looked at me with admiration in their eyes. If only I deserved it.

Over the next half-hour, Heather listened as I told her more stories from my travels. She was more interested in the people I'd met along the way than the places I'd visited, which I found to be telling about the kind of person she was.

As a cool summer breeze came in from the lake, Heather's mother appeared at the sliding door.

Heather took notice and said, "Mom, come join us."

"No. I just came out to take my pill. I'm going back to my room."

"It's a pleasure to meet you, Mrs. Chadwick," I said.

"Call me Alice."

I got up and extended my hand. "Noah Cavallari."

She took it. "I guess this is my opportunity to thank you for your help."

As I sat back down, I said, "No thanks needed. Like I told Heather, I actually enjoy physical labor."

"My daughter insists that you have no ulterior motive, but I'm not entirely sure I believe that."

Great. Fuck.

"I can assure you I don't."

"How old are you, sir?"

Shit.

I hadn't wanted to divulge my age, mainly because I knew Heather was so damn intent on knowing it. But I couldn't lie.

"Thirty-four."

Heather looked at me, and I knew exactly what she was thinking: that thirty-four wasn't *that* old. I'd told her I was old enough to be her father because a part of me wanted her to believe I was older than I am, so she wouldn't get any ideas.

"Well, that's too old for Heather, but she seems quite smitten with you."

Heather looked mortified. "Mom...please."

But Alice kept going. "The last thing she needs is to be taken for a ride and used by a man passing through town. She's vulnerable and wears her heart on her sleeve. Unless you plan to stay here in Lake Winnipesaukee, which I highly doubt, I suggest you proceed with caution."

Heather gritted her teeth. "Stop."

I needed to nip this in the bud. "I don't know how many ways I can say it, Mrs. Chadwick—Alice—but I don't have any romantic intentions toward your daughter. She's far too young for me. I didn't come here to make my life more complicated, just the opposite. So your worries are futile."

She looked at me skeptically for a few seconds. "Well, that's good, then."

I needed to get out of here *now*. Not only was this woman making me completely uncomfortable, but Heather looked ready to cry or explode. The longer I stayed, the worse this situation would get.

"On that note, I want to thank you, Heather, for a very nice dinner. I'm going to take my plate inside to the kitchen and let myself out."

Uncharacteristically, Heather didn't protest. In fact, she didn't say a word. That told me how upset she really was.

As I exited the kitchen and headed toward the door to put my shoes on, I noticed one of them was missing.

What the hell?

From the corner of my eye, I felt Fathead staring at me. Not only that, my shoe was in his mouth.

"Buddy, I need that."

He growled as I approached. When I held out my hand, he booked it upstairs.

Are you kidding me?

I wasn't going to chase him, so I decided to leave with one damn shoe on.

As I walked down the driveway, a strange feeling followed me back to the boathouse. And it wasn't my foot in a muddy, wet sock, either.

It was anger.

I was mad that Heather lived as a virtual prisoner to her mother's needs. She deserved to live her life, go to college, travel, and do whatever she damn well pleased. This had been going on for a while—since she was a teenager. But more than that, I was mad at myself. As much as I didn't want to admit it, I'd enjoyed sitting outside and talking to her more than I'd enjoyed anything in a *really* long time.

And that wasn't part of the freaking plan.

CHAPTER
FIVE

Heather

"How could you do that to me?" I scolded.

"I'm just trying to protect you," my mother said.

"By embarrassing the living hell out of me? That man has been nothing but respectful. First, you bail on dinner. Then you scare him away with bullshit."

"Every word that came out of my mouth is the truth. What does he want with you if he's leaving at the end of the summer?"

Now I was screaming. "He wants nothing! I already told you he isn't interested in me that way. Why can't you understand that? He hasn't tried a damn thing, and you just made a fool of yourself *and* me. You're acting as though I'm a child. I am almost twenty-one years old—an adult. I don't understand what part of that you don't get." I took my plate. "I can't do this. I need to go to my room."

"Heather...I'm sorry. I was just—"

"I can't!" I yelled as I walked away.

My mother was a lot to handle, but I loved her and knew she meant well. She truly believed she was somehow protecting me. But I still couldn't stand to look at her for the rest of the night.

After I took a shower to calm down, I texted Noah.

Heather: I'm sorry. I'm totally mortified.

A few seconds later, he responded.

Noah: Don't be.

Heather: I'm embarrassed about how she treated you.

Noah: You have nothing to be embarrassed about. You didn't do anything.

There was something I really wanted to get off my chest.

Heather: You don't have to feel sorry for me...for my situation. I can tell you do. I have a choice, you know. I could've left home. I made the choice to stay.

I could see he was typing a response.

Noah: I know that.

Heather: So...34, huh?

Noah: Yes.

Heather: That's not that old.

Noah: Still old enough to be your father.

Heather: Yeah, if you were 14 when you had me!

Noah: Technically possible.

Heather: You had me thinking you were in your forties, though I never thought you looked it. This makes more sense.

Noah: There's a world of difference between 34 and 20.

The only thing standing between thirty-four and twenty right now was the short walk to the boathouse. I couldn't contain what I was feeling. We'd been connecting out there tonight. I could feel it. I wanted to see him again.

Heather: Can I come over?

After a minute, he finally texted back.

Noah: I don't think that's a good idea.

I'd been bracing for that response, but it was still a bummer.

Heather: Ok.

I felt so defeated. Even if he wasn't interested in me romantically, I wasn't ready to say goodnight to him. Okay...maybe part of me still hoped he would change his mind about me.

Several minutes later, the last thing I expected was for my phone to chime again.

Noah: Unless...

My heart skipped a beat as I typed.

Heather: Unless what?

Noah: Unless there's leftover bread. We never touched it. Did you throw it out? I've been jonesing for it.

Heather: No! I forgot about it. It's still sitting on the counter.

Noah: Well, it would be a shame to let it go stale. You should bring it over and I'll throw it in the toaster oven.

Bread—and a side of you—would be great.

I couldn't stop smiling as I responded.

Heather: Be there in five.

I should've known he had no plans to invite me inside.

Noah was out smoking a cigar on the porch when I arrived. I guess I couldn't blame him. Aside from a small table, the entire boathouse was pretty much a bedroom. There wasn't even a couch, just the bed and a kitchenette. We would have had to sit on the bed, and I knew he wasn't having that.

"So..." I said. "Teddy brought me this as I was walking out the door." Noah's big shoe landed with a thud after I tossed it to the ground.

"Is that his name? I call him *Fathead* in my mind." He chuckled.

"He does have a really big head."

"Biggest one I've ever seen on a dog."

"I'd have to agree with you on that."

"Yeah, he had my shoe in his mouth when I was leaving, then took off with it. I didn't feel like chasing him upstairs, so I let him have it."

"I think taking your shoe was him trying to get you to stay. Why didn't you come get me instead of walking home with one shoe?"

"Sometimes you have to know when to walk away, even if it's without your shoe. You know what I'm saying?"

"Yeah. Unfortunately, in this case, I do. I don't blame you for booking it out of there." I sighed.

"Your mother is just looking out for you. I wouldn't trust me, either."

Why *did* I trust Noah so implicitly? It was a gut feeling, I guess.

"I'll put the bread inside," I said, squeezing past him and making my way into the house. After placing the loaf next to the toaster oven, I returned to the porch.

I sat right next to him, and he automatically moved a few inches away. He seemed very conscious of my closeness, and I could tell it made him uncomfortable. I just didn't know the reason why—whether he didn't like it, or he liked it but didn't think he *should* like it.

Noah blew out a couple of smoke rings. His hair was wet from the shower. Thinking about him taking a shower made my nipples hard as I imagined the water streaming down that carved back to his muscular ass.

He had changed into a fitted white T-shirt that hugged his chest. I looked down at his forearms and imagined him using them to lift me. I loved the way the veins protruded.

Since I'd also taken a shower, I chose my words carefully to gauge his reaction.

"Looks like we both had the same idea. We showered together tonight."

His Adam's apple moved as he swallowed. Had my comment created a visual?

There's definitely something there.

He remained quiet, so I said, "I don't know why, but I have this feeling there's more to you being here than you've said, that there's a reason you ran away from your life. It's none of my business, and it doesn't matter. I'm just glad you're here."

"You're right about that."

"That you're hiding something?"

"That it's none of your business." He blew out some smoke and ignored my quest for more information. "I assume you didn't tell your mother you were coming over."

"No, but it doesn't matter. I'm an adult. She can state her opinion, but she can't tell me how to live my life. I've given up enough by staying home with her and running things around here. I'm not letting her tell me who to spend time with on top of that." I gestured to his cigar. "Can I try it?"

"No."

"Come on. You don't buy me wine. The least you could do is let me have a puff. I've never tried a cigar before."

He flicked some of the ashes and let out a frustrated breath before handing it to me.

I wrapped my lips around it, noticing the wetness from his mouth. It made me long to feel his actual mouth on mine. His eyes were glued to my lips as I inhaled and coughed.

Handing it back to him, I coughed again. "Thank you."

Noah was amused. "What did you think?"

"Not for me."

He chuckled.

We were silent for a bit and then he asked, "Why are you looking at me like that?"

I hadn't realized I'd been looking at him funny. But I knew the answer.

"Because there's so much I want to know about you, but I'm afraid you'll chew my head off if I start prying."

"You're probably right." He stared down at the cigar in his hand before he turned to me. "What do you want to know, buttinski?"

"Everything. Too much." I sighed. "But for starters, why is a catch like you not married at thirty-four?"

"You're assuming I haven't been down that road already."

My heart nearly stopped. "You were married?"

He looked down at his cigar, then up at me. "Yes, I was."

Wow. "What happened?"

He blew out some smoke as he gathered his thoughts.

"Well, I could lie and tell you we grew apart because we got married young or some shit, but that wouldn't be the only reason. The truth is…I was a selfish bastard who put myself first. I chose to travel half of the time instead of being home, and I didn't give her the attention she deserved. She found what she needed in someone else. So, if that's your definition of a *catch*, maybe you should reassess."

Holy crap. Noah had been married. I was still trying to wrap my head around it.

"You're formally divorced?"

"As of three years ago, yeah."

"Do you regret how it ended?"

"I regret how I acted, that I was a shitty husband, but I'm not sure I regret that it ended. The experience made me realize I'm not really cut out for marriage, and she found someone who is. So it worked out in the end."

"Do you still speak to her?"

"Do you ever stop with the questions?"

"No." I grinned sheepishly.

He sighed. "Yeah, I just spoke to her today."

"Really?"

"We're friends. She's remarried now. But she still checks in on me from time to time."

"Well, that's nice, at least, that you're on good terms."

"We've known each other a long time, since we were kids. We started out as friends. I suppose we're ending that way, too."

"Wow," I said, soaking in everything he'd told me.

We sat in silence for a bit, and then I realized something. "We're both in the same situation now."

He lifted his brow. "You're divorced, too?"

"No, what I mean is...you like to point out that I haven't lived, that you've gone to college, traveled the world, and now, come to find out, you've been married. Our lives couldn't have been more different—up until this point. Yet, here we are in the very same place looking at the same moon by the lake, both single and uncertain of the future. Don't ask me how I know that about you—that you're in some kind of limbo—I just do. We're both in the very same place in life despite our past experiences and the years between us. Am I right? We're not so different, Noah. We're not. Maybe you were meant to meet me."

He just looked at me and mocked, "So deep, you are."

I laughed. "Asshole."

"I see I don't make you nervous anymore."

"I'm not nervous at this point in time, no."

"Good." Noah stared into my eyes. Maybe what I'd said about us crossing paths had resonated with him. He seemed to be pondering something.

"What happened to your mother?" he finally asked. "Not that depression needs a reason, but how long has she been that way?"

Do I tell him? "My sister killed herself."

It felt strange to utter those words aloud. This was the first time I'd spoken about it with someone other than my therapist.

A dark cloud crossed Noah's face. "I'm sorry, Heather."

"She was only twenty-five. Her name was Opal. She had some mental problems. She would act out when she wasn't taking her meds. Sometimes she was okay, and other times not. She ran away from home when she was my age."

I looked up at the night sky. "My sister was gorgeous, so it was scary to think she was out there on her own. We couldn't stop her from leaving. We tried. But she was an adult. She originally left with a boyfriend, but they broke up. Then she just wandered from city to city, taking odd jobs when she was on her meds and could hold one down. We'd beg her to tell us where she was, but all she'd do was call from time to time to let us know she was okay. We didn't realize how bad things had gotten until we received a call that she'd overdosed on pills at a motel off the highway in Connecticut. That was the worst night of my life. And my mother has blamed herself ever since for not doing more to make Opal come home. It's why she's so terrified of losing me. The whole situation just sucks."

Noah closed his eyes momentarily. He seemed very affected by my story. It made me wonder if he'd experienced loss, too.

"I'm so sorry," he repeated. "That had to have been hard."

Feeling emotional, I wanted nothing more than to distract from the sad thoughts. At the same time, thinking about my sister reminded me how short life is.

Yes.

Life is short.

Tomorrow isn't guaranteed.

All we have is today.

If you have something to say, say it.

"I'm very attracted to you," I blurted.

The words escaped my mouth before I could think about what saying them would mean.

Noah looked as if he didn't quite know how to respond, but he shot me down. "Don't…"

Despite his warning, I kept going like a runaway train.

"I know you think I'm too young for you. But I'm just gonna be honest. I don't live a very exciting life. I do what I have to do, then wake up to another sunrise on the lake each day. I go to work and take care of my responsibilities. But for some inexplicable reason, since you moved in, something has awakened inside of me. I wake up excited. I'm very drawn to you...and very attracted to you. I don't know if you feel the same way, or if maybe you're trying not to because you think my age automatically makes me immature. I can assure you I'm not. Never in my life have I admitted my attraction to someone like I'm doing right now. I've never done anything like this. I—"

"I can't, Heather." He lowered his voice and repeated, "I can't."

A brisk evening wind suddenly blew things around. It was as if Mother Nature was trying to help distract from my embarrassment.

We sat through a few seconds of awkward silence until he said, "I'm flattered that you feel that way about me. I really am. And I think you're beautiful...inside and out. But nothing can happen between us."

I felt nauseous.

Oh my God.

Why did I just do that?

I knew why. I wanted him so badly I was willing to risk looking like an idiot for the chance to experience being with him. And it backfired. Big time.

One thing about me, though? I didn't need to be told twice.

Okay, maybe this *was* the second time he'd made his lack of intentions toward me clear. But I didn't need to be told a *third* time, and I vowed never to make an ass of myself in front of Noah Cavallari again.

"Well...I guess I'll chalk this experience up to practice in putting myself out there and accepting rejection." I stood. "Today has not been my day. I think I'm gonna turn in."

"You don't have to go." Noah stood up, too. "Stay."

"I really need to call it a night."

He didn't fight me on it. "Alright..."

Disappointed in my impulsive behavior, I swore at myself under my breath the entire walk home.

And I was still feeling self-destructive when I got there, because when I returned to my room, I did the one thing I knew I would end up regretting.

Taking out my phone, I scrolled down to Eric's name.

Heather: I can meet you tomorrow night.

CHAPTER
SIX

Noah

With hard strokes, I took out my frustration on the house as I painted the next morning.

Heather's words from last night kept playing in my head as I rolled the paint over the wood of the boathouse.

I'm very drawn to you…and very attracted to you.

I'd felt like a piece of shit after she left. She'd taken my rejection personally, when that was the last thing I wanted.

I still had no clue if I was going to tell her why I'd left Pennsylvania to come here. But I knew I needed time without complications. And my twisted feelings for Heather were starting to become a complication.

Shit, if there's anything sexier than a woman who isn't afraid to ask for what she wants. But Heather wasn't exactly a *woman*. She had a lot of growing up to do. While she was old enough to know what she wanted *sexually*, she wasn't old enough to know what was good for her. That would only come with time and years of experience. I wasn't going to be the one to teach her about the kind of guy *not* to get involved with. She needed someone grounded, who would make a good husband to her someday, not someone messed up in the head who'd already proven incapable of marriage.

More than anything, she didn't know the truth. I could never take advantage of her advances—no matter how hard it was to resist. It didn't matter that she was drop-dead gorgeous, that I was horny as fuck, or that she seemed to be the only person capable of making me smile.

Though I continued to ruminate while painting, at one point, the sound of music playing registered. I got down from the ladder and took a little walk to see where it was coming from.

"MMMBop" by Hanson.

Sure enough, it came from Heather's room. It was like the nineties threw up in there. I was tempted to yell up to her window and tease her, but after last night, I didn't think she'd appreciate it.

So I bit my tongue, shook my head, and walked back to the boathouse.

Later that afternoon, I was back up on the ladder when my heart nearly dropped to my stomach. I looked over to see someone standing on the roof of the main house. The structure was three stories high, so anyone who fell off was going to be seriously injured.

It didn't take long for me to figure out it was Heather.

What the hell is she doing on the roof?

She was looking down as if she was...pondering jumping? I found it hard to believe she would ever do that.

Why then? Adrenaline pumped through me as I climbed down and ran toward the house.

With my heart pounding, I called up to her, "Heather! What are you doing?"

She put her hand on her chest. "Oh my God. You scared the shit out of me."

I held my hand over my forehead to block the sunlight. "I scared *you*? Get down! Are you crazy?"

"Why?"

"Because you could fall. Why are you up there?" I swallowed, terrified of her answer.

"It's an exposure exercise," she said.

"What? What the hell are you talking about?"

"I have a massive fear of heights. I've been listening to this podcast on facing your fears, and the doctor says to overcome any fear, you have to challenge yourself, expose yourself to it. I decided to climb up here and experience the fear for a bit, to habituate to it."

My mouth hung open. "That's the craziest thing I've ever heard, especially when you can fall and break your neck in the process."

She crossed her arms and looked down at me. "What did you *think* I was doing up here?" After a moment, her face changed. "Oh my God, Noah. You didn't think I was going to jump?"

I let out a long breath as my heartbeat started to return to normal. "I don't know what I thought. But what in God's name else would someone be doing up on the roof, standing there and looking down at the ground?"

"I can't believe you thought I was going to off myself. What—did you think your rejection last night put me over the edge?" She started to laugh.

As sick as it was under the circumstances, I was happy to hear her joking about last night. I'd been worried I'd hurt her.

"You *do* realize this is the second botched attempt at saving my life you've had since your arrival, right?" she shouted down.

I shook my head and couldn't help but laugh.

She climbed carefully down the ladder and walked over to stand in front of me.

"You're insane, you know that?" I said. "You scared me. I'm not gonna lie. But now I see how ridiculous the whole thing is."

Her face turned serious. "Do you really think I could do that to my mother after what happened to my sister?"

That question hurt my chest. "I wasn't thinking. I saw you up there, and I freaked out for a second. I had no idea what you were doing."

She reached out to pinch my cheek, letting her hand rest a bit on my face. "It's cute that you cared."

My body went rigid at her touch. I was way too aware of the fact that it was the first time I'd felt her hands on me.

"You headed into work?" I asked, trying to shake off this weird experience.

"No...ugh, I actually took the night off."

"Good. You deserve a break. Going anywhere?"

She looked down at her feet for a moment. "Eric is picking me up."

My stomach sank. *The asshole ex is taking her out?*

"Oh."

"Yeah, I decided to have dinner with him, to at least hear him out."

I knew I should stay out of it, but...

"You really think he deserves that?"

She shrugged. "I don't know. You're allegedly the more mature one here. You tell me. Doesn't everyone deserve a second chance?"

"A man who fucks around on his woman doesn't deserve jack shit. He's a coward."

"Did you cheat on your wife?"

This girl did not hold back.

"No, not physically. But there are other ways to hurt someone."

"Like how? Give me an example."

"Well, you can *want* something else. That's not quite the same as cheating, but in a sense, it's a form of betrayal."

"So you emotionally cheated on your wife?"

"I didn't say that. But the mere desire for something outside of your marriage—whether that be another person or another life altogether—that can be like a betrayal. You have to know how to walk away when it gets to that point—*before* you hurt the person."

"And that's what you did."

I hesitated. "Yes. Basically."

"How did we go from you trying to save me from jumping off the roof to talking about your personal life?"

"This seems to be the way with you. One second I'm getting involved in your asinine shit, the next you're sticking your nose where it doesn't belong. Wash. Rinse. Repeat."

She laughed. "Then it ends with me running home with my tail between my legs."

That made me chuckle. "Sounds about right."

"I'll take your advice on Eric into consideration," she said as she suddenly headed back toward the house.

I forced my eyes to the ground when I caught them lingering on her ass as she walked away.

"Stay safe," I called out.

It was past midnight, and she hadn't come home yet. I knew I should've just gone to bed and minded my own damn business, but my butt seemed glued to the porch. I told myself I needed to make sure she got home safely, and then I'd call it a night.

But with each passing minute, I became more convinced she'd decided to spend the night with him. Could I really blame her? It wasn't like I was giving her horny little ass what she'd asked me for. That meant she was going to get it from somewhere else, whether I liked it or not. I just wished it wasn't with an undeserving asshole who'd already hurt her.

A flash of light appeared from down the gravel road leading to Heather's house. I stood up to get a look and realized it was the same red Civic that had picked her up earlier.

I watched as he let her out.

When the car took off, she hadn't moved from the front steps. I struggled to see in the darkness, but thanks to an overhead light on her porch, I could make out her shoulders rising and falling. Her head was in her hands as she sank to sit on the step.

She was crying.

Fuck.

What did he do to her?

My blood was pumping.

Against my better judgment, I felt my feet moving, one in front of the other, as if they were going with or without my approval to the main house.

"Hey," I called. "Are you alright?"

She jumped. "You scared me."

"Second time today I did that."

She wiped her eyes. "I know."

"I was out on my porch having a smoke, and I saw you with your head down."

"I'm fine."

"You don't look fine."

"It's not what you think."

"What happened?"

She shook her head. "I'm not crying because he hurt me. I'm crying because I found the strength to turn him down when I was feeling weak. In the midst of my vulnerability, I found my self-worth. And it feels really good. These aren't sad tears." She sniffled. "You were right. Once a cheater, always a cheater. Even if he never cheated on me again, I wouldn't be able to look him in the eyes and fully trust him. Ever. I deserve better."

Damn.

Good girl.

"I'm proud of you."

I took a seat next to her on the steps.

She turned to look at me. "I'm sorry for putting you in an uncomfortable position last night. I don't know what came over me."

I hadn't expected her to bring that up.

"Don't even think about apologizing. There's nothing to apologize for. You were being forthright, and I admire your honesty. That's why I owe you the very same."

This was my opportunity to explain myself, so I took a deep breath in. "I need you to know that my turning you down has nothing to do with you. I'm wrong for you in so many ways, and knowing that, I can't take advantage of the situation—no matter how tempting it might be."

"Rejection stings," she said. "But I don't regret saying those things because I would never know how you feel otherwise. Now I do. You don't have to worry about me doing something like that again. I only have to be told once—or twice. The bottom line is, I heard it loud and clear. I won't be coming onto you again."

"I don't know...are sure you can resist?" I winked.

"I can manage." She laughed and wiped the remnants of her tears. "Can we be friends?"

I smiled. "Yeah."

The tension in the air was thick, but at least she didn't seem mad.

She looked up at the sky and yawned. "I'm tired, but I'm totally wired at the same time. I won't be able to sleep. Will you stay up with me for a little bit?"

Considering everything she'd just told me, that seemed innocent enough.

"Sure."

I liked hanging out with Heather.

"Did you end up eating the bread?" she asked.

I laughed. "No...but I'm pretty sure it's stale by now."

"Not if you toast it," she said. "Want to try?"

I stood up. "Sure. Let's do it."

Our shoes scraped along the gravel as we walked together back to the boathouse. Crickets chirped. It was another beautiful night on the lake with the moon casting a glow over the property.

Heather waited on the porch while I went inside to toast the garlic bread. She seemed to know the drill; I never invited her inside, so she didn't bother to try to follow me.

After I brought the bread out, I sliced a piece and handed it to her.

Heather moaned as she took it into her mouth. My traitorous dick twitched at the sound, and I did my best to ignore that.

She spoke with her mouth full. "Who knew day-old bread could taste so good?"

"It *is* pretty damn good," I agreed, taking a big bite. "It's *mmm*...bop. MMMBop."

I cracked myself up.

Heather stopped chewing. "That song was...um...it was just playing on the..."

"On your iPhone. It was playing on your phone because you put it there, because you like cheesy nineties' music. Nothing to be ashamed of."

"Hey, it's the decade I was born into. I have a special appreciation for it. I missed a lot of good stuff when I was too young to remember, apparently. So maybe I do enjoy the occasional *unique* song."

"I have a feeling it's more than occasional. In fact, I'd love to see what else is on that phone."

She bit into more bread. "You're never gonna find out."

I hoped she knew I was teasing. I mean, her taste in music was...*different*. But so was she—in a good way.

She leaned her head against the side of the house and closed her eyes, almost looking ready to fall asleep, but then she opened them and stared out toward the lake.

It hit me in this moment how comfortable she made me feel. (Well, she made me feel comfortable, and that made me *uncomfortable*.) Heather was the type of person you could just hang out with in silence. She gave the impression that you could tell her anything and she wouldn't judge. At the same time, it was okay to say absolutely nothing at all and just be.

Before coming to the lake, I hadn't known what to expect from this place. I sure as hell wasn't planning to feel so at peace here. It had crossed my mind that I could live this simple life forever. That wasn't an option, but it was a nice thought.

As if she could read my mind, Heather asked, "So, what's your next step?"

"Next step?"

"What will you do when August ends? Return to Pennsylvania, get back to work?"

"Yeah. I can't leave my business for too long. Or my father."

"Is your father ill?"

"No, but he's the only family I have there. My mom and my brother who's married with three children all live in Minnesota."

She grinned. "Uncle Noah."

"Yeah." I smiled, thinking about my two nephews and niece. "My mother moved there to be closer to my brother and his kids."

"Your parents are divorced, then."

"Yeah. Ever since I was about your age."

"Well, I'd say sorry, but sometimes divorce can be a good thing if the situation that preceded it was unbearable."

"That's very true. In my parents' case, though, it was amicable." I paused a moment. "What about your parents? You haven't mentioned your father at all."

"My father remarried when my sister and I were young. He has two daughters with his new wife, and I barely see him. They live in western Massachusetts. He returns to the lake once a year, stays at a hotel, and comes over for dinner. He mostly criticizes my mother and me, then leaves. I dread that visit because my mother is always a wreck the entire week before, during, and after. Well, even more of a wreck than she already is."

Shit. That couldn't have been easy for her—that her dad had another two daughters he spent all of his time with. Overall, he sounded like an ass.

"That must be hard for you..."

"Yes, but I can't change it, so I try to accept it. Aside from his yearly visit, I go to visit them a couple of times a year. I was always more accepting of the situation than Opal, but she had other issues affecting her reactions to things. She saw my father leaving as pure abandonment. I've tried to see it differently—that sometimes people don't get things right the first time around in life. He seems happy now. I know he regrets leaving us the way he did. He's told me so. Even though knowing that doesn't make it any easier, I forgive him."

"I admire how you handle what you've been dealt," I said.

"All I can do is my best. I try not to dwell on the sad stuff, and I try to find some happiness in every day, even if it's only one thing."

"What was your happiness today?"

She looked me straight in the eyes. "This...hanging out with you."

I cut her another piece of bread to deflect how that made me feel, which was all sorts of fucked-up inside. If she asked *me* that question, my answer would be the same.

I watched her chew on the bread. It was oddly sensual, giving her food piece by piece and watching her eat it. Or maybe that was my depraved mind wishing I could give her something more. Maybe in a different time, a different world, that would have been possible. But in this reality, Heather was too good for me, too innocent and pure.

Though I'd tried to convince myself I wasn't supposed to view her sexually, my body didn't agree. It thought Heather was fantastically beautiful. With her long, silky blond hair and laid-back attitude, she was sort of like Barbie's down-to-Earth cousin. She had an understated beauty and a personality to match—a great sense of humor. Her body, while athletic, had subtle curves in all the right places. As she stretched her long legs out on the porch, I had the urge to rub my hand along the blond fuzz on her thighs. She kicked her shoes off, displaying dainty feet.

My attraction to her would have to stay my dirty little secret, because I wouldn't be laying a hand on her.

She licked her lips. "So...Eric thinks something's going on between us."

"Oh yeah?"

"And I sort of...let him believe it."

"Good. Serves him right."

"I was hoping you'd be okay with that."

"Fuck yes, I am. If I'd known what he'd done to you when I met him that night at your house, I would have played it up, made him feel like the little shit he is."

"I appreciate that you would do that for me."

My feelings for Heather were complicated, but more than anything, I felt protective of her. I would do anything to make the prick who'd cheated on her jealous.

We stayed on the porch talking for a couple more hours.

After she left, I lay in my bed, staring out at the moon as my mind raced.

It felt like I had a mission, and I was running out of time. I needed to help her get out of this place. I could only do so much while I was in New Hampshire, but I needed a plan. I would fix as much around here as possible so she could put the property on the market. Maybe she could get her mother into some kind of retirement community where people could help look after her. Getting Alice into a different situation was gonna be the toughest part. But if that could happen somehow, then Heather could go to college and follow her dreams.

CHAPTER
SEVEN

Heather

About a year ago, I'd decided I really needed to talk to a professional. Remote therapy seemed like a good option since there weren't a ton of qualified therapists near me who took my insurance. I'd found a woman based out of New York who did.

In the beginning, we'd talked a lot about how Opal's suicide and my mother's depression were impacting me, but as of late, we were focused on my general well-being.

Dr. Vaughan popped up on the screen. "Hi, Heather. Can you hear and see me okay?"

"Yes. Crystal clear."

"Good. How have you been?"

"Pretty good, actually."

"Okay. Great." She looked down at her notes. "Let's see...the last time we spoke, you told me about a man who'd moved onto your property. It was nice to hear you excited about something. How are things going with that situation?"

When we'd spoken a month ago, Noah had just moved in. I'd described my attraction to him and admitted I was holding out hope that something might happen between us over the course of the summer. Things had changed.

"Well, unfortunately, my excitement was a bit premature. Noah has turned out to be a great friend and a huge help around the property, but he made it clear he's not interested in me romantically or sexually."

She took some notes, then asked, "How did he explain that to you exactly?"

"I...sort of took a chance and made an advance toward him one night, let him know I was attracted to him."

"That was very brave."

"Yeah, well, he was quick to explain that he doesn't see it happening. He thinks, among other things, that he's too old for me, even though I don't think thirty-four is too old at all."

"How do you feel about his rejection?"

"I've learned to accept it. Like I said, we've become friends. I'm still attracted to him and wish things were different, but it is what it is. I can't force him to want me that way."

"You seem to be taking it as well as could be expected."

"I don't have a choice. I still really like being around him. He's listened to me vent about a lot of stuff and is very encouraging. He wants me to find a way to go to college, and he's been fixing things around the property to help us get it into a condition where we can put it on the market."

"What are your mother's thoughts on that—potentially moving?"

"She doesn't want to sell, but she agrees we probably have to. Since the house is paid off, we could buy something smaller and use the money for the future. The fact that the property comes with the boathouse for rental income is a huge selling point. I'm hoping we can get a good deal for it."

"How does your mother feel about Noah helping out?"

"Well, she was very suspect of his intentions at first, but she's calmed down about that—especially after she got a look at the freshly painted boathouse." I chuckled. "He's started fixing things on the main property now—installed a new hot water heater, replaced a couple of windows, things like that. He's really a jack of all trades, used to work in construction. Mom still stays in her room most of the day, but she's come out once or twice to say hello to him, and she even apologized for being rude to him early on."

"It sounds like Noah's being there has turned out to be a really great thing."

"Yeah. Almost like he was sent from above."

My feelings for Noah had only grown over the past couple of weeks. I felt so safe with him around. We'd hung out a lot, talked a lot. The front porch of the boathouse had become our place. I'd watch him smoke his one cigar—never two—and we'd sit and talk about anything and everything, sometimes until the wee hours of the morning. Things had stayed platonic, and I was more convinced than ever about that not changing. But it still hurt a little. I wanted him more each day and couldn't imagine how I was going to feel after he left. I knew for sure he was someone I would never forget.

After I got off the phone with Dr. Vaughan, I opened my journal as I often did after clearing my head in therapy. While I typically wrote down my thoughts and feelings, today my head was in a totally different space. Maybe it was all that talk about Noah not wanting me, but all I could seem to focus on was how much I wanted *him* and ridding myself of some of this pent-up frustration. If I couldn't actually have him, I would let it all out on the pages of my journal. No holds barred, I wrote out my greatest sexual fantasy, including all the things I wished he would do to me.

Noah: It's 10PM. Do you know where your dog is?

That's a strange question.

Heather: Downstairs. I think?

Noah: Pretty sure that's not the case, considering I can't get him off my bed right now.

Oh my God. What?

Heather: Really? That's scary! How did he get out?

Noah: Well, I'd ask him but...

Heather: How long has he been there?

Noah: He showed up at my door fifteen minutes ago.

Heather: Be right there.

As terrifying as it was that Teddy had escaped, given his destination, I couldn't help but laugh as I ran to the boathouse.

Noah opened the door before I had a chance to knock. Just as he'd said, Teddy had completely taken over the bed. He looked so comfortable.

"I'm sorry about this."

Noah shrugged. "I don't mind."

"He must have remembered the time I brought him here when you first moved in. He knew exactly where to find you."

"He was sitting on the porch when I went out to have a cigar—like he was waiting for me."

"That's so cute. I'm glad he had the good sense to come here and not run away." I patted my thighs. "Come on, Teddy. Let's go."

"He can stay." Noah took a sip of his wine. There was an open bottle on the counter. I wished I could join him, but I knew how he felt about offering me alcohol.

"I figured you wanted me to come get him."

He waved his hand. "Nah. He's fine."

"Well, he doesn't exactly look ready to go anyway, I suppose."

I looked around, then removed my shoes. It was strange to be *inside* the boathouse with Noah for once. I could thank Teddy for this opportunity. I hopped up on the bed and rubbed my dog while Noah took a seat across from us and kicked his legs up on the foot of the bed. With his big feet facing me, I was tempted to press the bottoms of mine against his.

But I refrained, of course.

Teddy was the perfect buffer to keep my hanging out on the bed from being awkward. The scent of Noah emanating from his sheets surrounded me. Teddy definitely had the right idea.

Noah looked particularly hot tonight. He wore these gray sweatpants that hugged his crotch in a way that left little to the imagination. It was hard not to gawk at his amazing body.

Don't look down. He's going to catch you.

If not me...what was Noah's type? I often wondered about the woman he'd been married to.

"Do you have any photos of your ex-wife?"

He squinted. "Random much? Where did that come from?"

"Do you expect anything less from me? I laughed. "It just came to mind. I've always been curious as to what she looks like."

"Yeah. Hang on."

Noah pulled out his phone and scrolled through his photos. My heart sped up in anticipation. He handed it to me.

His ex had dark hair and dark eyes. She looked Greek or Italian. It came as no shock that she was absolutely gorgeous. Her Mediterranean features were the total opposite of my Scandinavian looks.

"Wow. I'm not sure you ever told me her name."

"Olivia."

Olivia.

Though I knew they weren't together anymore, I still envied her. She'd gotten to make love to him and experience everything with him, even if it wasn't forever.

"She's really pretty, but I didn't expect anything less." I handed him back the phone.

"She's a good person, too."

He looked a little down.

"Do you feel like you failed her?" I asked.

"For a while I did feel like my marriage was my biggest failure. But she's happy now, so that's all that matters. The idea of failure is subjective. Our marriage *failed*, but she ended up with something better in the end. So it was hardly a failure for her."

It made me sad that he felt that way. "Why do you sell yourself short?"

"I told you before...I wasn't a good husband."

"Yeah, but you've learned from your mistakes. Maybe she's missing out on the person you are now, and that might have been better than what she has with the other guy. You're older and wiser."

"Definitely older. I don't know about wiser." He chuckled. After some silence, he asked, "So, what about you...? What do you consider your biggest failure?"

"I'm pretty sure I've yet to have it, but I bet it'll be a doozy."

"I can't wait to find out what it is, for you to get it over with. I expect a phone call when it happens."

The thought of calling him sometime in the future kind of bummed me out, knowing he would be far away. I wondered if we would even keep in touch.

"I can definitely do that. By then, you'll be like...'Wait, Heather who?'"

He pretended to be holding a phone to his ear and talking to me in the future. "Oh...that crazy blond chick from New Hampshire? Yeah, yeah, yeah. I remember you. How the hell are ya?"

I held my hand up to my ear. "Yup, that's me! The loony one who dances in the lake and pretends to be getting ready to jump off the roof while listening to Hanson. That one."

"Yeah. The one who made me smile." He looked over at me. "That one."

An hour or so later, Teddy was finally ready to go. I went down to the basement to do laundry when I got home and noticed a full load of Noah's clothes still in the dryer. He must have put them in this afternoon and forgotten to come get them.

It wasn't often that I had the opportunity to do something for him, so I was happy to be able to fold his wash. I fluffed the load for a few minutes before taking it out.

Smelling each warm article of clothing, I closely examined them all. His shirts were size large. His boxer briefs were a mixture of Calvin Klein and Armani Exchange. I'd always found folding laundry to be relaxing, but folding the clothes of the man I was obsessed with was particularly enjoyable.

I was so turned on tonight. My body was in a constant state of alert whenever I was around Noah, and the feeling typically lasted long after I'd left him. Handling his clothing like this only made it worse.

After everything was neatly placed in the basket, I started to walk out of the laundry area. Then I stopped and turned back around.

Feeling impulsive, I reached under my skirt and pulled my black lace panties down my legs. Holding them in my hands, I paused, wondering if this was a good idea. Who was I kidding? I knew it was a very bad idea. After all, I'd vowed not to make any more advances toward him. This would be crossing the line.

But I wanted to mess with him, wanted to push boundaries and have some fun again. I'd been really good. Technically, this wouldn't be anything like a proposition. I could pretend I'd been folding my clothes and accidentally mixed up the piles—if he ever called me out on it, that is.

I folded the panties and tucked them in the middle of his laundry, running out before I could change my mind.

CHAPTER
EIGHT

Noah

I'd started doing some landscaping work around the property, and Heather would often come outside during the day to help pull weeds or throw down mulch. We'd joke around and bust each other's balls while working together. These were my favorite days.

One such afternoon, Heather was particularly chatty while we worked.

"Did I ever tell you the story of how I got my name?" she asked.

"No, I don't think so."

"I was named after an actress."

"Locklear?"

"No. You know the horror movie *Poltergeist*?"

"Yeah."

"The little girl who played Carol Ann—her name in real life was Heather O'Rourke. She died at the age of twelve. Anyway, my mom loved that film, so she named me after her."

"Wow. That's pretty cool and creepy at the same time."

"Yeah, especially since I looked a lot like her when I was little—with my light blond hair and the bangs I used to have. When I was younger, I was totally obsessed with that movie. I liked to pretend I was her. I would turn the TV to a snowy channel, put my palms on the screen, and play *Poltergeist*. To this day, I love horror movies. It's one way I take after my mother."

"Well, if I didn't think you were strange already, that pretty much seals the deal," I teased.

"Do you have any strange habits, Noah?"

"Nothing comes to mind."

"You want to know something else I do that's strange?"

"I think you're gonna tell me either way."

"I talk in my sleep."

"No shit? How do you even know that, if you're sleeping?"

"I've been told by various people. My mother…Eric… my sister."

Her expression dampened upon the mention of her sister. I tried to snap her out of it.

"So, what kinds of things do you say? Funny shit?"

"Weird things that don't make sense sometimes. Other times, embarrassing truths. I can only go by what they tell me I said. I have no recollection of it."

I remembered there was something I needed from my truck.

She looked up from where she was planting flowers when she noticed me walking away. "Where are you going?"

"Gotta get something from the truck. Be right back."

When I returned with what I'd purchased, she took one look at it and said, "Oh my God. What did you do?"

"What or *whooo*," I joked.

I dug the stick into the ground. Attached to the top was a fake owl that looked quite lifelike.

Heather had told me a story one night about her father planting a cherry tree shortly before he took off. Each year, the birds got to the cherries before anyone could pick them. Heather had always somehow related that to her dad leaving nothing for them. That made me angry, so I wanted to do something. I bought the owl hoping maybe it would save some of the cherries. Maybe Heather could finally have some for what could possibly be her last summer at the lakehouse.

"This guy here is supposed to scare away the birds. Might as well give him a try. Maybe we can salvage some of the cherries that are coming in. You said they're almost ready to pick around now."

"I can't believe you thought to do that." She flashed a gorgeous smile. "Thank you."

She kept staring at the owl, seeming deeply moved by my gesture. It didn't take much to make her happy. That was one of the things I loved about her.

Whoa.

Calm the fuck down.

"I'll tell you what," she said. "If this works, I'll make you the biggest and best cherry pie to celebrate. I don't have a clue how to do that, Noah, but I'll learn. I will."

I started singing the Warrant song, "Cherry Pie."

"What's that song?" she asked.

"You've never heard that song? I thought you knew all the old songs from the nineties!"

"No. I must be slipping."

It dawned on me that I was in elementary school when that song came out, which meant Heather hadn't been born yet. Damn, that made me feel old. I pulled the song up on my phone and cranked the volume.

Heather started shaking her ass around in her short little shorts, and I pretended not to love every second of it.

The music stopped, and we went back to work on the gardening and landscaping.

After a long while, she dropped a bomb. "I have to tell you something. It's important. Well, two things. I might need you to stop working for a minute."

Her tone made me uneasy. "Yeah...let me put my hoe down."

"Don't talk to her like that," she joked.

"Very funny," I said, digging the hoe into the dirt to stand it up. "What's up?"

Heather licked her lips. "I'm going to talk to a realtor tomorrow, to get the process started, find out what things I need to do to put this place on the market."

My heart beat faster. I wasn't sure why. I was the one encouraging her to sell this place, but something about her really going through with it put me on edge. I knew she would miss it here and would probably never be ready to leave it behind. Heck, I would miss it here, and I hadn't grown up here.

"I think that's a good idea," I said, ignoring all my conflicted thoughts.

"The other thing is...I've been thinking a lot about some of the stuff we've been talking about—how precious these years are. There's something I haven't mentioned, but I didn't think I could make it a reality until recently..."

"Okay..."

"I applied to the University of Vermont. I got into their nursing program, but it would be for the spring semester.

I applied knowing I might not be able to go, but I got accepted anyway. I think I'm going to do it."

Wow.

As much as I'd hoped for this outcome for her, I wasn't expecting it to happen so soon.

"Heather, that's awesome. Truly. I'm so happy you're gonna finally do it."

Why does my chest hurt so badly, then?

"I just have to figure out the situation with my mother. I don't want her living alone. I want to talk to my aunt who lives outside of Boston to see if she would be willing to move here, or take Mom in, or at least look out for her. There's a lot to figure out before I can make this happen."

"Does Alice know about Vermont?"

"Not yet. I haven't told her, because I want to be completely sure it's going to happen first. Part of that is seeing what the realtor has to say about how easily she thinks we can sell the property. Summer is a good time to put it on the market, and I'll need that money to fund school. So, if she doesn't think it will sell, then—"

"Don't let that stop you."

"What do you mean?"

"I mean...I'll lend you the money to start school."

Offering Heather help was a no-brainer. I'd always been smart with my funds, even when I was traveling. I'd often stay in hostels instead of fancy hotels. The bottom line was, I could easily afford to lend it to her.

"I can't let you do that."

"I have a good amount of savings. It wouldn't be an issue to lend you whatever you need to get started. You could always pay me back when the sale goes through. It's not a big deal."

"What if the house doesn't sell?"

"It will."

Her mouth hung open. "Well, I don't even know what to say. I'm not too proud to accept your generosity if it comes to that, and I'm completely blown away that you would offer. Seriously, thank you."

"It's no skin off my back. The money is just sitting in the bank doing nothing."

"I hope I don't have to take advantage of it, but I really appreciate it."

"You're welcome."

A mix of emotions ran through me. I was so incredibly proud of her for taking this step. I was envious of all of the people who had yet to meet her, envious of the lucky bastard she would choose to spend her time with there. Most of all, I knew I would miss her. I'd miss her smile. I'd miss talking to her. I'd miss everything about her and this place.

After her news, things were quiet for a while as we returned to work. Then Heather snapped me out of my thoughts.

"Hey, can we take a quick ride?" she asked, checking her phone for the time. "I didn't realize how late it was, and I need your truck for something."

"You need to pick something up?"

"Yes. I need you to take me to the pet store. I don't have room in my car for everything."

"Everything?"

"I'm sort of rescuing a couple of guinea pigs. They come with a lot of baggage."

Chuckling, I said, "Guinea pigs have baggage?"

"Well, their cage is really big."

"You're seriously bringing them back here?"

"Yes."

"Do you think that's a good idea if you're gonna be leaving for school at some point?"

"We don't have a choice. The pet store is closing tomorrow for good, and my friend Trish says if no one takes them, they could end up being euthanized. I'll figure something out. But this will buy them more time."

"There's no one else who can take them in?"

"She said she can't find anyone. Trish already has three of them at home."

Heather's life was about to be in limbo. She needed this like a hole in the head, but she had a heart of gold, and I knew there would be no talking her out of this.

Brushing the dirt off my hands, I said, "Okay, let's go rescue some guinea pigs."

An hour later, I was thinking I needed my head examined for agreeing to this. Those pigs took up way more space than I'd ever imagined.

I'd helped her bring the animals upstairs and set up their massive cage in the corner of her room.

It was my first time inside Heather's bedroom, and it was just as soft and feminine as I'd imagined it to be. I was as tense being in here as I'd imagined I'd be, too.

My eyes wandered to the top shelf in her closet. There were bags upon bags of stacked candy corn packages.

"I take it you like candy corn?"

"Well, you have to stock up, otherwise you can't find them all year. I can't live without them. So I hit the sales at the end of Halloween."

"And buy out the whole store?"

"Pretty much." She laughed. "I never told you Halloween was my favorite holiday?"

"No. Although based on your penchant for horror movies, I should've known."

She was clicking away on her laptop, trying to find information about caring for her new pets. Neither one of us knew a thing about guinea pigs.

"There's so much I have to learn. It's overwhelming."

"Like what?"

"Well, for one...I don't think we have enough hay. This says if they don't have enough of it, it can lead to malocclusion."

"Malo-what?"

"It's a misalignment of their teeth. Without hay, their digestive tract also shuts down. They could die." She buried her head in her hands. "Holy crap. What did I get myself into?" She seemed to be panicking. "They eat lettuce and kale? I don't have any of that in the house. I assumed the pellets she gave us were their food. These guys are supposed to be eating good stuff." She went back to the screen for a moment. "Crap. It says you need a lid for the cage if you have other pets. What if Teddy tries something? What if he accidentally murders them?"

As if on cue, the dog entered the room and began barking at the cage. The guinea pigs trembled. This wasn't good.

"No, Teddy!" Heather shouted, steering the dog away from the cage. "I can't believe I never thought this through."

"You didn't know how Fathead was going to react."

She shook her head. "This was a mistake. I won't be able to sleep tonight."

Heather led the dog downstairs before returning to the room and sitting down on the bed.

She continued scrolling for information. "Their toenails have to be trimmed from time to time. It says here you could break a blood vessel doing it." She kept reading, seeming unable to look away.

I must have been out of my mind, but I said, "Tell you what, I'll take them over to the boathouse for tonight. That will solve the dog issue until we can get a top for the cage. I think I have a little romaine lettuce, too, that I use for my sandwiches."

"I feel awful making you do that. We just set everything up here and—"

"It's really no problem. I'll move everything over. Tomorrow we can get more hay and buy some greens and stuff. They'll be fine."

Heather looked like I'd lifted a huge load off of her chest. "Seriously...I don't know what I would do without you this summer. You've done more for me in the six weeks you've been here than my father has in my entire life. I feel like you keep saving my ass. I owe you so much."

Saving her ass wasn't exactly where my mind had been lately.

She stood up, walked over, and wrapped her arms around my neck. It caught me off guard, and my body stiffened. But rather than continue to tense up, I closed my eyes and let myself experience the comfort that holding her brought me. Nothing had felt this damn good in a long time. With my nose buried in her hair, I took a deep breath in. She smelled so good it was almost too much to bear. I knew she had to have felt my heart beating. *Christ.* Now I could feel my cock stiffening. This wasn't good.

I pulled back. "I'd better get everything packed up."

After I returned to the boathouse and got the guinea pigs settled in their cage on my floor, I decided to wash up after the long day of working outside.

I jerked off in the shower and came in a matter of seconds, proving how much I really needed to get laid. If that was going to happen, it sure as fuck couldn't be with Heather, so I'd better figure out a plan B. Holding her tonight had felt way better than it should have. I almost wished she'd never touched me. I hated that my mind wouldn't focus on anything besides her beautiful face and body while I beat myself off.

The guinea pigs—who had yet to be named—stared at me as I walked out of the bathroom. If I didn't know better, I would have thought they were judging me.

"What are you looking at?" I chuckled.

Their little mouths moved in sync as they chomped on some hay. It seemed I now had an audience.

"Don't be so judgey."

After I got dressed, I realized I still had a basket of laundry to put away from, like, a week ago. Heather had surprised me by folding it, and I'd forgotten to thank her for doing that.

As I put things away in my drawers, I stopped short when my fingers landed on black lace.

Well, this definitely isn't mine.

The shock of realizing I was holding Heather's panties caused my fingers to spring open. Like a hot potato, the underwear fell to the ground.

I bent down to pick it up, holding it in my hands while my dick swelled against my jeans. My fists closed over the material as I willed myself to throw them back into the basket.

Don't do it.

Against my better judgment, I gave in to the need to smell them. Bringing them to my nose, I breathed in the hint of her scent that remained.

I'm so fucked.

CHAPTER
NINE

Heather

I t was set to be a busy day, so I got up earlier than usual to get things done before I had to go to the realtor's office later in the morning.

As I sat by my bedroom window, sipping my coffee, I noticed someone walking onto the porch of the boathouse.

It was my slutty neighbor, Kira Shaw.

My heart nearly stopped.

Then she disappeared inside.

It felt like all of the blood in my body rushed to my head.

No.

He never let anyone in the boathouse.

Unless...

I paced for a while, unsure of what to do.

You can't control what he does, Heather.

You're just friends.

He can fuck anyone he wants.

He can do whatever he wants with his life, and it's none of your business.

What part of that don't you understand?

He's a man. He has needs. What do you expect? Like Mom said, men are weak.

My imagination ran wild. I pictured him pulling her inside before they started going at it on his bed.

Did you really expect him to be celibate the entire summer?

Oh my God. I was going to be sick.

I *had* to know. I had to know if it was true. No way could I go about my day like I hadn't seen her enter the boathouse.

My heart raced as I threw on some clothes. I wouldn't do anything, but I needed to confirm. I vowed not to embarrass myself or him by making my presence known. Those days were over. But I would see if I could tell what was going on. Then I would leave. I wouldn't subject myself to watching anything more than necessary to get my answer. I could just peek inside the window and be on my merry way.

Yeah right, as if it would be that easy to get over Noah fucking Kira Shaw—or anyone, for that matter. But especially her.

This is devastating.

A cool mist in the air and light morning fog greeted me as I stepped outside. My stomach churned as I approached the boathouse.

What if he'd drawn the shades and I couldn't see inside? Then what?

As I stepped onto the porch, I made sure they wouldn't hear me.

To my surprise, when I peeked in the window, the bed was empty.

Where are they?

The only other room was the bathroom, and there was only one thing they could be doing together in there. That made me feel even sicker. Now things were almost certainly not going to go in my favor.

My legs felt wobbly as I walked around to the bathroom window on the other side of the house.

It was slightly open, and the shade was only lowered halfway, so I was able to peek inside.

The water was running, and the shower curtain was closed.

They're showering together.

Holy shit.

I wanted to cry.

But I wouldn't.

I needed to be strong. Maybe this was just the thing I needed to help me get over him.

I wasn't going to want him after he'd been with her. This was going to change everything.

My heart palpitated as I stared at the embroidered butterflies on the white shower curtain and listened to the sound of the water.

Then, as if the situation couldn't get any worse, the sound of Noah's groaning echoed through the bathroom.

That should have been my cue to leave, but I stayed frozen at the window, consumed by curiosity. My shock had paralyzed me.

Suddenly, out of nowhere, the shower curtain whipped open.

The sight of a stark-naked Noah flashed before my eyes. A very naked—but alone—Noah. His body glistened, and let's just say everything I'd imagined about his anatomy was all that and more. He was freaking huge.

I gasped.

I hadn't meant to make a sound. It just came out.

Then I ran as fast as I could back to the house.

Had he seen me? I was certain he must have heard me, but maybe he didn't know it was me.

And who was he, Houdini? Where the hell was Kira?

I'd seen her enter the boathouse. He was groaning! Yet he was alone in the shower.

Back in my bedroom, I prayed I'd dodged a bullet, that by some miracle he hadn't seen me running away.

When my phone chimed a few minutes later, I got my answer.

Noah: Something you want to tell me?

Heather: It wasn't what it looked like.

Noah: Oh good. What a relief. Because it looked like you were spying on me in the shower.

Damn it!

Heather: I can explain.

Noah: I'm just putting some coffee on. This outta be good.

I took this as a hint that he wanted me to get my ass over there and explain myself, perhaps while he sat back and sipped coffee, enjoying the show of my humiliation.

Swallowing my pride, I walked back over to the boathouse to face the music.

As usual, he opened the door before I had the chance to knock.

Noah's hair was wet. He'd put on a gray T-shirt that stretched against his muscles. He wore jeans, and his feet were bare.

He was silent. All you could hear was the sound of coffee percolating. What struck me was the lack of amusement on his face. He looked seriously concerned for my mental health.

I couldn't blame him.

I wanted to run for the hills, but instead, I came right out with it. "I saw Kira Shaw here. I was looking out my window, and I saw you open the door and let her in."

His brow lifted. "You did, huh?"

"Yes, I swear."

"You sure you saw me open the door?"

"Yes. At least, I think I did, but now I'm wondering if I was hallucinating."

The coffee made that loud bubbling sound it always does when it's finished brewing. Noah sauntered over to the pot and poured some into a mug.

"Cream and sugar?"

"I'm good. I already had some. I've had my fill."

"Apparently, in your wild imagination, so have I this morning."

Jesus. I was truly doubting my sanity.

"Want some quiche?" he asked.

Quiche?

"What?"

"Quiche. It's this egg pie with—"

"I know what it is, but no, I'm not hungry."

"Oh, that's too bad... Because unbeknownst to me, Kira entered my place while I was in the shower and left me an entire quiche."

My eyes followed as he walked over to the quiche on the other side of the counter. I hadn't noticed it until now. There was a little note on top of the pie dish.

He handed it to me.

Noah,

I knocked and there was no answer. Your door was open. Thought I'd catch you, but you're in the shower. I considered waiting but didn't want to startle you. I made you a spinach, tomato, and feta quiche. Figured since you haven't taken me up on dinner, I'd bring breakfast to you. I hope you enjoy. The dinner offer still stands. Or anything else you might desire.

xoxo
Kira

Noah stared at me as I looked up at him.

Handing him the note, I said, "Okay. So, I overreacted."

"You think?"

"It just seemed so real. I mean...I saw her come in. I could have sworn you let her in. I know it's not any of my business, but I just had to know. And then I heard the shower. Then I heard *you*...making sounds."

He closed his eyes and spoke under his breath. "Fuck."

It occurred to me all of a sudden that the sound was *him*...masturbating. I'd been obsessed with the idea that he was having sex with Kira. And now I'd just admitted that I'd listened intently while he jerked off in the shower. *Great.* This morning just kept getting better and better.

"I assumed she was in there with you. I'm sorry. There's no excuse. I guess old habits die hard. I feel like such an idiot."

Noah looked at me for the longest time.

I expected him to scold me, but he didn't.

"Tell you what...how about you stop beating yourself up about this, and we pretend it never happened?"

"You're gonna let me off that easy? No ridicule? No scolding about how it's none of my damn business?"

"Well, that's true. But you've got a lot on your plate. I'm not gonna add to it. Let's just forget about it."

I blew out a sigh of relief. "That sounds really good to me."

Noah nodded and kept staring at me in silence. I felt like I needed to leave while I was ahead.

Pointing behind me toward the door, I said, "I'd better go. I have an appointment with the realtor this morning."

He nodded. "Good. Keep me posted."

"I will."

When I was almost out the door, he called to me.

"Hey."

I turned around. "Yeah?"

Noah stepped forward until he was right in front of me. My pulse quickened, and to my shock, he placed his hand on my cheek. It was the first time he'd ever touched me like this, and my nipples stood at attention as I closed my eyes and savored every second.

What's happening?

"I told you I wasn't interested in her," he finally said.

Too flustered to speak, I simply nodded. He slid his hand down my face, and his fingers grazed my neck.

And that was the end of it.

He walked over to his coffee and sipped it as if he hadn't just rocked my world.

I somehow made it out the door and floated all the way home, unsure what to think.

Later that day, on my way home from the realtor's office, I was still thinking about the way Noah's hand felt on my face, about his need to assure me he wasn't interested in Kira. It felt different than just a simple admission for some reason. My body tingled at the memory of his touch and his words.

Now that I'd spoken to the real estate agent, I felt more confident about putting the house on the market. The next step was to break the news to my mother that this sale was happening. I wasn't sure if I was ready to tackle the Vermont conversation yet, so I decided to play it by ear.

Mom was in her room when I got home.

I sat at the corner of the bed and squeezed her feet through the floral bedspread. The shades were down, and it was dark.

She sat up against the headboard. "How did it go?"

"She says she thinks we should list it soon. The middle of the summer season will be the best time to show it because of the weather. She also thinks we should list it for between 800 and 900 grand."

My mother blinked a few times as she processed the information. "That's more than I thought."

"I know. Me, too. But she seems confident we can get close to asking."

"It all sounds too good to be true."

"You mean the listing price?"

"What aren't you telling me, Heather? You've been acting strange. Does it have to do with Noah?"

"No. Nothing has changed with Noah."

Except for the fact that he touched my face and made me forget my own name for half the day.

"But there *is* something…" she said.

I sighed. "Yes."

"What is it?"

It was now or never. I needed to tell her.

"So, um…remember I was telling you about the nursing program at the University of Vermont, and we talked about how nice Burlington is and all that?"

"Yes."

"Well, some time ago, I decided to bite the bullet and apply." I hesitated. "I got in. It's for the spring semester, though. So it wouldn't be right away."

She clutched her chest as if that news physically pained her.

"Are you alright?" I asked.

"I knew this was coming. I just…"

"I hope you know how hard this is for me. I promise not to go unless you're settled. You won't be alone. I will make sure of it. I've been talking to Aunt Katy…"

"Katy? You're gonna pawn me off on my flighty sister?"

"Katy may be flighty, but she loves you. She seems willing to move out here. She can do her art from anywhere. She said she wants to do this for me. It's a sacrifice for her, but she's willing to do it, and I'm extremely grateful. You have to be open to it."

My mother's sister, Katy, had been going through a messy divorce for the past few years. Now that everything was finally settled, she had the option to move. Katy was an oil painter who sold her work to small galleries across New England.

"I can live on my own," my mother said.

"We've already had this discussion. It's not that I don't think you could live on your own most days, but you need to be around people. You need to have someone looking out for you even on days when you don't need it. And there's no way I would leave you alone, because some days you *do* need it, so there's that."

"I can't stop you from going. I know that. I've kept you here long enough."

My eyes began to water. "It's really hard for me to think about leaving."

She reached her hand out to me. "I know. You're a good girl...my angel."

"We still have plenty of time. And thanks to Noah, it's looking like we might actually be able to sell this place. So everything is going according to plan."

We were quiet for a bit. Then she said, "Noah really has turned out to be a godsend, hasn't he?"

"I'm glad you've learned to trust him, Mom."

"I might trust him, but I still think he has feelings for you."

"I'm not sure what you're basing that on."

Actually, today was the first day I'd thought she could be right. But I wasn't a hundred-percent convinced I wasn't reading into things too much. He'd touched my cheek, not my clit, for heaven's sake. Maybe he'd just seen that I was upset with myself and was trying to make me feel better. Still, my gut told me there was something to the electricity I felt when he touched me, even if it *was* just my face.

"You do know you two have been gardening right outside my bedroom window, right? I've listened to your conversations. He genuinely likes you."

"He likes me, yes, but not in that way. He likes me like a little sister."

"No way I'm buying that, Heather. He might have chosen not to act on it, and in many ways, I commend him for that. But he most definitely has feelings for you."

What was wrong with me that hearing her say that gave me goosebumps? *Am I delusional?* Was this entire day one big hallucination? Even if Noah were developing feelings for me and somehow made it known *today*, he was leaving, and now so was I.

Besides, I still didn't think Noah would ever cross that line.

"You know...he's divorced," I said.

"Really? Some stupid woman let that man go?"

"I know, right?" I chuckled. "He takes a lot of the blame for their marriage ending. He said he put his career first a lot in his twenties and neglected their relationship. He recognizes his mistakes, though, and I have a feeling the lucky woman who nabs him next is going to reap the benefits of that."

That evening at Jack Foley's Pub, I was busy obsessing over Noah when an old, familiar face turned up in my section.

He seemed happy to see me. "Heather?"

It was a guy I'd gone to high school with, one I hadn't seen in a few years. He was one year ahead of me.

"Oh my God...Jared!" I hugged him.

Jared Mackenzie had always been smart, and everyone was super impressed when he'd gotten into Harvard.

"It's so good to see you," he said.

"You, too. You don't usually come home for the summer, do you? I haven't seen you since you graduated."

He frowned. "My father is sick, so I'm not working the usual summer job I keep in Cambridge."

"I'm sorry to hear that."

"Yeah, lung cancer."

My stomach dropped. "That's tough. I'm really sorry."

That reminded me things could always be worse. My mother was severely depressed, but at least she was physically healthy.

"It's been a rough summer, but running into you tonight is a nice surprise."

"Likewise." I smiled. "So, what's it like to be almost finished with school? One more year, right?"

"Yeah. It's surreal how fast time flies. I hope to stay in Boston for grad school. So, it'll be a while before I have to face the real world and find a job."

"What's your major again?"

"Neuroscience. I'd like to become a medical researcher."

"Right. I remember it being something easy." I winked and caught myself twirling my hair, which I often did when I was feeling flirtatious.

Jared laughed. "Listen, I've pretty much been sitting by my dad's bedside every day, and at night I just need a breather. I haven't wanted to hang out with the people from school or go drinking. But I would love to go somewhere and talk—have a good conversation and a good meal. Would you want to hang out sometime?"

I was surprised, but I couldn't find one reason to say no. "That would be great."

"Can I admit something?" he asked.

"Sure."

"When I heard you and Eric broke up, I might have done a little fist pump."

I covered my mouth. "Really?"

"I also might have had a pretty intense crush on you in high school, but you were always taken."

My heart fluttered. "I would've never known that. You were always so busy playing lacrosse or with your nose buried in books. I never sensed anything."

"You didn't have me pegged as a nerd, did you?"

"No. Just the opposite. I think intelligence is amazingly sexy."

Pipe down.

After I took his order, we exchanged numbers. Maybe a date with Jared would be exactly what I needed. He'd be going back to Cambridge, so there wouldn't be any obligation to continue things beyond the summer. And Lord knows, I needed a distraction from Noah. It would do me good to redirect my focus toward someone else.

CHAPTER
TEN

Noah

L ater that week, I was working outside Heather's house when a man I didn't recognize approached me. He was probably in his early fifties. My guard immediately went up.

"Can I help you?" I asked.

"I'm here to see my daughter. Who are you?"

This is Heather's father?

"I'm Noah Cavallari. I've been renting the boathouse."

He held out his hand. "Rick Chadwick."

I wiped the dirt off my palms and shook his hand. "Good to meet you."

Rick was stocky and wearing an oversized, brown Members Only-type jacket. If I weren't a big guy myself, I might have been intimidated by the way he was looking at me.

At that moment, Heather opened the door. "Hey, Dad."

"Hi, darling."

She looked between us. "I see you've met Noah."

"Briefly, yes."

Heather turned to me. "My father is in town for a couple of days."

I remembered she'd said her dad did a yearly visit.

It would've been nice if she'd given me some warning.

"Would you want to join us for dinner tonight, Noah?"

What am I supposed to say? "I don't want to intrude."

Rick intervened. "No intrusion at all. I'd prefer to get to know the man spending so much time on the property."

Great.

"See you at seven," Heather said before disappearing inside the house with him.

Had I missed the part where I'd said yes?

As I continued to work outside, my phone vibrated.

Heather: I'm sorry I didn't say anything about him coming. I didn't know until this morning. He wasn't supposed to visit until the fall. He sprung this on me. I think it's because he heard we're selling the house. He's against it.

This was going to be a real fun fucking dinner. A hoot.

Noah: I'm not sure I should be joining you.

Heather: I would appreciate your company. I feel like I need a buffer tonight.

How could I refuse that?

Noah: Okay. Can I bring something?

Heather: Do you even have to ask what to bring? ;-)

Noah: I'll pick up some garlic bread. Anything else you need?

Heather: New parents? LOL

Noah: They don't sell those at Stop and Shop.

Heather: See you at 7.

I smiled.

Noah: K.

The fact that Heather's father stayed at a hotel when they had this huge house with a couple of guest rooms really spoke volumes about the nature of his relationship with Heather and Alice.

When I arrived for dinner, it surprised me to see Alice out and about in the kitchen with Heather. It was as if she knew her daughter needed her. Somehow, she'd been able to get her shit together tonight.

Rick and I sat at the kitchen table as Heather and her mother chopped vegetables for the salad. He'd brought a six-pack of Corona and offered me one. I gladly partook. Anything to take the edge off this situation.

Heather and Alice refused my numerous offers to help, and I noticed Rick hadn't even offered once. So far, the only good thing about this guy seemed to be the striking blue eyes he'd passed on to Heather.

His voice startled me. "Noah, what is it exactly that you do?"

"I'm a photographer."

Heather looked over at us. "Noah is amazing. He's traveled the world and covered a lot of big events. You should see his website."

Rick didn't seem like he was buying what Heather was selling. "If you have such a great life, why would you want to spend the summer on Lake Winnipesaukee?"

His question pissed me off. I didn't like the way he'd said that, as if there was nothing of value here.

"Just looking for a change of pace."

"Actually, Noah's handiwork is the reason we're able to put the house on the market. He's been a big help," Heather said.

Rick gave me the stink eye. "Is that so…"

I couldn't figure out why he wasn't in favor of the sale.

Dinner was finally served. Heather had made a meatloaf that was really tasty. The way the ketchup cooked into the top of the meat reminded me of the way my mother used to make it.

She sat next to me, seeming really tense.

I leaned into her. "Good job on the meatloaf. It's delicious."

She smiled. "Thank you."

For the longest time, it was a quiet and awkward meal with clanking silverware the only sound. Her damn father hadn't said a thing as he scarfed down the food. I kept sane by sneaking bits of my meal to Fathead, who was hanging out by my feet.

Alice also looked very stressed. I had to say, I was

kind of proud of her. I knew it couldn't have been easy. Heather had told me she still had a lot of hang-ups about the divorce.

We hadn't even gotten halfway through dinner when Rick said, "So, we need to talk about this plan to sell the house."

Heather set her fork down and wiped her mouth. "What is there to talk about?"

"You know how I feel about this. It's not the right time. The market hasn't hit its peak, and I think you're going to be losing a shit ton of money if you don't wait."

"The realtor doesn't seem to think it's a bad time."

"What does she know? She wants to make a quick buck. You can't trust what she says."

"It doesn't matter if it's not the perfect time. We need to sell. I can't handle the upkeep anymore. I need the money for school."

"Why can't you take out loans like everyone else?"

"Well, I plan to continue working to help pay my tuition, but I don't want to have loans hanging over my head for the rest of my life. Plus, Mom has always said when the house sold, I could use some of the money for school."

"When did you even decide on school?"

"I was going to mention it. I got into the University of Vermont's nursing program. I plan to start in the spring semester."

I knew Heather didn't see her father often, but it was also becoming clear he was the last to know anything going on with her.

"When were you planning to tell me?"

"The next time I saw you, which is now. It's only recently become a possibility."

"Do you really think it's a good idea to abandon your mother?"

My fists curled into balls. I wanted to punch him. He was pushing this guilt on her when he was the one who'd abandoned *them*?

"I'm fine," Alice insisted.

"You don't look fine. You seem worse than you were the last time I saw you."

"Aunt Katy is moving here," Heather announced.

"Katy? She's gonna look after your mother? She can't even take care of herself. You're gonna leave so you can study how to take care of sick people when your mother is sicker than them all?"

Alice trembled. "Stop!"

Heather clenched her jaw. "Why do you even care about anything that happens here?"

I couldn't take it anymore. I had to speak up.

"With all due respect, Rick, I don't think you're being fair. Heather has done nothing but take good care of her mother for several years. It's time for her to have some freedom."

"With all due respect to *you*, I don't need to sit here and listen to someone who literally blew in like the wind five minutes ago. You don't know anything about this family."

"As of late? I guarantee I know more than you do."

"You have no right to an opinion here."

Heather intervened, "Well, you lost your right to an opinion the day you walked out on us."

"This house is half mine," he said. "I do have an opinion."

"What are you talking about? This house is Mom's."

"Alice? You want to break the news to our daughter?"

Heather looked confused as she turned to her mother. "What's going on?"

Alice was shaking as she looked at Rick. "You bastard. You promised you wouldn't go after that money."

Heather looked between them. "What are you talking about?"

"After your grandfather died, he left the house to your mother," Rick said. "But during our divorce proceedings, it was determined that when the property sold, I would get half of the money."

My heart sank.

Heather turned toward her mother. "Is this true?"

Alice looked like she wanted to disappear. "Technically, it is, but your father assured me some years back that he would sign over his rights to us if we ever had to sell, that he wouldn't take any of that money because he didn't feel he was entitled to it. This is the first I'm hearing that he seems to think he has a right to half of my father's house."

"Things have changed," he said. "My financial situation isn't what it used to be. My company is going under, and I'm going to need that money after all. It wasn't my intention to have to take advantage of it, but I'm afraid I do. Although, as I've said, I think waiting for the market to strengthen in a couple more years would be wise."

"Are you kidding me right now?" Heather cried. "You've made plenty of money, and you're so cheap, I bet you have a heap of savings. The money from this house is the only future we have. This house belonged to *her* father. *Her* name is on the deed, not yours. You abandoned us years ago. What right do you have to anything you left behind?"

"Well, you may not believe I deserve it, but the fact remains that I do have the *legal* right to half."

My blood boiled. I'd never wanted to annihilate anyone so much in my life.

Heather looked ready to collapse, and Alice's face was turning white.

Without thinking it through, I reached for Heather's hand under the table. I wanted her to know I had her back, that everything would be okay despite what her father was trying to pull.

Heather squeezed my hand as she spoke to him.

"We thought we lost everything when you left. But that was nothing compared to losing Opal. All we've been trying to do is get back on our feet ever since, to rise up from the guilt and pain. We've survived thus far, and we can handle anything else life throws at us. So if you want half the house, take it. We'll survive without it."

The room went quiet. I broke the silence when I couldn't hold my words in any longer.

"I've spent more quality time here in the past several weeks than you have in years. I see how hard your daughter works, not only to take care of her mother, but to make sure everything else gets done around here. You couldn't possibly understand what their life is like if you only come around once a year. A lot of bad shit has happened, but she still gets up every day and does the best that she can, keeps her mother alive and well and keeps this house running.

She's your daughter, and she's never asked you for one goddamn thing, least of all your love. All she's asking is that you keep out of what's not rightfully yours, so she can live her life. If you're legally entitled to something, I suppose you can take it. But you can never get back your daughter's trust."

I looked over at Heather and she mouthed, "Thank you." I grasped her hand tighter. I just wanted to protect her.

She let go of me and stood up. "I need to be by myself for a while."

She took off up the stairs, and Teddy followed her, leaving me alone with her parents. I needed to get out of here.

"Thank you for dinner, Alice," I said as I got up, refusing to even look at Rick.

I made my way out the door, getting angrier by the second as I walked back to the boathouse.

CHAPTER
ELEVEN

Heather

It took me a few hours before I had the energy to come out of my room. My father had gone back to western Massachusetts. He'd texted to let me know. His leaving didn't surprise me. After what he'd pulled, I didn't want to see him, and he was smart enough to figure that out. I wondered if he planned to take that money or if it was an empty threat to keep us from selling now. I suspected he had every intention of taking it.

My mother was back in bed, probably totally mentally exhausted, just as I was. I needed to check in on her before I went over to Noah's to thank him for standing up for me. When he'd reached for my hand under the table, I'd grabbed it like a lifeline.

Mom sat up in her bed when she noticed me at the doorway. "I'm so sorry I never told you about the divorce settlement. He assured me he wouldn't come after that money."

"It's not your fault," I said, rubbing her legs.

"Even if he takes half, there's still plenty for your schooling. It will be tight, but we can manage. Promise me you won't let this stop you."

I nodded. "I have to rethink things. Maybe I'll take out some loans."

Her eyes flitted back and forth as she seemed to search for a solution. "I have lots of jewelry from your grandmother. I'll sell it."

"I just can't believe he's putting us in this position. I never thought he'd do something like this."

"Your father has always been a selfish man. I've tried not to badmouth him too much over the years or taint your view of him...but this doesn't really surprise me at all."

"His actions have always proven his selfishness," I said. "I'd forgiven him for abandoning us. I'm not sure I can forgive him for this, though. It's one thing to not give us anything. It's another to take from us."

"I'm so sorry, honey."

Picking some lint off her bedspread, I asked, "How long did Noah stay after I went upstairs?"

"He left right after you went to your room."

I couldn't blame him. I'd left him alone in the middle of a shit storm.

"I can't believe how he stood up to Dad."

"He's very fond of you."

"I need to go thank him."

"Bring him the dessert we never ate. It's the least we can do."

I'd love to give him more than that tonight.

Carrying the chocolate cake, I walked carefully over to the boathouse.

As I approached, a flicker of a flame caught my eye; Noah was on the porch smoking a cigar.

When he spotted me, he stood. "Are you okay?"

"I am. Sit. I'm just gonna grab two forks so we can have some cake." I entered his kitchen and grabbed the utensils.

When I returned, he said, "It's a no-plates-needed kind of night, huh?"

"Yes." I spoke with my mouth full. "Have some. Don't make me feel like a pig."

"Fine. You twisted my arm." Noah dug in. "Did he leave?"

"I guess he left shortly after you did. He went back to Massachusetts."

"Good."

I stuck my fork in the cake. "Thank you for standing up for me."

"Please tell me what he pulled isn't going to deter you."

"No. It won't. I don't care what I have to do. I'll make it work."

He stopped eating for a moment. "I hope you don't take offense to this, but I wanted to kill your father tonight."

I sighed. "I can relate." Looking up at the starry sky, I said, "You know, Opal used to ask me how I could forgive him so easily for leaving us. I never could come up with an answer that pleased her. But the truth was, for me, it wasn't that complicated. He's my father, and therefore I've always loved him—maybe when I shouldn't have. All I ever wanted was his love and support. He never gave us anything but the bare minimum required by law. That didn't matter to me, because I just craved his attention.

It's not the money, you know? It's the message that his wanting to take it sends. It's the realization that I don't mean as much to him as I thought I did." A tear fell from my eye.

Noah reached out and wiped it with his thumb. "He's a fool. You deserve so much better than that. He doesn't even know you. That much was clear to me."

"Well, I never really let him in."

"Don't make excuses for him. It's not your fault. He's the parent. You're the child. It's his responsibility to make you feel safe and loved, and he's doing a damn shitty job. He doesn't realize how lucky he is to have you. My father would've killed to have a daughter like you."

I rubbed my eyes and smiled. "Really?"

"Yeah. He ended up with two cruddy sons, but he always wanted a little girl."

"He can adopt me." I laughed. "Nah. Then I'd have an awkward crush on my stepbrother. That would be weird."

He closed his eyes for a moment.

"I'm kidding," I said. *I wasn't.*

Noah dipped his finger in the chocolate frosting and dabbed it on the tip of my nose.

Once again, a point in time with him had become my happiest moment of the day.

CHAPTER
TWELVE

Noah

I was becoming more cognizant of the fact that my time at the lake was limited. The property was officially on the market, and today the very first potential buyers were taking a tour.

I ended up clearing the entire kitchen table so I could get the guinea pig cage off the floor. Their cage was a little unsightly for visitors, but they were damn cute. I never had brought them back to Heather's. I was probably crazy for taking them in permanently, but I was growing attached to their little rodent asses.

I'd told Heather to let me know when someone was coming to see the property, that I could leave the boathouse during the showings. So when she'd called me earlier to tell me someone had made an appointment, I took a ride to a local discount furniture store to kill time.

One of the things missing from the boathouse was a place for people to sit. I thought it might look nice for potential buyers if there was a small sofa there—something other than just the bed to make the space seem like a home, rather than a glorified bedroom. There was barely space for anything else, but there was just enough room to make it work if I moved the bed a certain way. It also crossed my mind that one of the main reasons I never invited Heather inside was because there was no comfortable place for us to sit together except for the bed. By adding a piece of furniture, I could invite her inside without it feeling awkward.

I picked up a small loveseat from the furniture store and loaded it in the back of my truck.

By the time I returned to the boathouse, the showing was over. I could tell they had already been inside because a chair was misplaced.

"How did it go?" I asked the guinea pigs.

I grabbed some chopped cucumbers from the fridge and fed my furry friends with chopsticks. That was always calming for me.

Afterward, I went back out to the truck and set the loveseat up in the corner of the room, right across from the television.

Plopping myself down on it, I remembered it was Heather's night off. I wondered if I should ask her if she wanted to come over and watch a movie.

Why does the thought of that make my pulse race?

Ever since the morning I'd caught her snooping on me, I hadn't been able to shake it. As crazy and inappropriate as the whole thing was, her little voyeur act had made it into my fantasies several times since. I couldn't step into the shower anymore without imagining her outside that window, listening in or even watching while I took care of business. The whole thing was kind of freaky to begin with, because while she had thought I was screwing Kira in the shower that morning, I'd actually been getting off to thoughts of *her*. Pretty freaking ironic.

I'd almost messed up that day, too. Though I wasn't going to act on my impulses, I somehow needed her to understand she didn't need to worry about me and Kira. As fucked-up as it may sound, even if I had an interest in Kira—which I didn't—I would never do anything to hurt Heather while I was here.

I had needed her to know that, and in the process, I'd lost control of my feelings when I touched her—a poor judgment call that likely confused her. I'd been trying lately to act as "normal" as possible to reverse whatever mixed signals I'd sent her that day. Part of that meant not avoiding her or acting any differently. So I suppose that could be an argument in *favor* of inviting her over for a movie tonight.

After a half-hour of going back and forth about it, I picked up the phone and dialed her.

"Hey, Noah," she answered.

"You around tonight?"

"Yeah. What's up?"

Why am I sweating?

"You feel like watching a movie?"

"That's strange..." she said.

"What's strange?"

"You're inviting me inside the boathouse. You never do that."

No shit.

"Well, I have a spot we can sit now."

"What do you mean?"

Rubbing my temple, I said, "I bought a small couch." I intentionally refrained from using the word *loveseat*.

"You did?"

"I figured it would be nice to have one. You know…for the showings."

Right.

For the showings.

There was one reason and one reason alone why I'd bought this damn couch, and it had nothing to do with comfort. I wanted more time with her before we went our separate ways. Some nights, it was too muggy to sit outside with all the mosquitos. Even if we couldn't have more than this platonic friendship, I wanted to be around her for the short amount of time we had left. She made me happy.

"You didn't have to do that."

"It's fine. I got it for a steal."

"Well, yeah, a movie sounds great. Can Teddy come? He's been standing by the door wagging his tail. I think he wants to see you."

"Yeah, Fathead can come, too."

The dog had been to the boathouse a couple of times since the guinea pigs' arrival. It seemed he no longer cared about them because the barking had ceased.

"Okay. We'll be right there," she said.

The moment I opened the door, I regretted asking her over. Heather looked beautiful—too beautiful to be merely watching a movie. She wore a pink dress with spaghetti straps that left little to the imagination; her nipples pointed through the fabric.

Christ. This is a bad idea.

"Why are you all dressed up?" I asked as the dog jumped all over me.

"It's my first formal invitation inside the boathouse. I figured it was a special occasion." She laughed. "No. I was at a baby shower for one of the waitresses earlier. They held it in the back room at Jack Foley's."

Relieved, I nodded. "I see."

She ran over to the new sofa and sat down. "I love it. It's so plush and comfy!"

Her dress rode up a little as she lay her willowy legs across the length of the loveseat. She was graceful even when casually lounging around.

Yeah. Not sure what I was smoking, thinking having her here like this was going to be okay.

Fathead raced over to join her.

"Teddy approves, too," she said as she sat up to make room for him. "What are you in the mood for?"

Going down on you.

I swallowed. "What do you mean?"

"What do you want to watch?"

"Oh...haven't really thought about it. What about you?"

"Something light and funny without sex so I don't blush watching it with you." She laughed.

Damn good idea.

"Alright."

But as she sat there enjoying the new piece of furniture, I couldn't take my eyes off her. Those nipples piercing through her dress taunted me. How I wanted to bite into them, taste her skin. *What's wrong with me?* I normally had better control over my thoughts—maybe not in the shower, but at least in her presence. Tonight, though, I couldn't seem to stop them. Maybe holding everything in for so long had finally made me crazy. I imagined her spread eagle beneath me, screaming in pleasure as I rammed into her tight, little pussy. I imagined my cock down her throat. I imagined my tongue in her asshole while I rubbed her clit and brought her to orgasm over and over. Licking my lips, I could feel myself getting hard. I needed to refocus my brain before she noticed.

When she seemed to catch me staring, I pulled a question out of my ass. "Is that your natural hair color?"

What the heck did I just say?

"Yeah. My father had blond hair before he lost it all. I get it from him." Her eyes narrowed. "Why do you ask?"

"No reason. It's nice."

"Thanks."

We ended up choosing some Reese Witherspoon movie. Even though Heather was looking at the screen, she seemed preoccupied. I knew that, of course, because I still couldn't take my damn eyes off her.

She nearly caught me again when she suddenly turned to me. "Are you sure I'm doing the right thing?"

I sat up straighter and lowered the volume a little. "About selling the house?"

"Yeah. Now that people are starting to look, it's getting so real."

"You don't have to sell if you really don't want to, but I do think it's best for your future."

"We'll never get it back. You know?"

"You'll always have the memories. Happiness shouldn't be about a particular place anyway. It should be something you take with you everywhere you go—transferable. If you really miss it, you can always visit the lake. It'll always be here."

"*You* won't be here."

My eyes widened. "No, I won't."

She stared long and hard into my eyes before asking, "Are *you* happy, Noah?"

Heather had been trying to figure out my deal since the moment I moved in. Maybe I could afford to open up to her a little.

"I'm working on it. Being here has been good for that. It's been exactly what I needed."

"You needed to work your ass off for no pay?" she teased.

"I've gotten plenty out of it. Believe me."

She turned her body toward me and rested her head on her hand. "Are you ever gonna tell me what you're running from?"

Heather had really good intuition. But she was wrong in thinking I was running away from something. Whenever we spent time together, I was tempted to tell her the truth, but I was never quite sure it was the right thing to do.

"Why do you assume I'm running? Maybe I needed to run *toward* something else. I was looking for a change of pace, something different—and I found it here."

"You were looking for something profound, and you got me instead?" She smiled.

She had no clue how much she'd changed me.

"It wasn't until I got here that I realized *why* I was here. Something outside of myself sent me here to help you. I truly believe that. I feel like once I leave, my job will be done. I've helped set you on the right path."

I'm a better person when I'm around you.

Heather didn't seem satisfied with my answers. "What about you? I sell the house, go away to college, start my new life. What happens to you?"

I blew out a breath. "I go back to my life in Pennsylvania. Taking photo assignments. Looking after my father. I don't really know what's next for me. But I'll go back home feeling more fulfilled because I was here."

She nodded slowly. "I really like you, Noah." Her face turned red. "I don't mean that in the way I did when we first met, so don't worry. I really like *you*. You try to remain a mystery, but I can see right through you—to your heart. You show people with your actions what kind of a person you are. You live your life with purpose, just like I try to. I think that's probably the biggest thing we have in common."

"I can agree with that."

"I can also tell you live with a lot of regret. I can sense it. Whatever guilt you're carrying around—about who you were in the past, the mistakes you made with your ex-wife, whatever it may be—let it go, because you deserve better than to live like that."

Her words both healed me and amped up the guilt inside of me all at once. *She doesn't know everything.* "I'll try. Thank you."

She looked over at the television and joked, "Well, this was a good movie."

"It was for the first five minutes when I was paying attention." I chuckled.

Heather looked back at me. "I like talking to you better."

"I like talking to you, too. We're definitely good at that."

We're good together.

That realization stung, because *being* together wasn't a possibility.

131

Our eyes lingered. Fuck, if I didn't want to kiss her. Her skin was so soft and flushed. I wished I could have bit into it and watched it change color some more. It felt like she could see right through me. I wondered if my feelings for her were obvious.

She looked down at the sofa and rubbed her hands along the fabric. "This was a really nice gesture. Thank you."

"I'll take it back to Pennsylvania with me, so you don't have to worry about moving it." I rubbed the dog's head. "Fathead seems to really like it."

Teddy was out like a light.

"Either that or he's asleep because we bored him to death."

When the feelings creeping up inside of me felt like they were becoming too transparent, I stood up and said, "I almost forgot, I bought some bread. Want me to heat it up?"

"That sounds yummy. Yeah."

I couldn't go past the bakery in the supermarket anymore without buying a loaf of garlic bread.

Slicing some pieces, I said, "Bonnie and Clyde always look pissed when I'm making real food."

Heather looked perplexed. "Bonnie and Clyde?"

"The guinea pigs. I finally named them."

"Aw, that's so cute."

"Yeah, but they get angry when they see me eating—especially meat."

"They're bitter vegans." She laughed.

We ate the bread in comfortable silence as Fathead continued to sleep.

For a moment, I considered asking her why she'd left her panties in my damn laundry a couple of weeks ago. But then I'd have to admit what I did with them and why she'd never get them back.

The following afternoon, while Heather was at work, Alice let me into the main house to fix a few things. The last window that needed to be replaced was the one in Heather's room. I hadn't told her I would be coming in to do this work today, so I hoped she wouldn't be mad when she found out I'd been in her bedroom.

It took me about an hour to put the window in. After I finished cleaning up, I was headed out when I tripped over her bedside table, knocking a notebook to the ground. When I picked it up, I noticed my name written amongst a bunch of other words.

I couldn't stop thinking about Noah all day. It was hot out, so I decided to sneak over to the boathouse to use the outdoor shower. After taking off my clothes, I let the water stream down on me. My backside was fully exposed.

When I heard footsteps, I covered my chest and turned around to find Noah standing there. I expected him to yell at me for sneaking into his outdoor shower. Instead, he said nothing, just flipped me around so my ass was facing him. I could feel how hard he was as he—

"Noah?"

I dropped the notebook at the sound of Alice's voice coming down the hall.

I was panting. "Yes?" I moved quickly to the window. I had to hide the erection I was sporting thanks to Heather's little porn diary. I hadn't even gotten to the good part, and I was hard as a rock.

"Are you finished in here?" she asked from the doorway.

I pretended to be trying the window out, opening and closing it, as I turned only my head toward her. "Just finishing up now."

"I need to talk to you about something important when you're done."

"Sure. I'll meet you downstairs?"

"Yes. That's fine."

After I heard her at the bottom of the stairs, I picked up the notebook and put it back on the table. Despite how curious I was about the rest of the story, I was clearly never meant to see it. It was better that I didn't read any more. Anyway, I was pretty sure how it was going to end. And that would torment me all night.

Fuck, Heather. Seriously? You're trying to kill me.

After visiting the bathroom to talk down my hard-on, I went downstairs to find out what Alice wanted.

Still flustered as all hell, I found her in the kitchen. "What's up?" I asked.

Her expression made me a little uneasy. "It's about Heather."

Shit.

"What about Heather?"

"Tomorrow is her twenty-first birthday."

Oh. Wow. Wasn't expecting that.

"Really? She never mentioned it."

"She doesn't talk about her birthday. She tries to forget it."

"Why?"

She looked away. "It's also the day her sister died."

No. My heart broke in two.

"Anyway...this is a big birthday for her," Alice said. "I wish I felt up to doing something, but I don't know how to celebrate it without upsetting her. She's been particularly off since her father's visit, too. I wanted you to know in case you can think of anything that might brighten her day. I know she won't tell you. Heather stopped celebrating her birthday when...you know."

"Thank you for telling me. I'll definitely try to come up with something."

After Alice thanked me for my work and went back to her room, I went home, but I couldn't stop thinking about what she'd said. The fact that Heather's sister had died on her birthday haunted me.

If Heather didn't want to celebrate her birthday, I couldn't make her. At the same time, her twenty-first would only come around once. She'd never get it back.

I had to try.

CHAPTER
THIRTEEN

Heather

Noah: Meet me in the lake.

I had to look twice to make sure it was actually Noah sending me this message.

Heather: IN the lake?

Noah: Yes. IN the lake. Wear a bathing suit and meet me in the lake across from the boathouse.

Did he really mean *in the water,* or was I misinterpreting? I hadn't seen Noah Cavallari so much as dip his toes in the lake since the day he thought I was drowning.

In any case, I needed to know what this was all about, so I did as he asked. Rummaging through my drawers, I couldn't decide which bikini to wear. I normally didn't overthink such things, but the man I had a massive crush on had just demanded that I get into a bathing suit. I couldn't lose this opportunity to make him sweat.

Today was a sucky day—as all my birthdays had been since Opal died. I'd stayed in my room most of the morning, sipping tea and reading. This message definitely changed my outlook.

After slipping on my favorite black bikini, I flew out the front door and ran toward the lake, still wondering why Noah wanted me to meet him there.

When I saw him, he waved frantically to me from the waist-deep water. Then he started dancing.

What the?

He swayed his hips and pumped his fists, and it was the most ridiculous yet adorable thing I'd ever seen a man of his size do. He was totally mocking my water aerobics, but it was hysterical.

As I approached, I noticed he was holding a bottle of champagne.

"Why are you dancing?" I shouted.

He stopped moving and lifted the bottle into the air. "We're celebrating your birthday."

What? How does he know? "Who told you?"

"Never mind. I have my ways." He waved. "Get over here."

His demanding tone made my pulse speed up as I trudged through the water to get to him.

"I can't believe you didn't tell me you were turning twenty-one today," he said.

"There's a reason I don't—"

"I know."

He knows? "Did my mother tell you?"

"Yeah. She did. So you don't need to explain any of it. Today is not gonna be about sad stuff." He handed me the two glasses he'd been holding. "Take these." He unwrapped the foil covering on the bottle. I smiled when he stuck the trash in the waistband of his shorts rather than litter.

"It's your twenty-first fucking birthday, Heather. It's not okay to let this day pass you by. You only have one twenty-first birthday in your entire life."

Without further ado, Noah popped open the bottle of champagne, which sort of exploded onto his bare chest. "Well, that didn't exactly go as planned."

We both got a good laugh, and then he licked some off of his arm. He looked so sexy as he flashed a crooked smile with champagne dripping down his body. I so badly wanted to lick that champagne off of his chest and abs. And that was just for starters...

He took the flutes back and poured me a glass, then poured himself one as well.

"This feels surreal. You're serving me alcohol."

"Well, you're legal now." He winked.

"Wow. I really am, aren't I?"

"Cheers." He smiled.

We clinked our glasses together, and I took a sip of the bubbly. It was ice cold and delicious.

I looked over at a boat in the distance, and when I turned back to Noah, he moved his eyes quickly away. I'd caught him red-handed looking down at my breasts. That made me feel damn good. *Nice work, black bikini.*

"Were you really gonna pretend this was just another day?" he asked.

"Yes. I was," I said.

I specifically didn't make plans, specifically didn't want to celebrate my life when my sister had lost hers on this day.

"Well, not anymore. Not this year."

"Is this what I have to do to get you in the water? Turn another year older?"

"Pretty much. Otherwise I only jump in when I have to save people from their own bad dancing."

"You were so mad at me that day. Talk about getting off on the wrong foot. I'm glad that happened, though."

His brow lifted. "Yeah?"

"Yes, because if it wasn't for that, we might never have had that conversation. It might have taken weeks before we interacted, if ever. Life is made up of little moments that don't seem that important at the time, but in retrospect they're what get you to where you are."

"So we can thank Kris Kross for the fact that we're standing in this water drinking champagne."

"Yeah." I smiled. "Timing is everything."

At that moment, the sky opened up, dropping rain on us.

"Speaking of timing…" Noah laughed. "You okay with staying out here, or do you want to go inside?"

"I'm not gonna let a little rain ruin my very first surprise birthday champagne party."

"Good."

Noah smiled at me, but more than that, his *eyes* were smiling. It was genuine happiness that made me realize he was just as glad to be hanging out here with me as I was to be with him. It was the kind of smile that gave me a false hope about where things stood with us.

We stayed in the lake for a while, sipping champagne in the rain. After a few minutes, the sun peeked out again while it was still raining. Sun showers were always so cool, so rare. So were moments like this.

The alcohol was definitely going to my head.

"I'd better slow down. I'm starting to feel it."

"That's the point."

"Yeah...but I have to work tonight."

He emptied his glass and shook his head. "Huh-uh. No, you don't."

"Yes, I do. What do you mean?"

"I had lunch over at Jack Foley's Pub today. Spoke to your friend there—Marlene, is it? She's gonna get someone to cover for you tonight."

"Are you serious?"

"Yes."

"What are we doing?"

"Don't worry about it. Just go home and get dressed. Nothing too fancy. I'll pick you up in a couple of hours."

Noah wouldn't tell me where we were going. We rode with the windows down, and the warm summer evening air blew my hair around. It felt amazing to be next to him in his truck. I stole glances over at his profile and wondered if this feeling of wanting him would ever subside. I wished he would touch me again, even just my face. There wasn't much I wouldn't give for a taste of something more with him.

Finally, we pulled up to Tito's Cantina, a popular Mexican place. Noah had taken a roundabout way to get here. It was almost like he'd driven in a circle.

"Tito's! How did you know I love this place?"

"You told me once Mexican is your favorite. This is supposed to be the best place in town, so…"

"You're good. You listen." I grinned.

As we walked into the restaurant, he placed his hand on the small of my back, which practically lit my insides on fire.

The feeling was quickly replaced by shock, which then transformed into pure joy.

My heart filled up fast as I spotted my mother, Chrissy, and Marlene sitting at a table surrounded by balloons.

My mother is here?

They were all wearing sombreros.

"Surprise!" Chrissy shouted.

The real surprise was seeing my mother out and about. I couldn't remember the last time she'd left the house other than to go to a doctor's appointment.

"Mom?"

She smiled. "Hi, honey. Happy birthday."

I turned to Noah. "Now I know why you drove around for a while. How on Earth did you get her out of the house?"

"She loves you. It didn't take much."

"Happy birthday, my beautiful daughter."

I bent down to kiss my mother before moving over to hug Chrissy.

"You took tonight off?" I asked.

Nurse Chrissy was supposed to be working a twelve-hour shift starting at seven.

"Yup. Got someone to cover for me. I couldn't miss your birthday."

"And who's covering for *me*?" I asked Marlene.

"Are you kidding? When they found out it was your twenty-first birthday, Kel and Leah were fighting over who got to fill in. I can't believe I didn't know. Thanks to Noah, I can celebrate with you."

After we sat down, I leaned into him. "I can't believe you pulled this off."

Noah winked and grabbed a sombrero, placing it on my head. "Happy birthday, beautiful."

A rush of heat ran through me. I wouldn't read into it, but it felt damn good to hear him say that.

Dinner was everything I could have wanted. My mother laughed at Marlene's stories. Noah was by my side. As far as I was concerned, everyone at this table was family to me—Noah included. I didn't know how else to characterize him. He was a friend, for sure, but also a big brother figure, and someone I still had a massive crush on no matter how hard I tried to deny it.

It was very emotional to be sitting here with the four people who mattered most to me, especially knowing how many changes were on the horizon. I shook those thoughts from my mind, because tonight wasn't supposed to be about that. I needed to enjoy this moment with the people I cared about.

We all stuffed ourselves. And after polishing off two margaritas, I felt completely tipsy.

Chrissy ended up taking Mom home early, and after Marlene left, it was just Noah and me at the table. His eyes lingered on my lips as I licked the remaining salt off the rim of my glass.

I took my hat off and placed it on his head. "It's a good thing you're driving, señor."

"That was always part of the plan."

Moving my straw around, I smiled. "Thank you again for doing this."

Noah grinned mischievously. "I might have one more surprise up my sleeve."

"You're just full of them tonight, huh?" My cheeks hurt from smiling. "What is it?"

"It's back at the boathouse. Wanna get going?"

I nodded. "Sure."

He led me inside. "You need to close your eyes for a little bit, so I can get something set up."

I laughed. "Okay."

Making myself comfortable on the loveseat, I covered my eyes with my hands.

"Okay, you can open them now."

Noah had lit two candles that formed the number twenty-one. This wasn't just any cake.

"Holy shit," I said.

"You like it?"

"Who made that?"

"You know Evie's Cakes in the center? I told her what I wanted, and she did it."

The top of the cake was a little girl with her hands on a snowy television set—a replica of the famous scene from *Poltergeist*, the one I'd told him I was obsessed with as a child.

"This is the most awesome cake I have ever seen in my entire life."

"I think we should try it."

"Are you kidding? I don't even want to touch it. We can't ruin it."

"We can cut around the bottom, leave the top intact. But eventually you're probably going to have to destroy that, too."

"No way! I'm freezing it."

"You're gonna leave a *Poltergeist* cake in your mom's freezer while you go away to school?"

"Yes. I'm keeping it forever and ever. Someday, when I'm old and gray, I will still have that thing in my freezer. You think I'm joking, but I'm not."

"That's crazy. I hope you know that."

"Well, so am I—a little."

"This is true." He winked. "Well, then I'd better not accidentally destroy it."

Noah sliced us two pieces of cake from the bottom part, being careful not to touch the top.

"I almost brought it to the restaurant," he said. "But I was afraid something would happen to it. Plus, it would've ruined the surprise of everyone being there if you saw me carrying a cake."

"You really did surprise me, and I'm kind of glad it's just us now."

I knew that comment was a bit too honest, that it bordered on crossing the line. But it was the truth. I wanted him all to myself.

"This is the best birthday I've had in a long time," I said. "I know my mother told you my sister died on my birthday. This was the first one I've had since then where I didn't think of her all day. I'm not sure how I feel about that."

"You shouldn't feel guilty."

"I've always felt I don't deserve to celebrate my birthday if she can't have them anymore."

"The day you were born is something to be acknowledged. Your sister would want you to celebrate your birthday."

"I know that rationally. But you can't always help how you feel." I took a bite of cake, which was chocolate with a pudding filling. Yum. "I just wish I could have done something to help her. I was young and never thought things were as bad as they were."

He nodded to himself as if he'd just figured something out. "That's why you want to become a psychiatric nurse, isn't it? Because of your sister."

"Yeah. I want to help people feel better."

He licked frosting off the corner of his mouth. "You know, sometimes that's not possible, right? Not everyone can be saved."

"I do realize that. But I can try."

"Yes. You absolutely can, but you can't blame yourself for not being able to succeed every time—not for anything that happened with your sister or anything that may happen in the future to someone else. We don't have control over others' actions, no matter how hard we try."

"Of course. I know that. And I have a long way to go, right? Before anyone can trust me with their mental health?"

"You're a strong person, and you have a lot of personal experience dealing with mental health issues from the people around you. So I'd say that's a huge advantage over most people going into the field."

"Wish that weren't the case, but it's true." I stared off. "I'm sorry...this night has taken a dark turn, hasn't it?"

"We're eating a *Poltergeist* cake. It fits the mood," he said.

"That's true."

"Hey, have you ever considered becoming a writer?"

"Not as a career, but I've dabbled in it. Why do you ask?"

"No reason. I just have a feeling you might be good at it."

Hmm.

Strange.

Noah looked down at his plate and played with the remnants of his frosting. It seemed like he had something on his mind.

Finally, he said, "I found out today that Olivia's pregnant."

Wow. His ex-wife is having a baby.

"That's pretty big news..."

"Yeah."

"How do you feel about that?"

"She and her husband had been trying for a while. I'm happy for her."

I wasn't sure I believed him. "Really?"

"Yeah...really."

"But it must be weird."

"It's a little surreal, but not in a way that takes away my happiness for her. It's a lesson that life moves on with or without you, a reminder that I should probably figure out my own life at some point."

"Do you want kids?"

Noah sighed. "I wasn't a very good husband, not sure I'd be any better as a father."

I shook my head. I knew in my heart he was wrong. You know how sometimes you can see things in other people that they can't see in themselves?

"I absolutely beg to differ," I told him.

"Oh, yeah?"

"Yes. You've taught me so much about believing in myself and about the world. You've lived a diverse life, and you have a lot to offer a child from your experiences. And you're protective. Plus, you know how I really know you'd be a good dad?"

"How?"

"It's how you treat the guinea pigs, feeding them with chopsticks and always making sure they have enough water and hay. You make sure they each get an equal amount of food. Also, how you treat Teddy. He can be really overbearing sometimes, not to mention he's super big. Yet you let him climb all over you, slobber on you, because you know it makes him happy."

He chuckled. "I don't do anything. I don't know why he likes me so damn much."

"I can relate to how he feels."

Shit.

Noah stared at me, eyes wide.

Quick. Say something to distract. I cleared my throat. "So...I sort of have a date next weekend."

CHAPTER FOURTEEN

Noah

My mood went from hot to cold in an instant.

"Oh, yeah?" I said, trying to seem calm about it even as I felt sick to my stomach. "With who?"

It didn't matter what I told myself—my feelings, my reactions when it came to her didn't lie. I wondered which shade of green I was turning.

"This guy Jared I went to high school with. He's in town for the summer because his father is sick. He goes to Harvard."

"Harvard...pretty impressive."

"Yeah. Neuroscience major. So clearly we have a lot in common." She rolled her eyes.

It was getting hotter in here by the second.

"You like him?" I braced for her answer.

"Well, he's attractive and nice. But I don't know him too well. We weren't really in the same crowd in high school. I was always with Eric—who wouldn't have liked me hanging out with Jared."

I swallowed. "He's picking you up here?"

"Yes. Why?"

"I might want to check him out, make sure he's legit."

"No. You'll scare him away. Either that or I'll have to explain you to him, which won't be easy."

"That *is* easy. You tell him, this is my friend and bodyguard, Noah. He'll kick your ass if you do anything to hurt me."

She laughed. "Bodyguard?"

"Sure, why not?"

"I don't think saying that will go over real well."

"Is he a big dude?"

"Not as big as you."

"Perfect, then." I chuckled. "I'm kidding. I won't embarrass you in front of your little friend."

This whole thing felt like a test. It was the first time she'd be going out on a date since the time she'd gone out with her ex. I didn't remember feeling like this, like I wanted to kill someone. Anyway, this was my problem, not hers.

Then, I pulled something I had no right to pull. For completely selfish reasons, I asked, "You sure you should be getting involved with someone who's gonna be leaving soon?"

You're a dick, Noah.

"Well, actually, I was thinking it might be perfect— no strings—since I can't do anything serious right now, either." She shrugged. "I'm leaving, too, so…"

And that's what you get, asshole—a nice visual of Heather spreading her legs for a no-strings-attached relationship with some guy who's not you. That came back to bite you in the ass, didn't it?

"I see," I said.

"I'm sure you had lots of those after the divorce? Sex-with-no-strings relationships?"

Is she fucking with me? Or is she seriously considering boning this guy?

"A couple," I answered. "But I don't prefer them. In my experience, if a woman likes you and tells you she doesn't want anything more than a hookup, she's lying. Even those relationships eventually turn into something else. I've had so-called no-strings relationships that turned out to be hardly that. It's a bit of a catch-22, though, because any woman I don't want more than sex with is probably not worth my time anyway. Maybe it comes with age, but I need to feel something more than just physical attraction to truly enjoy being with someone."

Her face turned red. "Have you been with anyone since you've been here?"

"I think you know the answer to that. You've seen me almost every night."

"I guess that's true. And I intercepted the one whore who wanted to change that."

"There was nothing to intercept, because as I've told you before, she's not my type."

She cocked her head. "So, what *is* your type, then?"

I wanted to tell her the truth, that lately I only had one type, and that was Heather Chadwick—beautiful, young, wide-eyed, honest Heather Chadwick, whom I wanted to protect with every ounce of my soul as much as I wanted to taint her.

"I don't have a type."

"You just said Kira *wasn't* your type. That means you have a type."

Shit.

I did say that, didn't I? I was losing my mind, and I knew exactly why.

"I don't know what my type is...but I know what my type is *not*. Her."

"Okay, fair enough."

I'd thought she was done with her inquisition, but then she asked, "So, you haven't been with anyone in a while?"

"That's an interesting way of asking me the last time I had sex."

Her cheeks pinked. "You don't have to tell me."

She's fucking adorable. And nosy.

It felt like forever. I actually had to think about it. "May."

"So the month before you came here..."

"Yes."

"Who was she?"

"It wasn't anything serious. Just someone—"

"Someone you fuck."

Jesus Christ. Hearing her say that word made my dick go rigid. I hoped to God she didn't say it again. At the same time, I *wanted* her to say it again.

"I haven't had a serious relationship since the divorce. She was someone I thought I had an understanding with, but like I said, in my experience, that's a slippery slope. She started to expect more from me. It's hard to find someone who's not interested in something more."

"Because the women end up falling for you."

"Or just wanting more, yeah."

"They fall in love with you, Noah," she said matter-of-factly.

She could see right through me.

I needed to change the subject, but I was curious about her, too. This might be my only opportunity to bring it up. *Fuck it.*

"Since you've given me the third degree, I think it's only fair I return the favor. What about you?"

"I've only had sex with Eric."

Wow. Given how sexually charged she was, that kind of surprised me. But I suspected she wasn't the type of girl who gave it up to anyone if her heart wasn't in it—which was why I wasn't sure I believed her little sex-with-no-strings act at all.

"So it's been a long time."

She smiled. "Are you thinking the drought explains some of my behavior earlier this summer? Because that wouldn't be entirely true. I've never acted like that before, never asserted myself like that with anyone."

That made me happy inside, which was messed-up. Whatever I was feeling, I had to get over it. I couldn't be anything more than a friend and mentor to this girl, especially now that she was finally on the right path. She looked up to me, believed in me. She didn't need a grown man who couldn't control his feelings or his dick messing with her emotions right now. I'd be leaving at the end of the month, and regardless of how strong my feelings had grown toward her, I had to stick it out, not get carried away, and stand my ground, even if I felt that ground crumbling beneath me.

Oh! I hadn't given her the present I'd bought for her. Presenting it now would be a good way to escape this conversation about sex. After our talk earlier, I'd worried it might make her sad if it reminded her of her sister. But ultimately, I needed to give it to her.

I walked over to a drawer and took out the box. "I got you something."

"You didn't have to do that."

I handed it to her, and my heart raced as she opened it. I'd searched a long time for the right one.

When she took the figurine out of the packaging, she covered her mouth. "Oh my God."

"I know you said you stopped collecting them some years back. I assumed it was because whatever hope they gave you disappeared after your sister died. Am I right?"

Seeming a little choked up, she nodded. "Yes."

"This one is called Merry Wanderer."

Heather ran her fingers along the ceramic. "Oh, I know. It's famous. I've always wanted it."

I smiled. "Really?"

"Yes."

This particular Hummel featured a little boy with a suitcase and umbrella, headed out on an adventure.

"I figured he could remind you of me, the wanderer who passed through town that one summer. So my choosing it was a little selfish."

"This is so perfect." She hugged it to her chest.

"Don't ever feel guilty about being happy. Your sister would want you to be happy. Collect the Hummels. Live your life."

Tears sprung to her eyes as she leaned in and wrapped her arms around me. Just like the last time she'd done this, my heart hammered against my chest. I was completely aware of her soft breasts pressed against me, completely aware of my body reacting in a way that was absolutely opposite of what should have been happening. I prayed my erection would subside. Heather was too damn astute. She would notice that shit.

She pulled back to look in my eyes. "This really means a lot. Thank you for this entire night. I'll never forget it as long as I live."

I'd never wanted to kiss anyone so badly in my life. "You're welcome," I told her.

She suddenly yawned, and small beads of spit sprayed out of her mouth.

"Oh my gosh! I just squirted."

The moment she realized what she'd said, her entire face froze before it turned beet red. It was like time stopped for a few seconds.

I sure as fuck wasn't going to touch her "squirting" with a ten-foot pole, although I couldn't say I totally minded the visual it brought on.

"Can I use your bathroom?"

Ah. She's going to escape the embarrassment.

"You don't even have to ask."

"Thanks."

After a few minutes, she emerged. "I think all of the alcohol and sugar did me in. I'm not feeling so great. Do you mind if I lie down for a bit?"

"No. Of course not."

Heather made her way over to my bed and sank her head into the pillow.

My chest tightened at the sight of her. I longed to curl up behind her.

Instead of dwelling on it, I lifted my ass off the loveseat and forced myself to clean up the paper plates we'd left out.

I carefully lifted the remaining cake into the refrigerator so it wouldn't melt.

After cleaning everything up, I returned to the loveseat and put the TV on very low volume. Heather was completely out. It was late. Not wanting to disrupt her if she didn't wake up tonight, I'd just sleep on the loveseat with my legs dangling over the end.

At one point, Heather moaned. "Noah..."

I sat up. "You okay?"

She didn't respond, so I walked over to her and saw that her eyes were still closed. I'd almost walked away again when she repeated, "Noah..." It was more like a whisper.

"What's up, Heather?" I murmured.

She didn't respond. I realized she was probably talking in her sleep. She'd mentioned she did that from time to time.

"Noah..."

I stayed standing, a foot away from the bed, and looked at her for a while. Just as I'd turned around to return to the couch, I heard her again.

"Noah...fuck me. Please...fuck me."

Oh.

Shit.

I froze, unsure what to do. This felt like a violation, because I wasn't supposed to hear her say those words. Yet they'd exited her mouth and were meant for me, in a sense. *Do I wake her up?*

Her voice shook me yet again. "Fuck me, Noah."

Jesus.

She did it again. "I want you so bad. Please fuck me."

This time I spoke back.

"I want to. Believe me." My words came out louder than I'd intended. I didn't want to wake her up.

"I want to tickle your ass."

Hold up. *Say what?*

Did she just say she wanted to *tickle* my ass? Or was it...*dick in my ass*? I couldn't be sure. Maybe I was just hearing things.

"I want to tickle your ass, Noah."

Nope. Not hearing things. *Tickle*. That's exactly what she said. Unable to help it, I lost it and started laughing.

"God, girl, you're something else."

My laughter must have woken her, because she stirred.

Then she opened her eyes. She stared at me, looking dazed and confused.

She scrubbed her hand over her face. "Hey."

My heart pounded. "Hi."

Heather blinked. "Wow, I dozed off, huh?"

As she sat up against the headboard, she didn't seem to have any knowledge of what she'd been muttering—or what I'd said.

"Yeah. You sure did."

"Did I miss anything exciting?"

I bit my bottom lip. "Nope."

156

CHAPTER
FIFTEEN

Heather

Even though I knew it was a possibility, I never expected to get an offer on the property so soon.

When I got off the phone with the realtor on Friday afternoon, my mouth hung open. A man who had come to see the houses yesterday offered five thousand over asking. It was just a matter of us accepting, and then the realtor said he'd likely schedule an inspection. If all went well, it would be a done deal.

We'd told prospective buyers we wouldn't be able to vacate until September. But now that this was becoming a reality, I felt a little panic.

I needed to calm down before I told my mother the news. I needed to talk to Noah.

I raced over to the boathouse, only to find he wasn't home. Sadness washed over me. I knew he wasn't gone yet, but his not being home in this moment when I really needed him reminded me that soon he *would be* gone. Soon, my world as I knew it would be different.

I sat on the porch of the boathouse and called him.

He answered, "Hey."

"Where are you?"

"I'm picking up some supplies from Home Depot. What's up?"

"I'm sort of freaking out."

"Why?"

"We got an offer on the property."

He went silent for a few seconds. "No shit. Already? Really?"

"Yes."

"Wow. Congratulations."

"Thanks." I was getting teary eyed.

"That's fantastic. Are you going to accept?"

I sniffled. "I think I should. It was a little over asking."

He paused. "Are you crying?"

"Yeah. It's stupid. I know."

"It's okay to be emotional about it. Shit...I'm feeling emotional about it, and I didn't grow up here."

"We'll still have until the beginning of September to figure things out, but I feel really overwhelmed all of a sudden. Not sure I was expecting this to happen so quickly."

"That's understandable. It's getting very real." He sighed into the phone. "Heather, listen. Take a deep breath, okay? We can start looking for a new place tomorrow. Is the thing with your mother's sister a done deal?"

His using the word *we* made me even more emotional. There was no way I could have done any of this without him.

"My Aunt Katy assures me she's moving here, yes."

"Maybe you should see if she can come up here soon, so she can look, too. If she's going to be living there, she should have a say."

"That's a good point. I'll get on that." Fear still bubbled inside me. "What are we gonna do with all of our stuff? I thought I'd have time to go through everything. My mother has so much crap."

"Well, maybe we can hold a yard sale. Some of it might have to go into storage for a while."

When I went quiet, he seemed to realize I was back in freak-out mode. His voice snapped me out of my thoughts.

"Things are working out as they're supposed to. It's totally normal to feel overwhelmed. It would be odd if you didn't. Change is scary, but it's the only way to get to the next step."

I let out a shaky breath. "Yeah."

"There are big things ahead for you. I just know it."

Closing my eyes, I said, "Thank you."

"What are you doing tonight? We can celebrate."

My brief excitement over that was squelched when I remembered I had plans.

"Oh...um, tonight is my date with Jared."

He was silent for a bit. "I didn't realize that. I thought it was tomorrow."

"Yeah. We were originally going out Saturday, but he asked if we could switch it. He's picking me up at eight."

He paused. "Gotcha. Well, maybe another night."

Things suddenly felt awkward.

"Yes. Definitely."

"You want anything from McDonald's? I shouldn't be eating that stuff, but I'm driving through on the way home."

I smiled. It was nice of him to ask. He was always so considerate.

"No. I just had an early lunch, but thank you. I'll come by and say hello before I leave tonight."

"Yeah...okay...I'll be home."

Home. A part of me loved this life so much, living here on the lake and having Noah nearby. I wasn't ready for that to change.

"Thanks for listening."

"Don't worry, Heather. Everything's gonna be okay."

Later that afternoon, Chrissy sat on my bed as I got dressed for my date with Jared.

"Damn. You look hot in that dress," she said, bouncing a little.

"Jared said to wear something nice, so I figured I'd go all out. I didn't think we were going anywhere dressy until he said that."

"What else would you expect from a Harvard boy?" She narrowed her eyes as she took a look at my face. "Is everything okay? Are you feeling weird about the offer on the house?"

Actually, all I could think about today was Noah.

"Can I tell you something in confidence?"

"Yeah, of course."

"It's about Noah."

She nodded. "I should've known."

"Should've known what?"

"That something was up there."

"Nothing is actually up there. I mean, not really—other than in my head."

"You have feelings for him. I could have told you that."

"So, it's obvious, then?"

"I picked up on something the night of your party at Tito's."

"You did?"

"Oh, yeah. I just couldn't figure out if it was my imagination or if it was real. Like, I *wanted* it to be real, you know? You two are both insanely attractive people, and even though he's older, I don't think that's a big deal. You'd make a great couple. He's clearly very fond of you. I can tell from the way he looks at you. And the way he treats you."

"He's fond of me...but not in *that* way."

"You know that for a fact?"

"When he first moved in, he treated me like a kid. I think now that he's gotten to know me, he doesn't see me as so young anymore. I've earned his respect. But he still says nothing can happen between us. Although...lately, I've been feeling a shift. I'm getting this vibe I didn't get in the beginning. I've been feeling like maybe he *does* like me as more than a friend, but he's afraid to do anything. Maybe it's just wishful thinking. Anyway, it's a moot point. He wouldn't try anything, even if he did feel something for me. He's been the biggest supporter of my going away to school, and he wouldn't do anything to interfere with that."

She bit the corner of her mouth. "But you wish he would...interfere."

"I can't seem to shake these feelings for him no matter how hard I try. Regardless of what's about to happen in my life, I just...want him. And the feeling is getting worse the closer we come to the end of his time here."

"Wow. How come you didn't talk to me about this before?"

"I've been hoping to get over it."

"Thus, the date with Jared."

"Well, yeah, I mean, Jared's a great guy. But Noah... Noah takes my breath away—always has from almost the very beginning. Now that I've gotten to know him, it feels so much stronger than physical attraction. We undoubtedly have a connection. I've come to depend on him, to trust him. I'm just...really gonna miss him."

Chrissy offered a sympathetic smile. "If something is meant to happen there, it will. If not now, then maybe someday."

"Like what do you mean? Years down the line?"

"Sure, why not? Maybe you go away to school, get settled in your career, and reconnect with him somehow when the time is right. You don't know what life has in store."

"Or he could be married with kids by then."

"Well, that's true." She seemed at a loss for what to say. "Have you hinted at how you feel?"

"I've more than hinted. I flat-out told him I was attracted to him a while back. He shot me down. So there's that."

"Ouch. You did?"

"Yeah, shortly after he moved in. I vowed that would be it. I'll never make the first move again. I haven't dropped any more hints, aside from not-so-accidentally dropping my *panties* in his laundry. Other than that, I haven't done anything else."

"Holy crap. You didn't..."

I put on my earrings. "I did. And he hasn't even acknowledged it. It's the most bizarre thing. It's like my undies disappeared into the Bermuda Triangle."

"Wow." She laughed. "That's so nuts."

"Anyway...I just have to get over this."

"Trust in fate. What's meant to happen will. In the meantime, have some fun with Jared. You deserve it."

As much as I appreciated Chrissy's advice about enjoying my date with Jared, deep down, I knew who I had really dressed up for tonight. As I walked over to the boathouse, my heart thundered in my chest.

I'd told Noah I would stop in before my date. As I knocked on the door, I took a deep breath in, then exhaled.

I knocked a second time.

He wasn't home.

Feeling disappointed, I wondered if I wouldn't get to see him before I left.

Then his deep voice vibrated through me. "Quit knockin'. I'm not buyin' what you're sellin'."

I turned around. "You scared me."

My nipples stiffened at the sight of him. Noah had grease on his face and his T-shirt. A shimmer of sweat glistened over his forehead. He was dirty, but for some reason he'd never looked hotter to me. And my body's immediate reaction never ceased to amaze me.

He swallowed hard as he looked me over. I knew beyond a shadow of a doubt that he liked what he saw. His eyes landed on the cleavage I'd very intentionally created by adding extra padding to my bra. My breasts were already pretty big for my frame—a full C—but I wanted to show them off tonight.

"Why are you so dirty?" I asked.

That was a dumb question, but I didn't know what else to say as his eyes continued to wander over me.

"I had to do some work on my truck." He didn't look happy right now.

"Is it all set?"

Instead of answering, he looked me up and down. "You're not going out like that, are you?"

"I was going to, yes."

"It's too much."

"I don't look good?"

"I didn't say that. It's just...too much." He moved past me and entered the boathouse.

I followed him inside. To my surprise, Noah went straight to the cabinet and took out a shot glass. He poured himself a scotch and drank it down before slamming it on the counter. He was angry. Something about that was damn sexy.

"Can I have one?" I asked.

"No."

"Why not?"

"Because you shouldn't be going out on a date impaired. You need to be alert."

"One shot is not going to impair me. It'll relax me."

He repeated, "No."

"Are you forgetting that I'm not underage anymore?"

His eyes traced over my body. "That's painfully obvious right now." He grabbed the bottle and put it away. "You don't want to drink that shit anyway."

"It's good enough for you but not me?"

"It's too strong."

"Can I taste it?"

"No."

"Why did you drink it if it's too strong?"

He spoke through gritted teeth. "Because I need to take the edge off tonight."

"Why?"

He refused to answer me, but his eyes told me everything I needed to know: Noah Cavallari was jealous, and he was finally coming undone.

CHAPTER
SIXTEEN

Noah

Heather had painted on bright, fire engine red lipstick. It felt like a knife to the heart for some reason. That look just wasn't her. She was sexy as hell in that dress, but something about the lipstick bugged me, like she was trying to be something she wasn't. That lipstick invited trouble. She didn't need a drop of makeup; she was so incredibly beautiful without it.

I was doing a terrible job of hiding my feelings tonight. But it was either take that shot of scotch or swallow her whole. Taking the shot was the right thing to do.

She stared at me now with her beautiful blue eyes, her hair draped over her cleavage in waves. Her body looked too damn good in that dress, and I had the urge to kiss off all of that red paint on her mouth. Come to think of it, maybe another shot was in order.

I took the bottle out of the cabinet and poured myself a second but didn't drink it. I needed to know it was there if I needed it.

"I've never seen you wearing lipstick that bright."

"Chrissy lent it to me. Does it look stupid?"

"It doesn't look stupid. It just isn't *you*. It kind of hides your lips. Why would you want to do that?" *All I want right now is to suck on them—lipstick or not.*

I'd been in a funk all day, and this moment was the culmination. The offer on the property had put me in a strange mood. I'd been once again second-guessing whether I'd made the best decision in steering her to sell. It had to be the right thing, but anything that made her sad at this point really got to me. And now, watching her get ready to go out with some guy who was likely just looking for a summer lay had put me in a *really* shitty mood.

I was acting like a jealous prick. You'd think I was, well, her age—not mine.

Her voice barely registered. "Should I take it off?"

I was in a daze. "What?" *Take off what?*

"The lipstick."

Oh, the lipstick. What the fuck else would she be taking off?

"Does it make me look like a clown?" she asked.

Instead of answering her, I walked over to the kitchen sink and ran some water over a paper towel. I squeezed out all of the moisture and came to where she was standing. I began to wipe the lipstick off of her lips. She remained still, seeming shocked. I could relate to the feeling. I had no right to do this. I didn't own her, even though at times I wanted to.

When most of it was off, I dumped the paper towel in the trash. "Much better."

She licked her lips, and I could feel my dick twitch.

"You think so?" she asked.

"Yes. You have beautiful lips. You shouldn't hide them."

But I don't want them on anyone else.

Her cheeks turned pink. "Thanks."

"Hang on."

I walked over to my bed and reached under it for the camera bag.

"I thought you said you didn't bring your camera here."

"No, I said I didn't come here to take photos, but I never leave home without my camera. You never know when you're gonna need it. The sun is setting now. It's the perfect lighting. Let's go outside. I'll take a few shots of you in that dress."

"The famous Noah Cavallari is going to photograph me? I feel so special," she teased. "Seriously, this is cool."

Seeing the smile on her face made me wonder why I hadn't thought of this sooner.

Once outside, I showed her where to stand but didn't have to tell her what to do. She was a natural in front of the camera, smiling organically and laughing as I snapped away. The remaining sunlight cast a glow around her blond locks.

At one point, her hair was in her face, so I reached out to move it to the side and noticed my hand fucking shaking. I was seriously losing my marbles.

After I'd stopped taking photos, Heather asked, "Will you send them to me?"

My mind was still in a haze. "What?"

"The photos. Will you email me some?"

Nodding, I said, "Yeah, of course."

"Are you alright, Noah? You seem out of it."

"I'm fine."

She looked back toward the main house. "I have to go. He's gonna be here any minute."

What are you doing letting her go out with this guy?

"I'll see you later," she said. "Thank you for taking the photos."

She lingered even though she'd said she had to go. She was waiting for me to say something. But I couldn't find the words.

We stood there on the porch facing each other until she stammered, "Have a nice night."

Despite how much I wanted to stop her, I let her walk away.

The farther she got from me, the more I just felt...sick.

Suddenly, it seemed like the switch that had been controlling my sanity flipped.

"Hey!" I shouted.

She turned around. "Yeah?"

"Come here."

She walked back until she was in front of me again.

"Why did you put your panties in my laundry?" I asked.

Her face turned as red as her dress. At a loss for words, she muttered, "I...uh..."

Taking a few steps forward, I stopped just inches from her. "If you knew how much it affected me, you wouldn't have done it."

She leaned in, just a hair away from my face. "I wanted to get a rise out of you. I wanted to send you a message without having to say it."

I could feel her breath on my face.

Placing my hand on her cheek, I said, "You're so fucking honest."

She closed her eyes briefly. "I can't help it."

I looped a piece of her hair around my finger. "You could have just said they accidentally fell in."

Her breath was shaky. "Yeah, but that would have defeated the purpose. I wanted you to have them. And I wanted you to think of me in them."

My breath hitched as I pulled on her hair. "Christ, Heather. You don't think I feel the same things you do? You think I'm superhuman, that it's easy to resist you? I'm just trying to do the right thing."

"I wish you would stop trying."

The scotch must have gone to my head, because I asked, "You want to know what I did with those panties?"

"Yes," she whispered.

"I put them over my face to smell you. I couldn't get enough. Then I wrapped them around my cock while I jerked off and came all over them. I got so angry at myself for doing it, that I ripped them to shreds. That's how crazy you make me."

Her chest rose and fell. "I knew you wanted me."

I gritted my teeth. "I never said I didn't want you. Did I? Not once. I *wish* I didn't want to fuck you."

Her breathing was heavy. "Let me taste the scotch."

"I said you can't have any."

"I don't want you to pour me one. I want to taste it on your tongue."

Fuck. Me.

That sentence obliterated the last resistance I had. I gripped her waist and pulled her into me, giving her exactly what we both wanted. My lips smashed against hers before my tongue sought entry.

Her hot, hungry mouth was everything I'd ever imagined it to be, the moans emanating from it making me so rock hard that my dick physically hurt, aching for more.

I kissed her harder as she worked to keep up with the pace. Neither of us broke away long enough to even breathe.

Heather's fingers raked through my hair as I devoured her mouth. I didn't even recognize the damn sounds I was making, the sounds of a long starvation finally satisfied. Anyone who drove by would have seen me practically attacking her, and I didn't care.

Her lips, her mouth, her tongue tasted so good I thought I might never come up for air. I ran my hands through her soft, silky hair. It felt surreal. But this was wrong. So damn wrong. I was stealing something I had no right to, but fuck if I knew how to stop. Nothing had ever felt this good. It took everything in me not to carry her inside the boathouse and take everything else, too. I knew she'd give me whatever I wanted. And that scared the hell out of me.

As if she'd read my mind, she spoke over my lips, "I want to feel you inside of me, Noah."

Her words were like a slap in the face, a reality check.

You have no right to do this.

I pried myself off of her. It felt unnatural—downright painful—to pull away when all I wanted was to disappear into her. But nevertheless, I somehow managed to do it.

Licking my lips to salvage what was left of her taste, I closed my eyes and caught my breath, intentionally looking away from her. I knew if I looked into her eyes, this would be too difficult. But it had to be done.

I could ruin her life with one bad decision. I wasn't going to be responsible for that. I wanted to own her body, but I cared about the soul within it a hell of a lot more—more than anything. I needed to get myself in check before I ruined everything for her.

When I finally met her stare, she looked distraught, with glistening eyes.

"Why did you stop?" she asked.

"I have to, Heather. You have no idea how badly I want you, but I have to stop this before we go too far."

Tears formed in her eyes. "I don't understand you. I never will."

At that moment, a car pulled up to the front of the main house in the distance.

She glanced over to look at it. "Shit. He's here." She wiped her eyes. "Tell me not to go with him, Noah, and I'll stay. I want to be with you. I don't want anyone but you, don't want *anything* but you. I'm so crazy about you. I—"

"You should go." That sentence might have been the hardest thing I'd ever had to push out of myself.

Her pupils darkened. Now she looked pissed. "Really? You want me to go?"

My mind was in turmoil. The words were right there but wouldn't come.

Don't go.

Stay with me.

Be with me.

I wouldn't let them out.

"Go," I barked.

I'd never seen her face so red with anger as she turned away and headed toward her house. As her date exited the

172

black beemer to open the door for her, I couldn't even bear to look at him.

I went inside and slammed the door. I sat on the edge of my bed with my head in my hands. My ears were ringing.

It's the right thing to do.

You need to ignore these feelings.

This is not what you came here for.

Maybe you should go back to Pennsylvania.

Bouncing my legs up and down, I needed a reality check. There was only one person I could trust enough to talk to about this. While my father knew why I'd come here and knew about Heather, he didn't know about my feelings toward her. I needed to confide in someone who had enough sense to talk me out of a huge mistake. I needed someone to talk me out of doing what I wanted to, which was to run after her and stop her damn date.

Dad sounded surprised to hear from me. "Noah?"

"Hey."

"Is something wrong?"

"Yes. I need your advice."

"That's not something I hear very often."

I got right to it. "I fucked up."

"Are you in some kind of trouble?"

"Depends on how you define trouble. I'm not in danger, but I'm pretty sure I'm in trouble."

"What's happened?"

Running my fingers through my hair, I said, "Things here have gotten out of hand."

I spent the better part of the next ten minutes admitting my feelings for Heather to my father—without going into the specifics of what I'd said to her tonight. I prayed he'd be able to knock some sense into me.

"You kissed her, and now she's out with some kid?"

"Yes. A *kid* her own age."

"You do realize that when I met your mother, I was thirty-five, and she was twenty-three?"

"That didn't exactly work out, did it?"

"It worked out plenty for a very long time, wiseass. Got two great sons out of it. For the record, I'd take that woman back in a heartbeat. She's the love of my life, and I don't regret a thing. But I digress—the age difference never mattered. You're beating yourself up for something that has happened to men throughout the ages. You fell for a beautiful young woman—who's of legal age. That's not a crime."

Pulling on my hair, I said, "This wasn't supposed to happen. You're not supposed to be encouraging it."

"It's not enough to believe you're not *supposed* to fall for someone. It doesn't matter what you believe is wrong or right. It's already happened. You've already fallen. Am I right? It's not a crime to care about someone or to covet them."

"I was supposed to help her, not complicate her life even more. This trip was supposed to be about *her*...not me."

"No matter what I say, it's not gonna change how you feel. Stop trying to change something that's out of your control."

"Maybe I should just leave."

"You're going to walk away now? Never look back? Never see her again?"

My chest hurt just thinking about leaving any earlier than I was supposed to. Leaving was inevitable, but I wasn't ready to say goodbye.

"I'm so damn confused. Tell me what to do."

"How about be honest with her? There's a novel idea! And I mean *really* honest. Tell her everything. Stop carrying this burden around with you."

"You think I should tell her *everything*? It's gonna shatter her, particularly the fact that I've been hiding it in the first place. She trusts me."

"I think that's part of the problem. You're walking around with all of this guilt, trying to be some kind of saint. You're only human. Tell her the truth. Then once you've let that go, just let life happen naturally without trying to manipulate everything."

"What if she hates me?"

"From everything you've told me, she seems like she's a pretty smart girl—and tough, too. Hopefully, she can handle it."

That was true. Heather was tough. But she wasn't prepared for this. My father was right, though. My biggest problem was that I didn't feel I deserved how she felt about me because she didn't know why I was here.

I hung up with him, still torn over how to handle things.

As the night wore on, I felt more and more like telling Heather the truth.

As much as I was tempted to find out where she was and go to her, I didn't want to be a dick and interrupt her date. I had no right to do that after I'd kicked her out.

I just needed to let her know one thing—the one thing I was certain of.

So I sent her a text.

Noah: I made a mistake. I shouldn't have let you go.

She didn't respond, and I couldn't blame her. I had behaved like an erratic teenager tonight. I was a grown man and needed to start acting like one. I owed her the truth. I owed her brutal honesty—not only about why I was here, but also about my feelings for her. But the latter couldn't come without full disclosure first.

A long while after I'd texted her, a response finally came in.

Heather: Well, I could have told you that.

I couldn't help but crack a smile, relieved that she was even responding.

Noah: Are you okay?

Her answer was immediate.

Heather: Let me in and I'll tell you.

My heart pumped as I rushed to the door.

Heather stood there getting drenched, her red dress stuck to her body. I'd been so preoccupied, I hadn't even realized it was raining.

One look at her, and I was done for again.

"I couldn't stop thinking about you all night," she said. "I owe you a huge apology for the way I acted."

Her hair was dripping. "I don't want to want you either, you know. The thought of you leaving and possibly never seeing you again is so scary. I wish I didn't feel this way."

She smelled even better wet from the rain. I really tried not to kiss her again, but the need was even more intense now that I knew what it felt like. I needed to taste her one last time before what would be one of the toughest conversations of my life.

Wrapping my hands around her cheeks, I brought her face into mine and devoured her lips. This kiss was different than the last. While the first had been frenzied and desperate, this time I kissed her slowly and passionately, my tongue stroking hers gently. Her fingers tangled in my hair as she pulled, seeming desperate for more. My eyes closed as I cherished every second, every little moan that escaped her.

After several minutes, I gently bit her bottom lip before forcing myself back.

"Please don't stop."

"I have to."

"Why?"

Taking both of her hands in mine, I led her over to the spot next to me on the sofa.

"I have to talk to you. I don't want to put it off anymore. It's something I wasn't necessarily going to tell you, because I wasn't expecting to be in this deep. Now that I am, I feel like I owe you an explanation for why I'm here."

"Why you're here? You're scaring me. What's going on?"

"Please don't be scared."

"What is it? Are you sick? I've always had this scary feeling that maybe—"

"No. Nothing like that. I'm fine. Healthy as a horse."

Heather sighed in relief. "Okay…"

"I've been keeping something from you. While you may not fully understand why I didn't say anything, I need you to know that I came here with the best of intentions."

"Intentions?"

"My choosing this place wasn't a coincidence."

Her eyes narrowed. "What are you talking about?"

There was no easy way to say it. "Heather…" I took a deep breath and braced myself. "I knew your sister."

CHAPTER SEVENTEEN

Heather

My eyes wouldn't stop blinking.

Did he just say he knew my sister?

The only thing that would come out of me was, "What?"

"I knew Opal."

A rush of panic hit me.

Noah...and my sister?

"Did you...did you and my sister..."

"No!" he said adamantly, seeming to realize where I was coming from. "No...God, I need you to know that. Nothing *ever* happened between us. We were not romantically involved in any way, shape, or form. So please don't think that. But I did meet her, and I need to tell you the story."

The room felt like it was spinning.

"I can't believe this. What..."

"Your sister, she was living in Pennsylvania for a while. She walked into my studio one day, wanting a portrait shoot."

Okay.

That made *some* sense.

Noah squeezed my hand. As confused as I was, his touch calmed the shock a bit. I looked at him, waiting for more.

"She said she was trying to get into modeling and needed a full portfolio." He paused. "Anyway, we scheduled it. She came back about a week later, and we did the shoot."

"You took photos of my sister..."

"Yes. They were all tasteful, a mix of headshots and simple poses. She was fully clothed. It wasn't anything crazy. My studio at the time was attached to my house. I have a different space now. Anyway, she met Olivia and everything. I was still married then." He took a deep breath, seeming to gear up for more. "Despite knowing that fact, your sister started to message me after our business had concluded. You have to believe me when I tell you we never had any contact besides that one shoot. But in her messages, she said really inappropriate things."

Oh no. "Like what?"

"Like she couldn't stop thinking about me and she felt we had some kind of cosmic connection—also some sexual things. She just kept contacting me through my business email, professing her feelings for me and suggesting we meet up. The first couple of times I responded very simply and dismissively, and after a while, I stopped responding at all. Her messages kept coming anyway. I didn't know what to do. It was bizarre and unlike anything I'd experienced before. Even after I asked her to please stop contacting me, she kept doing it. It was all very *Fatal Attraction.* I think she was delusional."

Holy shit.

My sister was without a doubt not well. But when she was taking her medication, she would have good patches. The problem was, you never knew when she would randomly stop taking care of herself. As much as I didn't want to believe it, this story sounded like her.

I let him go on.

"Olivia saw some of the messages, and it really tested us. She knew I was telling the truth, that nothing had happened with Opal, but it was hard for her to accept that a woman was sending me sexually explicit messages and professing her love. It agitated an already bad situation."

"So Opal kept emailing you? Then what?"

He nodded. "Then one day it just...stopped. There were no more messages. At the time I was really relieved, because I never knew if she would eventually try something crazy."

"That was it? It stopped, and you never heard from her again?"

"Not exactly." He squeezed my hand harder. "That was it for a while. I thought it was over. But one day several months later, I received a call from an investigator in Connecticut. It was...after they'd found her. She'd left a letter at the motel. It was addressed to me."

Covering my mouth, I gasped and whispered into my hand, "Oh my God."

I had managed to keep my composure up until this point, but now my tears fell. Noah wiped them away with his thumb and went over to the counter to grab a tissue for me.

I sniffled. "What did it say?"

"In the letter, she wrote how sorry she was for upsetting me. But that wasn't the purpose of her writing. She was reaching out to me for my help."

"Your help?"

"She listed your address here on Lake Winnipesaukee and asked me to look after her sister—you—when she was gone. Even in her state of mind, she was worried about you."

My heart felt ready to shatter. My lip trembled. "That's all she said?"

"Pretty much. She explained that she couldn't handle life anymore and needed me to help look after you. It wasn't very long. I have the letter, if you ever want to see it. I didn't bring it because I wasn't planning to tell you why I came. But I can easily get it."

Still in shock, I shook my head. It was hard to believe, but I knew it was true.

"I have no idea why she chose me, Heather. I hadn't heard from her in months, but for some reason, she chose to write to me in those last moments and ask for *my* help, and it's haunted me more than you know. Maybe it was part of her same delusional idea that I'd played some important role in her life. I will never know the reason she picked me."

I stared out at the rain pelting the window. "I'm still confused."

"Ask me anything."

"She died six years ago." I turned to him. "Why now? Why did you come now?"

Noah let out a long breath. "That's the question, isn't it?" He looked down at my hand in his for a moment. "I've lived with a lot of guilt over not getting her help. Despite how crazy it was that she messaged me like that, I never dreamed her issues were as serious as they were. I never thought to try to find her family or get her to a doctor. I had just wanted it to stop. In retrospect, I absolutely should have done something. When I found out she had taken her own life, it fucked me up. I became even more withdrawn from my marriage and fell into a depression."

I could relate to that guilt. So often I'd blamed myself for not doing something more to find my sister and help her. I'd never imagined she would take her own life, and that was a very naïve way of thinking.

"I'm sorry you had to go through that," I said.

"I learned a lot from it." He threaded his fingers with mine and looked down again at our hands. "Anyway, to answer your question, despite the fact that in her letter she asked me to look after you, I never considered doing it, because it didn't make any sense—some strange guy you've never met showing up at your door, asking if you're okay? You didn't even know me. I didn't see how that would help you. So I decided against it."

"What changed?"

"As the years went on, I still couldn't shake what happened. I couldn't change anything about the past. One day I woke up and realized maybe the only way to rid myself of the guilt was to do what she'd asked. It felt like the least I could do for her. So, I looked you up more than a year ago and found out about this rental situation. I planned carefully so I could book my stay far enough in advance to get a spot this summer. I was pretty shocked when I was able to reserve it for the *whole* summer, but I decided to go for it."

I couldn't make my brain work. "So, you came here on a mission to what? Make sure I wasn't a mess? To save me?"

"Honestly, Heather, I didn't know what I was going to do when I got here. I just came because I felt I owed it to Opal. I felt like my lack of action in getting her help had contributed to her death somehow. And I couldn't live with that. The time was right for me. I had no real commitments anymore. So I bit the bullet."

Finally, I nodded. "Now it makes sense—all the work around the house, helping me get it on the market, encouraging me to go away to school..."

"Well, that's the part that makes sense to you, but so much of this doesn't make sense to *me* anymore. What I didn't expect was that almost immediately, I felt very connected to this place—to you. Despite that, I was adamant that I wouldn't get emotionally involved. That's why I was so standoffish with you in the beginning. From the second I got here, I felt more invested than I ever imagined, and I've tried to fight that. I never meant to interfere with your life, to insert myself into it. My goal was to honor your sister's wishes, to make sure you were okay, and to set you on the right path before I left. I figured three months was enough time to make that happen. But I never expected to connect with you the way we have, to feel what I'm feeling. And I certainly never planned to tell you the real reason I came."

My God. I still had so many questions.

"Was this the reason for your divorce?"

"No. All of the mistakes I told you I made happened before Opal. My relationship with Olivia was already in shambles by the time I received the letter. But my depression really kicked in after that. So it certainly didn't help, but it wasn't the main reason. We wouldn't have lasted anyway."

"Does Olivia know why you're here?"

"Yeah. That's partly why we've been in touch a lot lately. She's been checking on me because she knows everything. My father, too. They're the only ones who know why I came here."

"Did they encourage it?"

"Olivia thought I was crazy. My father got it, though. He didn't see the harm in it, if it alleviated some of my guilt." He searched my eyes. "Tell me what you're thinking."

Feeling numb, I told him the truth. "I don't know how to feel right now. I'm in shock. Total shock."

"I was so worried you'd be angry at me."

Anger wasn't the right word. As much as this floored me, I couldn't be angry at him when his intentions were good. As bizarre as this story was, I could understand how it happened.

"I can't be mad at you for this. None of it is your fault. You've always told me not to blame myself for anything when it came to Opal's death. Well, the same goes for you. You couldn't have known what would happen. I didn't realize Opal was capable of taking her own life, and I was her sister. I knew her a lot better than you did. We tried to help her, but she wasn't letting us. I'll never know if I could have stopped her death if I had tried something different." I paused to take a breath. "The point is, if her own family couldn't help her, there's likely nothing she would have allowed you to do to help her, either."

He took a moment, seeming to let those words sink in.

"Are you mad that I kept my reason for coming here from you?" he asked.

"Well, what were you supposed to do? Announce it when you got here? I get why you kept it to yourself, why you didn't come right out and tell me. I probably would've wanted to send you packing. It's better that I got to know you first before you laid this on me."

He placed his head on my shoulder. "Fuck, Heather. You have no idea how relieved I am to hear you say that. I seriously doubted my decision."

"I just wish you didn't see me as a charity case."

He sat up to look me in the eyes. "Listen, I had my reasons for coming here, but this experience has been nothing like what I expected. You're not a charity case. You're strong, confident...amazing. You've taught me just as much as I could ever teach you. I'm drawn to you and finding it damn hard not to show it. My actions are scaring the hell out of me...because the last thing I meant to do was complicate your life."

I sat back on the couch and rested my head. The story he'd told me played through my head from start to finish like a movie as I tried to imagine how everything had gone down.

"Do you have the photos you took of her?"

He pursed his lips for a moment to think about it. "They're on my laptop, yeah."

"Can I see them?"

"Of course. Now?"

"If you don't mind, yes."

"Just give me a minute to pull them up. I keep everything I've ever shot on a special drive."

I watched as Noah logged in. It took him about three minutes to locate the file containing the photos.

When he placed the computer on my lap, nothing could have prepared me for the emotions I felt looking at image after image of my beautiful, smiling sister. We looked more alike than I remembered. Now that I was getting closer to the age she'd been in these photos, I could really see the resemblance.

Wiping a tear, I asked, "Did she seem off the day you took the photos?"

Noah moved closer to me. "Not at all. That's why it was so strange when the messages started coming in."

"That was typical. She was like two different people in many ways, depending on whether she was taking care of herself."

"Yeah. None of it made sense."

Not taking my eyes off the images, I said, "I really want to see the letter, too."

"I have it at home. I know where it is and will have my dad scan it. I should've brought it with me. I just really wasn't anticipating telling you."

The questions kept coming to me in waves. "Why did you decide to tell me tonight?"

"Because I couldn't hold it in any more, couldn't stand the thought of keeping anything from you. A lot has changed between us, and I don't know how to handle it. I just know I never want to be anything less than completely honest with you. That goes for my feelings about you, too."

A part of me wanted him to elaborate on that—his feelings for me—but I knew I couldn't handle anything more tonight. I needed to absorb this.

"Can you download these photos for me?"

"Of course. I'll buy a thumb drive tomorrow."

"Thanks." I continued sifting through the photographs, starting again from the beginning. "I don't think I'm gonna tell Mom about this. I don't know how she'd handle it. I don't want her to view you differently—not that I think there's any reason to feel differently about you, but I don't want to upset her."

"That's up to you. I get it. I'm okay with anything you decide, but I think that's a good call. There's too much going on right now as it is."

I stared at the screen. "I'm still in shock."

"It would be strange if you weren't."

I needed to be alone to process this.

Getting up off the couch, I wiped my eyes and announced, "I'm gonna go home. I just need to be alone for a while."

He stood. "Yeah. Of course."

I handed him the laptop and headed for the door.

Noah looked concerned. "Are you sure you're okay?"

I nodded, then walked home in a daze.

CHAPTER
EIGHTEEN

Noah

Heather hadn't come by since my revelation. An entire day had passed. Even though I was tempted to go over to the main house, I tried to give her space. My news was a lot to take in.

I couldn't help but text her, though, to ask if she was okay. She assured me she was, but I didn't entirely believe her, because it wasn't like her to stay away. I'd told her I made her a thumb drive of the photos she'd requested and asked if she wanted me to bring it over. She said no. I'd also had my father scan the letter from Opal and added it to the memory stick. The fact that she didn't even want to see me long enough to receive it confirmed that she was still processing.

At least I hoped that was it.

I'd done nothing all day but pace and drink coffee in between feeding the guinea pigs. As the afternoon turned into evening, I decided to call my father and fill him in on what happened.

After I told him the story of my conversation with Heather last night, he tried to convince me I'd done the right thing in telling her.

"She said she wasn't mad, but it's going to hit her later—or maybe that's what's happening now, why she's staying away."

"What does she have to be mad about?" he asked.

Is he serious? "Oh, I don't know...the fact that I came here under false pretenses? The fact that I could've potentially done something to save her sister's life if I'd gotten her help? She has a number of options."

"No one knew what was going to happen, Noah. You were a married man getting explicit messages from a strange woman. You had no idea what it was. A lot of delusional people aren't suicidal. You didn't know her, God rest her soul. Stop blaming yourself for something that's not your fault."

I wanted to believe his words, especially since they echoed Heather's, but I still struggled. I still wondered if removing myself from the situation might be best all around.

"I feel like the right thing to do now might be to go home early."

"You're gonna be able to walk away from her?"

"The longer I stay, the harder it's gonna be. Leaving is inevitable. Why prolong it?"

The thought of leaving now made me sick to my stomach, but maybe it was best for both of us. The property was under contract. Heather was enrolled in college, and she'd have the money for it even if her father took half the real estate proceeds. There was nothing stopping her. I'd be leaving in a few weeks anyway. Staying would cause nothing but more confusion for both of us.

"By the same token," Dad added, "you could look at it a different way. It's only a few more weeks. Why rush to say goodbye? What's the real reason you want out of there so fast?"

I knew the truth. "Because I can't control my feelings for her anymore. I know if I stay, they're gonna explode. I need to go home so she can leave and live her life without any complications."

"You think *that's* gonna make her feel better? To see you drive away when she's upset and clearly cares for you?"

"She doesn't know what's good for her, and honestly, she's been avoiding me today. She hasn't wanted to see me. This is probably the best time to make a clean break."

"I can't force you to stick it out if you're intent on leaving. But I don't get the sense that's what you want."

It wasn't what I wanted at all. I'd never been happier than these past couple of months. But sometimes, doing what's better for others trumps what makes you happy. It felt like the responsible decision.

"I think I'm gonna do it. I'm gonna pack up and tell her after everything is loaded, to make it easier."

"You sure about this?"

"It was gonna happen anyway. This will be like ripping the Band-Aid off." I looked over at the cage on my table. *Jesus. I have to figure out how to travel with guinea pigs.* "The only complication is the guinea pigs."

My father was rightfully confused. "Guinea pigs?"

"Yeah. Bonnie and Clyde. Long story. Let's just say I'm not coming home alone."

After we hung up, I started packing my things. I didn't have a lot of stuff, so it only took me about a half-hour. Then I Googled "how to take a road trip with guinea pigs" and realized I'd have to stop somewhere in the morning to get two, soft-sided animal carriers.

Even with that, packing was the easy part.

The hard part was going to be telling Heather I planned to leave in the morning. Maybe after last night's bombshell, she wouldn't fight me on it. Maybe she'd see why this was best for both of us.

Even though I'd been cutting back on the cigars lately, I needed to calm down, so I decided to light one up on the porch. As I gazed out at the lake, I thought about how much this summer had changed me. Most of my life, I'd wanted to be any place I wasn't. The grass was always greener. But not here. At the lake, I was content. I didn't feel so alone anymore. I was happy just...being. I'd heard about the practice of mindfulness but had never been able to implement it until recently. Here, I listened to the rain, tasted my food, and felt so many things going on inside of me, especially whenever Heather was around. Being able to enjoy the present moment was a blessing, one made easier by being somewhere that made me happy.

I wasn't kidding when I said I could have lived here the rest of my life. I wondered how much of that had to do with the lake and how much of it had to do with a certain girl who'd infiltrated my soul. That question scared the shit out of me, making me even more sure I needed to leave tomorrow.

I looked out over the water and chuckled to myself, thinking about the first time I'd interacted with Heather. I'd learned that day what a spirited firecracker she was. Thrown off by how alive she'd made me feel, I'd tried everything to scare her away. But it hadn't worked. Thank

God for that, because I never would have gotten the time I had with her, never would have learned I have the capability to be happy after all. For years, I'd thought I was a lost cause. But Heather's believing in me, and all her kind words about second chances, had resonated.

Darkness eclipsed the daylight, which was fitting as my thoughts turned from happy to sad. It was time to break the news to her.

I was just about to go inside and call her when I noticed her walking toward me in the distance. My body stilled.

She was holding something. As she got closer, I realized it was a pie. My heart squeezed at the sight of her.

I lost my ability to speak, let alone the courage to tell her my plans.

She looked at me for several seconds before she finally spoke.

"So, I know I've been quiet. I needed to ride it out for a day. I've been processing everything you told me, but I'm okay. I need you to know that. I didn't quite know how to express my feelings, how to convey everything to you, so I decided to bake that cherry pie I promised you. The cherries from the tree weren't good, and there weren't even enough of them anyway, so I had to go to the store and buy some. It took me all afternoon to figure out the best recipe—one I couldn't screw up. I think I actually did it. You'll have to be the judge. The candy corn smiley face on top is my personal touch."

Her smile was killing me. My mouth wouldn't move.

"It's okay, Noah. I want you to know it's okay. I need you to believe me when I say I don't hold anything against you. How could I?"

Her assurance gave me the comfort I desperately needed. It also complicated my plans. I no longer had any clue how to tell her I planned to leave in the morning.

Before I could think any further, she brushed past me into the boathouse.

I cringed when she stopped to look around.

"What the hell is going on?"

"I was gonna come over and talk to you tonight. I—"

"You're leaving?" Her voice cracked. She held her hand over her chest. "Oh my God. Let me put this pie down before I drop it."

I tried to find words to articulate my decision. The effort was futile. "Heather, I—"

"I can't believe you were just going to drop this on me."

"I thought it would be easier this way."

"Easier? Do you have any idea what you mean to me?"

It couldn't have hurt more if she'd ripped out my heart. Seeing her tears brought home how much she cared about me. It made me doubt everything again.

"This was gonna be happening in three weeks anyway," I said, although it seemed like a sad excuse right now.

"I know. And I was going to cherish the fuck out of the time you had left here. The next three weeks mean everything to me. You're just going to throw them away?"

"I don't think it makes sense to prolong it," I said weakly.

Her voice grew louder. "You're a coward. Don't think I don't know what this is really about. You're starting to feel something for me, so you're going to run away."

I laughed angrily. "*Starting*? I've been feeling it for so fucking long it's not even funny."

"You have an odd way of showing it."

"I upset you last night. It isn't going to be any easier to walk away from here in a few weeks. It seemed like the right time."

"I was upset. But not at *you*. The more I thought about what you did in coming here, your intentions, the more I admire you. Sure, I was sad earlier, but now? Seeing you ready to walk out of here? Now I'm *devastated*."

I swore under my breath. "It's not my intention to hurt you. That's not what leaving early is about—it's just the opposite. It's to avoid doing something to hurt you."

"You've kept your cool with me, kept your hands off me all summer with the exception of yesterday. Suddenly you don't think you can last another three weeks?"

She didn't get it. "Another three weeks? I can't last another *second*."

She looked stunned. That made two of us.

Heather took a step toward me. "Nothing has ever hurt as badly as the pain of wanting you and not getting to have you, trying to hide my feelings from you. I don't want to hurt *like this* anymore. I don't care about next week or three weeks or next year. All I care about is now. I know damn well what will happen between us if you stay. That's *exactly* why I don't want you to leave."

Fuck.

So many thoughts swirled through my brain. I took a moment to see her, this beautiful young woman who wanted to experience being with me. And I wanted nothing but to be with her. If I turned away now, would I look back at this moment for the rest of my life with regret? Would it haunt me—the moment I had an opportunity for something I wanted but threw it away? The moment I stopped us both from experiencing what we so badly wanted?

My head battled my heart and body—two against one. I knew with every ounce of my soul that if I moved toward her right now, it would be over. And it wouldn't be my head that won.

The pain in her eyes was like nothing I'd ever seen, not even when her father had pulled the rug out from under her.

For the first time, I realized I might be hurting her more by denying her. Or maybe that's just what I wanted to believe. Maybe it's what I *had* to believe, because there was no turning back.

My mind went blank as physical need overtook it. I no longer knew wrong from right. I no longer had a sense of time. I just *needed* her.

"Come here."

"Are you gonna send me away?"

"No. Not gonna do that."

She walked to me and fell into my arms. I held her tightly. For the first time, I let myself breathe her in, hold her the way I wanted to without resisting.

I was a goner.

CHAPTER
NINETEEN

Heather

When he lifted me into his arms and placed his lips on mine, I thought about how many times I'd imagined him doing this very thing. Feeling weightless, I wrapped my legs around his body, holding on to him for dear life.

Don't leave.

Please don't leave.

I'd been with one other person in my life, and he'd been a boy in every sense—mentally and physically. Noah was a man, larger than life in both body and mind. Getting to be with him like this incited unprecedented sensations within me. His sheer size rendered me powerless, and I'd never been so happy. I wanted him to own every inch of me.

I hoped I wasn't embarrassing myself with how eagerly I was kissing him, tasting him—basically humping him. It felt so good to be swept up by this man and kissed with everything he had in him, to feel the warmth of his breath filling me. I felt out of control—like a feral cat.

Moving my hips, I rubbed against the massive bulge in his jeans, his heat resonating between my legs. Knowing

I'd made him hard like that gave me immense satisfaction. I needed him to enter me.

"Don't hate me for my weakness," he groaned through our kiss.

"I'll hate you if you stop."

He smiled over my lips. *Thank God we're on the same page.*

"I've never wanted anything like I want you, Heather. You make me so fucking crazy."

I couldn't even wait for him to undress me. I broke away from our kiss long enough to lift my shirt over my head and throw it on the ground. Staring into his eyes, I unsnapped my bra and let it fall to our feet.

His breathing was labored as he took in the sight of my bare breasts for a few seconds before bearing down on them with his mouth. The wetness of his tongue and the heat of his breath on my nipples practically caused me to orgasm. I could feel my clit throbbing as Noah sucked so hard I wanted to scream. It hurt so good. He used to treat me like a little girl, but he was handling me like a woman tonight; I was grateful for that. I may not have been that experienced, but I knew I could take whatever he had to give. My body was ready. It had been gearing up for this moment from the first time I'd laid eyes on him.

He took my nipple gently between his teeth. "So, so beautiful..."

I pressed his head deeper into me, raking through his hair with my fingernails as he sucked on my neck. I knew there would be marks on me tomorrow, and I didn't care. Starving to taste him again, I guided him back up to my mouth. I kept expecting him to be bossy, tell me to slow down, scold me for my eagerness. But he never did.

Noah was just as lost in this as I was.

He walked us over toward the wall and propped me against it. He had no idea how many times I'd fantasized about this very thing.

Our kiss grew even more intense, and I wanted him to lift my skirt and fuck me right here. Instead, he suddenly put me down. Worried he'd changed his mind, I grabbed his shirt and pulled him back to me. He resisted.

He could see the fear in my eyes.

"Don't worry, baby. I'm not going anywhere, okay? But I need to stop for a second."

My heart pounded. *Why is he stopping?*

"I need to lock the door," he said before cupping his hands around my face and pulling me in for a reassuring kiss. "We can't take a chance on someone coming in."

Relief washed over me. I leaned against the wall as he went to the front door and turned the deadbolt. He drew the shades. Then he walked over to his backpack and took something out—a strip of condoms. He threw it on the nightstand and returned to me.

"I want to look at you," he rasped, sliding his hand down my chest to my stomach.

He pulled at the button of my denim skirt and undid it. He nudged it down until it fell. I kicked off my shoes. Left in nothing but my thong, I watched as he gawked at me with glassy eyes.

"You're so fucking hot. You have no idea how long I've dreamed about this. I'm so hard just looking at you."

"What do you want to do to me?"

He let out a long breath and caressed my cheek. "Everything you can imagine."

I needed to touch him, to feel how much he wanted me. I reached out to rub my palm over his cock, which was bursting through his pants. Its heat penetrated his jeans. His breathing became erratic as he closed his eyes and bent his head back to enjoy my touch.

"Fuuuck...stop." He placed his hand on mine. "Turn around."

Doing as he said, I placed my hands on the wall.

"Holy shit," I heard him whisper as he got a look at my ass.

His hand felt rough as he slid it down slowly, caressing my back. I felt his fingers looping though my G-string. He pulled on it and brought me toward him.

Showering the back of my neck with slow, firm kisses, he spoke against my skin, "It's almost too much."

I felt the air between us for a moment. When I looked over my shoulder, he was taking off his shirt. I leaned back against his bare, muscular chest, his erection right up against the crack of my ass. Wetness seeped through the material of my thong as I squeezed the muscles between my legs to curb the intense need building there.

He wrapped his arms around me, my entire body enveloped in his. The skin-to-skin contact felt so good. His heart beat against my back, and I wanted to weep for all the nights we'd wasted not doing this very thing.

He flipped me around and gazed at my body. Placing his hands on my waist, he lowered my thong. Completely naked before him, I felt goosebumps cover my body.

He knelt down and took my pussy into his mouth, lapping at my clit with his tongue before inserting it all the way inside of me. He kept at it for a few minutes as I bent my head back. The pleasure felt like shockwaves of electricity pulsing through my core.

"You taste so good." He spoke over my skin. "I can't decide how I want to take you first."

"Just take me," I breathed, desperate to feel him inside of me.

Noah stood and brought me to his chest. "I feel like the luckiest man alive right now. I don't deserve you." He swept me off my feet as he carried me over to the bed and laid me down.

I watched as he pulled his boxer briefs down. When his cock sprang forward, I marveled at how long and thick he was. In my experience from watching the occasional porn, you typically got one or the other. But Noah's cock was perfect. The tip was wet, and I had the urge to lick the precum off of it.

He lowered himself over me and began to rub his slick shaft across my taut stomach, sliding it up and down, over my belly button as he looked into my eyes. It was so erotic. Feeling his hot arousal on my skin turned me on to no end.

I couldn't take it anymore, though. I reached over to the nightstand and grabbed the strip of condoms, breaking one off and handing it to him.

"You trying to tell me something?" he teased.

"I want you so bad," I breathed.

"Easy, beautiful girl. You're gonna get me. I'm trying to take it slow, so I don't come all over you right now."

"I'm sorry if I'm too eager."

"Don't apologize for that. I've never been wanted by anyone so beautiful, so precious, in my entire life. I *love* how you want me. It makes me insane."

"*You* make me insane, Noah."

He ripped the condom package open with his teeth.

My heart raced with anticipation.

"Spread for me wide," he said as he rolled the rubber onto his engorged shaft.

He lowered himself over me. The weight of his body was overwhelming. I stretched my legs apart to make room for him. As he kissed me, I could feel his cock teasing my entrance. My legs quivered.

"I can feel how wet you are, and I'm not even inside of you yet. Holy shit."

Without warning, he pushed inside in one thrust. It burned in the best way. I hadn't had sex in over two years, so it was more painful than I'd expected. But after a few times of him moving in and out, the pain turned to pure ecstasy.

Holy shit. Noah is inside of me.

What started out as gentle soon transformed into raw fucking.

My fingernails dug into his back as he pounded into me rhythmically. With every movement in and out, I felt like I could orgasm if I let myself.

"Heather...you...oh my...fuck...you feel so good. So good, baby."

The headboard banged against the wall, and I was pretty sure the guinea pigs were having heart attacks. With every creak of the bed, I felt more grateful that the boathouse was set so far back from the main house.

Talk about being properly fucked.

I held on to his muscular ass and bucked my hips to meet his thrusts, desperate to stop myself from coming, because I didn't want this to be over.

"Look at me, Heather."

The intensity in his eyes was all it took for me to lose it. When my legs started to shake, he knew I was climaxing. I shrieked louder than I'd intended when my orgasm pummeled through me.

His body trembled seconds after, and his mouth fell agape as he came hard, pounding even deeper into me as he emptied his load into the condom.

He kept moving inside of me long after there was nothing left.

"So fucking good." Noah collapsed onto me. "I'll never be the same again."

He'd taken the words out of my mouth. He was still inside of me, and already I had no idea how any other man could measure up. I didn't want to find out.

CHAPTER
TWENTY

Noah

I couldn't remember the last time I'd woken up feeling so completely at peace, yet in turmoil at the same time. In the present moment, I was more content than I'd probably ever been. But as soon as my mind wandered into the future, dread crept in to ruin it.

Heather was still sleeping. Her beautiful bare ass faced me, and her gorgeous blond hair was a mess of spun gold falling down her back.

I had no idea how I'd gotten so lucky. She'd surrendered her body to me last night—several times. I should have been exhausted from the amount of sex we'd had. It was, bar none, the most incredible night of my life. On a physical level, we fit together perfectly. But even with her eagerness, even as I felt her orgasm pulsate against my cock—multiple times as I fucked every hole in her body—I still didn't feel I deserved her.

The guilt would set in as soon as this high was over. For now, I was still blinded by euphoria. I was living the moment I'd always feared: knowing what it was like to have her and still feeling as though I needed to let her go.

That wasn't going to be happening today, though. I knew that for sure. I needed her again and again—and wondered if she'd be up for another round.

Kissing the back of her neck, I hoped she'd wake up.

Her body stirred, and she pushed against my cock.

"Good morning," she said as she teased me with her ass.

The urge to slip inside her raw was intense. I grabbed the last condom from my nightstand and sheathed myself before I could give in and do something reckless.

I sank into her slowly until I was balls deep. Being inside of her already felt like home to me. She was so wet despite the fact that she'd just woken up.

Seeing her ass from this angle as I fucked her totally did me in. After only a minute of pumping into her hard and deep, I lost control and came. You'd think I would have built up some resistance over the past twelve hours. Instead, this was the first time in my life I'd ever prematurely blown my load.

"Shit. I'm sorry. This angle...it was too much for me."

"Don't pull out yet," she said.

She started to play with her clit, and my dick actually began to gear up for another round. Within seconds, she was bucking her hips and coming against her hand with me still inside of her.

If that wasn't the hottest thing I'd ever witnessed...

I pulled out of her slowly and got up to discard the condom.

Heather gawked at my naked body as I returned to the bed.

My eyebrows lifted. "Keep looking at me like that, and I'm gonna have to find another condom."

I lay facing her and planted a kiss on her beautiful lips.

After a few minutes, the plethora of worrisome thoughts returned. She noticed my change in expression.

"Do you regret what we've done?"

"Not one bit."

"I can see worry on your face."

"It has nothing to do with regret. I wouldn't change last night or this morning for the world."

"But you *are* worried."

I caressed her face, not wanting to ruin this time together. "We don't need to talk about this now."

Heather moved back a little bit, and suddenly it felt cold in the bed. "Just last night, you were about to walk out of my life. I feel like talking about this now. I want to know what you're thinking."

She was right. Things had gone from one extreme to the other. Even though I wanted to stay in this sexual fog, that wasn't fair. She deserved honesty, even if I didn't have all the answers.

"There's so much going on in my head right now that I'm not even sure how to express it."

"Try."

I pulled her in closer to me. "I'm confused," I finally said.

"About your feelings toward me?"

"My feelings toward you are the only thing I'm sure of. You make me happier than anyone or anything has in a very long time. And last night was the best sex of my life."

"Why do I feel like there's a *but* in there somewhere..."

Tightening my squeeze on her waist, I said, "I'm scared shitless to hold you back, Heather. You already know that.

You're getting attached to me. Instead, you should be focusing on going away to school and starting your life. I'm afraid to interfere and derail everything."

"Why does it have to be a choice? Why can't I have both?"

That was a fair question—without a simple answer.

"You can. But whether you'll still *want* that in six months or a year is very dependent on what you find when you get there, how you feel when you're on your own for the first time. I'm not sure you can know how you're gonna feel right now."

"I beg to differ... But let me ask you a question. What would *you* want if my schooling wasn't in the way?"

I didn't have to think about that. "I'd want to be around you every day."

"You wouldn't consider a long-distance relationship?"

"With you? I'd consider anything. I'd have to know you were fully ready for that, though. And I don't know if you can determine that now. This is a very emotional time in your life. You've relied on me a lot to get through it, and I'm so happy I could be here for you. But you might feel differently when you move away, when there's distance between us. Summer will turn to winter. You might not want to be tied down in a relationship with a thirty-five-year-old divorcé. You might want your freedom."

She seemed desperate to get her point across. "I want *you*. You're all I want. I can't imagine ever not wanting to be with you. I don't care if I'm here or in Timbuktu."

"I know you mean that with all of your heart right now."

"But you don't think I'll still feel that way when I get to school? You think I can just switch my feelings off that easily?"

We were blinded by infatuation. I'd experienced enough already to know what I wanted. I wanted *her*. But she was still evolving. How could I make her understand that if she didn't want to hear it?

"Heather, you're so damn young. You've never even lived away from home on your own. You have this amazing opportunity to go away to school and to have your freedom, and I think it's best for you not to be tied down before you even get there."

She started to cry.

Fuck.

Fuck.

Fuck.

"What you just said feels like you're breaking up with me, but that's silly because we're not even together. In reality, we only fucked."

My tone grew angry. "It wasn't *only* fucking, and you know it."

"Then what *does* it mean if we can't be together? It then becomes...just fucking."

"I didn't say we *can't* be together. I just—"

"I just had the best night of my life, and now you're pushing me away."

"Please don't think that. I'm *not* pushing you away. You asked me what was on my mind. I'm trying to be honest with you." It felt like my heart had suddenly burst open as my voice grew louder. "I'm scared, okay? What we have... it's intense. In some ways, it's the most intense thing I've ever experienced. There's no halfway with you. When you were out with that guy the other night, I felt physically ill." I realized I'd never heard anything about how her date went. "Whatever happened with him anyway?"

"I was so preoccupied after leaving you, I barely heard a word he said all night. I apologized for seeming out of it and asked him to take me home early."

Good.

"Well, I was a basket case the whole time you were gone. I've never felt that possessive over anyone in my entire life, not even the woman I was married to. But that reaction is very telling. It means I need to make sure my feelings toward you aren't impeding your freedom, that I'm not steering you in a certain direction for selfish reasons. The thought of losing you hurts. But what hurts me even more is the thought of you ever regretting choosing me. I don't want you to have any regrets. I don't want you to resent me."

I finally seemed to be getting through to her a little. Her eyes softened.

"I understand what you're saying. I just don't know what it means for us. Are you telling me to forget about you and date other people when I go away to school?"

That made my stomach turn. "Honestly? I have to think about what it means. We took things to a different level last night, one I wasn't mentally ready for and one we can't easily come back from, either. You asked me to open up. That's what I'm doing. I just don't have all of the answers yet. Right now, these feelings are very raw. I'm still so fucking high off of you I can't think straight."

She just kept blinking and nodding. She didn't know what to make of this conversation any more than I did.

Suddenly, she got out of bed. "I think I should go back to the house for a bit."

"Don't leave yet. Let's keep talking."

Heather started putting her clothes back on. "I can't think straight around you, either. Plus, my mother is probably wondering where I am. She knows I've fallen asleep here before. But I'm pretty sure she'll take one look at my face and figure out what happened this time. I'm not a very good liar."

The thought of Alice finding out about this made me panic a little. "Are you gonna tell her the truth if she calls you on it?"

"I'm not sure."

"Well, if you don't plan to, you'd better cover your neck. I left marks all over you."

The thought of that made me want to fuck her again. What was wrong with me? Even after all of the concerns I'd just shared, I wanted nothing more than to carry her back to bed, bury my head between her legs, and make her scream again. Forget about everything else.

"Let me get you something to put on." I threw on my pants and zipped them up.

Opening the suitcase I'd packed, I took out a turtleneck, cable knit sweater. Don't ask me why I'd brought that with me in the middle of summer, but I was thankful I had.

She pulled it over her head. "Thanks."

Practically swimming in my sweater, Heather lingered at the door.

I cupped her face. "Last night was incredible. I'm not going anywhere. I'm staying until you tell me it's okay to leave or until I'm kicked out of here by the new owner...

or by you. And I'm here all day when you're ready to talk more."

"Okay." She leaned in and placed a chaste kiss on my lips.

I watched her walk back to her house. *Well, Noah, you've finally done it. You've gone and fucked things up real good.*

CHAPTER
TWENTY-ONE

Heather

She knows.

My mother isn't stupid. She'd seen me leave with that pie last night and knew where I was going. So it didn't take a genius to figure out why I hadn't come home until now.

She was sitting in the dimly lit kitchen waiting for me when I arrived. The fact that she'd come out of her room to sit there and wait meant she was definitely looking for a confrontation.

She crossed her arms. "Where have you been?"

"You know the answer to that."

Tilting her head, she said, "I assume that's his sweater..."

"I fell asleep there. He let me borrow it. It's a little chilly this morning."

"Right."

I tried my best not to look at her as I fumbled in search of a K-cup to make some coffee.

"I understand, you know," she said.

I froze.

I turned around to face her and was now one-hundred percent sure she knew I'd fucked Noah.

As much as I didn't want to admit what had happened last night, a part of me needed my mother right now. I needed to talk to someone I trusted. I was used to being the one looking after her, but sometimes a girl needs to be taken care of by her parent. And it was really rare to have her attention like this.

I resumed making the coffee and finally coughed out the words. "I only went over to give him that pie. Things just...it was a mistake."

"There are no mistakes in life. Everything you do is a choice. Some of them are good, and others contribute to our personal growth, teach us lessons. Choices lead us to things we were meant to experience. I may be depressed, but I'm still your mother, and I've still garnered some wisdom over the years."

"You're not disappointed in me, then?"

"Why would I be? Noah is a great man. My trepidation about him early on had nothing to do with him and everything to do with me. I was afraid to lose you. I've since come to terms with the fact that you're leaving, so my feelings toward Noah have evolved, too. I've always sensed the attraction between the two of you. You know that. So, no, this isn't a surprise, and I'm not disappointed. I just don't want you to get hurt."

"Wow." I took a sip of my coffee and sighed. "I was expecting you to give me hell."

"Do I think he's too old for you? Yes. But the fact is, you're an adult. I've tried hard over the past couple of months to learn how to let you go. That means not questioning your decisions anymore. It hasn't been easy."

"I'm pretty sure I might be in love with him, but I would never tell him that. That would freak him out."

My mother didn't seem all that surprised to hear me say that either. "I know he cares about you, too."

"He cares about me, yes, and because of that, he didn't want to cross the line. But I've made it very difficult for him to resist me. I've practically thrown myself at him all summer. So, eventually he gave in. But...now I sort of regret my actions. I was careless, thinking I could handle anything. Maybe I can't."

"What is he telling you?"

"He doesn't want to tie me down right now. He's afraid I'll regret it. Which means I'm pretty sure his plan is to go back to Pennsylvania and go on with his life without me."

My mother looked pensive as she stared out the window toward the boathouse. "I do believe he has your best interests at heart. And I do believe he's right in some ways. But I also believe that if two people are truly meant to be together, they'll find a way to make it work. Sometimes you have to be apart first to figure that out."

Throughout the afternoon, I could still feel Noah between my legs. The harsh reality of our last conversation, though, clashed with the post-coital haze. As confused as I was, my body craved him.

I thought a lot about what my mother had said, about people sometimes needing to be apart to figure things out. There was a reason for that old saying about setting someone free if you love them. If they don't come back, they never belonged to you in the first place.

In my heart, I knew Noah wasn't going to let me cancel my plans to go to Vermont. It was important to him that

I experience living independently. So I had to figure out how I was going to handle these remaining days with him, considering that moving ahead with my plans was inevitable.

He'd texted a few times to check on me. I'd avoided going over there long enough.

I forced myself to shower and get dressed.

The weather was overcast and drizzly as I made my way back to the boathouse.

Noah opened the door right away, looking concerned, like he was already anticipating that my mood would be off.

"Hey," he said, his tone sullen.

"Hey."

There was an awkwardness in the air, like we didn't know whether to argue, kiss each other, start fucking again, or what.

The smell of something cooking invaded my senses as I entered.

Walking over to the stove, I asked, "What are you making?"

"It's cooler out today. I made this stew. Will you have some with me?"

"Yeah. That sounds great." I peeked into the pot. "What's in it?" The steam hit my face.

"Carrots, beef, onions, spices...a lot of things. A mish-mash, kind of like my brain today."

"I can relate."

Our eyes locked. His stare fell to my lips. He looked like he wanted to kiss me. I wanted him to, but at the same time, I prayed he didn't.

He stirred the pot. "My dad used to make this stew, actually. It's one of the only things he knows how to cook. One day I asked him to teach me how to make it. We call it man stew."

"That's funny." I chuckled. "Well, I'd love to try some of your man stew."

That most certainly sounded sexual.

Noah set two bowls out and poured some of the concoction into each. He carried them over to where I was sitting at the table.

I blew on it and took a bite. "Mmm...it's good. Hits the spot."

Jesus. Everything that came out of my mouth reminded me of sex.

He licked some of the stew off his lips. "Tell me what happened when you got back to the house."

I paused and put my spoon down. "My mother knows. She knew right away. I didn't even have to spell it out."

He froze for a moment. "Great. Okay. Thanks for the heads up." Expelling a long breath, he said, "I need to stay far away from the house."

"No. She's okay. We talked a lot. I don't want to get into all of what was said, but the bottom line is she accepts whatever decisions I make and doesn't blame you for anything. She won't treat you any differently."

He looked skeptical. "I've fucked her daughter. You'd better believe she'll be looking at me differently."

"She's not going to make your life miserable."

"Well, that's good to know." He muttered, "Jesus. I'd want to kill me if I was her. I looked her in the eyes and vowed to never touch you."

A long moment of silence ensued. Then we both started to talk at the same time.

"You first," Noah said.

I tried to gather my thoughts. "The entire day I've been thinking about our talk this morning. My mind has been alternating between that and fantasizing about last night."

His eyes seared into mine. "I can't stop thinking about last night, either."

This was the part where I really needed to swallow my pride.

"I'm sorry for overreacting to your concerns. I know you have my best interests in mind. I think you're right... about everything, even if I don't want to accept it. Even if I tell you my feelings won't change when I go away, you won't believe me until that's proven. As much as I feel like hanging everything up and chasing you back to Pennsylvania, I know you would never let me make such a rash decision. So, I am still going to Vermont, and you're still leaving. Last night isn't going to change that, but it still breaks my heart."

He rested his head in his hands for a moment before looking up at me. "Don't think for one second that last night didn't have a profound effect on me. It's made things ten times harder, which was always what I was trying to avoid."

"I know. That's why as hard as it is—and I can't believe I'm saying this—I don't think we should do it again. I don't think we should have sex any more while you're here."

His face told me he wasn't expecting that. Perhaps he figured me for a weaker person?

"Yeah...okay...I agree," he said.

"I don't regret what we did and wouldn't change it, but I feel so much more attached to you. Given everything that's going to happen, I can't afford to make that worse. I'll never be able to let you go."

Noah stared down into his stew a moment. "For the record, I don't regret it, either."

I grinned. "Maybe we should go back to just hanging out on the porch."

That made him laugh. "Sadly, I don't think you're kidding."

"No, I'm not."

"We can do that. Whatever will make it easier."

I exhaled. "Is this what it's like to be an adult? Making mature decisions, even if they don't feel right?"

"Bonus points if it feels like your heart is being ripped out, yeah."

It pained me to ask, "Have you decided when you're leaving?"

"No. I don't have a set date, aside from the thirty-first being the last day I'm paid for."

"Would you consider staying a little bit beyond that?"

"I'll stay as long as you need me."

"Thank you. That's a huge relief. I have so much to do. It's overwhelming."

"Take a deep breath. We'll get it done." His eyes lingered on the marks he'd left on my neck. "Fuck. It hasn't even been a full day, and this is already hard."

Need burned within me just from the way he looked at me. Maybe this would get easier as the days went on, but right now I just wanted to leap into his arms.

I totally chickened out when that feeling got to be too strong. Pushing my chair out, I said, "Thank you for the stew. I'm gonna head back to the house and start putting some stuff aside for the yard sale. I was thinking of having one next weekend."

"Are you sure you don't want to stay for some pie? We never touched it last night."

"No. That's okay. You enjoy it. You can tell me how it came out."

"Okay." He stood. "Let me know if you need help with anything."

"I will. My aunt Katy is coming next weekend. I was going to ask you if you'd come with us to see some properties. I'd love your input."

"Anything you need," he said as he walked me to the door.

But what I *needed,* I couldn't have.

CHAPTER
TWENTY-TWO

Noah

The next Sunday afternoon, Heather's aunt Katy had come up from Boston, and we'd made appointments to see five different houses in nearby towns that were close, but not exactly on the lake. Alice had opted to stay home. Too overwhelmed by the idea of moving, she'd decided to let Heather and Katy make the decision.

Debbie, the realtor, opened the door to the last property of the day: a modest but newly renovated one-level home.

Her heels echoed on the hardwood floor. "They're asking two-seventy-five. It's priced to sell. I think we can get them down a tad because the owners are eager to be done with it. They're already down in Florida. The good thing about this one is it was recently updated, so it's pretty move-in ready."

We were exhausted. The day before we'd held a massive yard sale outside the main house, which Heather had spent the entire week preparing for. We'd sold about half the stuff. I'd packed my truck with the rest and took it to a donation facility. It would probably take more than a month to empty out the main house completely, so it was a good thing they had until mid-September to vacate.

Heather wanted to go out to Vermont early, find an apartment and job, and get settled before the spring semester started. Once Alice was in her new place, Heather would be able to leave anytime to get a head start out there.

I knew this whole process was difficult on her, from parting with sentimental belongings to the stress of packing. But it had to be done. Since Alice was virtually useless a lot of the time—aside from slowly packing up some small things—the responsibility of this transition, as usual, fell on Heather's shoulders. She was a trooper, spending every waking moment that she wasn't at work doing something to prepare for the move.

The realtor led us to a back room that had been added onto the house. "Katy, I think this space would be perfect for your art room. The windows let a lot of sun in."

Katy brushed her fingers along the wall. "It's a little small, but it might work."

Heather had been giving her aunt first choice on a place. I think she was just so grateful Katy had agreed to look after her mother. She wanted Katy to be as happy and comfortable as possible here. It was a pretty damn good deal for Katy, since she wouldn't even be paying rent, although I supposed having to keep an eye on Alice would make up for that.

While Katy and Debbie ventured out to the backyard, Heather and I found ourselves heading to the other side of the house. We ended up in the master bedroom, which was pretty small.

"How are you holding up?" I asked.

"I'm tired."

I wanted so badly to hold her.

"I know. But at least it's been a productive weekend."

"Yeah. I just want her to pick from these choices so we can be done with it. The sooner we can start moving stuff in, the better."

I'd hoped my feelings for Heather would wane since our vow of celibacy. We'd been careful not to put ourselves in a position where we could end up losing control. But all the time we'd spent working this past week was only a reminder of how good we were together, how happy I was by her side. Nothing was getting any easier. Not to mention, holding myself back from touching her was slowly killing me.

She went to look out the window. The sunlight shone on her hair, bringing out the platinum highlights. I wished I had my camera to capture it.

I knew she was still mixed up about a lot of things, including where we stood. I gave in and placed my hands on her shoulders, resting my chin on the back of her head. I immediately felt her breathing change.

"Don't let go," she whispered.

Squeezing her shoulders, I kissed her head and spoke into her hair. "This is not easy."

She turned around to face me, and I almost leaned in to kiss her.

Our moment was interrupted when we heard Katy and Debbie's footsteps. We pushed back from each other, my heart going a mile a minute.

"I see you've found the master," Debbie said as she entered the room.

"Yeah. It's really cute," Heather answered, although I could tell her mind was elsewhere.

Katy looked between us suspiciously.

"I think this one has a lot of potential. It's my favorite by far," Katy said.

Debbie's face lit up. "Enough of a favorite to make an offer?"

"Well, that's up to my beautiful niece, but yes, I think this may be the one."

Heather looked around the room. "I think we should do it."

Debbie clapped her hands together. "Fantastic! Let's go pick up your mother and head back to my office to draw something up."

Later that evening, we returned to Heather's house to await the seller's decision on the offer, which was three thousand under the asking price. Heather was prepared to go up if they turned it down, though.

Katy and Alice left us alone downstairs.

Heather's eyes widened when she finally spotted the empty shelf in her living room. "Where are my Hummels?"

This morning, when she was out running some errands with her aunt, I'd come to the house to do some packing. She hadn't been back here since.

"You mentioned that the idea of moving the Hummels was stressing you out. So I snuck in here earlier and wrapped them—each one has tons of bubble wrap. They're safely in that box in the corner."

She walked over and knelt down to inspect them. "That was incredibly thoughtful of you."

"I figured it was one less thing you'd have to worry about."

"It really is. That project was daunting." Heather stood up and came over to me, her eyes filled with emotion. "I wouldn't have gotten through any of this without you."

I reached out to touch her cheek. "Happy to help."

She briefly closed her eyes. "Will you stay and have dinner? Maybe we can watch a movie? I just want to unwind tonight, eat some bad food and have a drink."

We both knew it was dangerous to be completely alone, so I'd been spending more time here; Alice's presence ensured we wouldn't slip.

"Yeah, that sounds good. I'm getting pretty hungry. You want to make something together or order out?"

"I bought stuff to make enchiladas the other day. I have a rotisserie chicken we can use for the meat."

My stomach growled. I'd been ravenous lately, eating more to compensate for my other hunger, which wasn't being satisfied.

"That sounds good," I said. "Let's do it."

I placed my cellphone and keys on the kitchen counter. "Be right back. I need to take a leak."

I returned from the bathroom to a noticeable change in energy.

When I looked over at Heather's face, all the color had drained from it.

"Are you okay?"

She didn't answer me. Instead, looking like she was about to hyperventilate, she leaned against the counter.

She handed me my phone. "You got a text."

I looked down. It wasn't just *any* text, but a photo of a woman's bare breasts, along with a message.

It was from Lindsey, the woman I'd been with before leaving Pennsylvania. This was the first time she'd contacted me since.

Oh fuck.

Lindsey: I miss you. Thought I'd send you this reminder. Wouldn't want you to forget me. Hope you're enjoying your vacation. I would love to see you when you get back.

My heart sank and words vomited out of my mouth. "I'm sorry you had to see that. She's not anyone important. This is—"

"She seems to think she's important enough that you'd be interested in a photo of her tits."

How could I explain this? It didn't look good no matter how you cut it.

I took a breath in. "Okay, remember when I told you there was someone last May, who I thought I had an understanding with?"

She folded her arms. "Yeah."

"This is her. I haven't spoken to her since I left. I don't know what possessed her to send this photo to me tonight, but I sure as hell have no interest in it."

"I take it you didn't exactly end things?"

"There was nothing to end."

Heather's face had gone from white to red. "That's right. She's just your fuck toy. She's clearly expecting to take up where you guys left off when you get back."

God, this sucked. The future of our relationship may not have been clear, but as long as I was here, I needed to respect Heather. This was nothing but disrespectful, and the worst possible timing. She was already under an enormous amount of stress. We were both exhausted. But there was no good time for her to see something like that.

Suddenly, she covered her face. At first I thought she was crying, but then she shook her head and did a total one-eighty. "God, what's wrong with me? I'm sorry. I can't blame you for this. Hell, I'm not even sure I have any right to be mad."

I looked at her a moment, trying to keep up. "You have every right to be mad. I would've lost my shit if the roles were reversed." I swiped my finger along the text and deleted it. "It's gone—where it belongs."

"I'm sorry for overreacting."

I took a breath in. "The guy she thinks she sent this text to? He doesn't exist anymore. That man was empty. I'll never be the same after this summer. I'm grateful for that."

Before she had a chance to respond, her phone rang.

I watched as she picked it up and spoke to someone I assumed was Debbie, the realtor.

"They did?" She looked at me and smiled.

She got the house. I gave her a thumbs up.

"That sounds great. Okay...thank you for letting me know."

She hung up and beamed. "They took the offer."

"Fuck, yeah!"

When she hugged me, I lifted her and spun her around.

"I heard the phone ring."

226

Katy's voice startled us, and I put Heather down.

"Was that the realtor?" she asked.

Heather ran to her aunt and embraced her. "Yes! We've got a house."

"Such great news!" Katy beamed.

"Wanna join us for a celebratory dinner?" Heather asked.

Katy looked over at me. "I don't want to intrude. You two should be alone."

Heather insisted, "It's no intrusion."

"I'm not too hungry," Katy said. "You two go ahead, and if there are leftovers later, I'll partake if I get my appetite back."

"Okay."

"I'll go tell Alice the good news," she said before disappearing upstairs.

That news shifted the mood to a better place. Heather and I spent the next hour making the enchiladas. Things lightened even more once we opened a bottle of wine. We enjoyed each other's company, and the drama over the text I received faded considerably.

After dinner, we retreated to the living room to watch a Melissa McCarthy movie. Teddy curled up on one side of me, and Heather was on the other. This was so much better than going back to the boathouse alone.

She lay down and put her feet on my lap. I took them into my hands and massaged them.

"Look how little my feet are in your big hands. This feels so good after standing up all day."

"You do have tiny feet."

I wanted to kiss them but refrained.

"Have I ever told you that you have huge feet?" She winked.

"You might have mentioned that once or twice, yeah."

She chuckled.

Her attention turned to the movie, but I remained preoccupied, thinking about what had happened earlier tonight. I wondered if she was really as understanding about the text from Lindsey as she claimed to be. Heather was strong and had the ability to catch herself when she got upset before things got out of hand. It was like she'd trained herself to brush things off. She never held grudges or let an argument go on for too long. I considered it a positive trait most of the time, but I wondered if that was good for *her* in the long run. Maybe she needed to let it all out sometimes, get angry before she had a breakdown.

I stared down at her feet and pressed on each of her toes. "You know, it's okay to be mad at me."

She sat up a little. "You *want* me to be mad?"

"No, of course not. But if you ever feel like you need to let it all out, it's okay. For example, that text earlier— it clearly upset you. You were angry, but just when you were about to lose it on me, you stopped. It was like you told yourself you *shouldn't* be mad, so you suppressed it. I just wonder if you deny your feelings sometimes as a protective mechanism."

She pondered my theory. "Maybe I do that without realizing it because I don't want conflict."

"It's okay to let out your frustration. I can handle it. If you're mad about something, I want you to know you can take it out on me."

Only after I spoke did I realize what that sounded like.

She lifted her brow. "You want me to take it out on you...in what way exactly?"

I should have known she wasn't going to let that one slide. And that was most definitely what I wanted. I squeezed her feet even harder.

When Katy joined us in the living room a little while later, I went back to the boathouse to give her and Heather some alone time. I knew they had a lot to discuss about the new living arrangements and the logistics of Katy's move from Boston to New Hampshire.

Just before midnight, I was just about to turn in when there was a knock on my door.

When I opened it, Heather stood there in a thin, white nightgown. I could pretty much see right through it. She scooted past me into the house, leaving a wave of her delicious scent.

"I wasn't expecting a visit from you this late."

She started to pace. "I couldn't stop thinking about what you said. I wanted to let you know that I *am* really mad."

The floodgates were about to burst open, and that was fine. This needed to happen.

"Talk to me, Heather."

She unleashed everything. "I'm mad at my father for making me sweat over that damn money. I still don't know if he's serious or not. But more than that, I'm so angry that I spent half my life trying to convince myself he loved me as much as his other kids. Deep down I never believed it was true. And that hurts."

229

When she started to cry, I took her in my arms. "Tell me more. Let it all out, baby."

She stayed like that for a while. After I let her go, she continued to pace.

"I'm mad that no matter what I try, I can't make my mother happy. It has to come from within herself and the right dose of medication." She wiped her tears. "I'm angry that my sister is dead, and I never had the opportunity to have a normal relationship with her. But I'm not angry that she brought you into my life. And while I'm not mad at you for the reason you came here, I have been keeping some of my feelings inside about it. It hurts to think about what Opal did and the fact that you knew her at all. The truth is, I do block out thoughts about my sister as a habit. They're just too painful."

I nodded. "Keep going."

Heather spoke through gritted teeth, her voice growing louder. "I'm mad about that text you got from Lindsey—not at you, though. I'm mad because it made me worry that I won't be there when you need a warm body. I'm extremely jealous. While we're on the topic, I'm jealous of your ex-wife, too—that you still talk to her and confide in her when I want you to confide in me." Her tone softened. "I'm mad about a lot of things, but most of all I'm *sad*, so fucking sad, Noah. Because I don't want to lose you."

Her last statement was like a punch to the gut. I could relate to that fear.

Placing my hands on her shoulders, I looked into her eyes. "No matter what happens in our lives, no matter where I am, if you *ever* need me, I will always be here for you. I can promise you that."

Her eyes glistened. She'd heard me. I wanted to hold her again, but I was afraid to lose control. I wanted to rip that nightgown right off of her.

Heather wiped her eyes. "Thank you for listening, and thank you for encouraging me to let it out."

"You're welcome. I—"

Before I could even finish my sentence, she ran to the door and disappeared into the night.

I didn't stop her, because then what? I did, however, stand on the porch to ensure she got home.

Five minutes later, while I was lying in bed, a text came in.

My heart raced as I realized what it was. A photo of the most beautiful set of tits lit up the screen—breasts I wished more than anything I could taste just one more time.

Heather: I figured I owed you one after all that.

My head sank into the pillow as I typed.

Noah: You've just made things ten times harder.

Heather: I hope so. ;-) You've been too good. Plus, I'm not there, so I can be bold without getting into trouble, right?

Noah: Did you see how much I ate tonight? I've been eating like crazy to make up for the fact that I can't touch you. Don't think I'm not dreaming about your body 24-7. And dreaming about that thing you do.

Heather: That's a good song.

Noah: What?

Heather: That Thing You Do, one-hit wonder from the 90s.

Noah: Ah. Figures you'd know that. I bet it's on your iPhone.

Heather: No comment.

I laughed. Pretty sure I woke the guinea pigs up.

Noah: LOL

Heather: What actual thing do I do, though?

Noah: I don't want to even think about it right now. It'll put me over the edge.

Heather: Come on. I need to know.

This conversation was veering into territory I'd been trying to stay away from. But she wasn't physically here, so how much trouble could I get myself into?

Noah: I thought it was a one-time deal, but by the third time you did it, I knew it was a thing.

Heather: What is it?

Just thinking about it made me harder.

Noah: When you know I'm about to come, you squeeze your pussy around my cock. It feels fucking amazing. Drives me crazy.

Heather: Well, I can assure you the song isn't about that.

Noah: Probably not.

Heather: And I know I do that thing. It's on purpose.

Noah: So, you WERE trying to kill me.

Heather: Yup. Death by pussy spasm.

Noah: Not a bad way to die.

Heather: LOL. I'll let you go to sleep.

Noah: You think I can fall asleep after this talk and that photo you sent?

Heather: Well, if you do...dream of me.

Noah: You can bet on that.

CHAPTER
TWENTY-THREE

Heather - One Month Later

August ended—and Noah was still here. He'd agreed to stay an extra two weeks to help get us settled. I greatly appreciated that.

It was now the middle of September. We'd made it completely out of our house just in time for the new owners to move in. Noah had rented a huge truck and took our remaining stuff to a storage facility.

Crisp fall air had replaced the summer heat in New Hampshire. We were living in our new house surrounded by stacks of boxes. It would take several more weeks to get fully organized.

Since the new place had only two bedrooms, Noah had spent the past few nights sleeping on the couch while I slept in bed with my mother.

Between Teddy, our boxes, and the guinea pigs, it was mass chaos. However, today I was too preoccupied to care about any of it, because tomorrow was the day I'd been dreading since June.

Noah would be going back to Pennsylvania.

It was completely surreal, and my heart was broken. All the unpacking was going to have to wait, because I didn't plan to do anything today but spend time with him.

I woke up super early to make coffee for us before my mother and aunt woke up. As I entered the kitchen, I realized Noah had beaten me to it.

"Good morning," I said, breathing the nutty scent of the java.

"Good morning, beautiful." Noah pulled me into an embrace and held me so tightly I could barely breathe.

Speaking into his chest, I said, "I can't believe this day is finally here. I don't feel ready."

"I'll never feel ready."

Things were still unclear between us. Noah refused to put a label on what we were or make any promises aside from his general vow to "always be there for me if I needed him." That didn't define whether or not we were in a relationship. He'd be there if I really needed him *someday*, but whether he'd be there for me during all the days in between was still unknown.

The lack of definition was intentional; I knew that. And I didn't want to waste our last day pushing the issue or analyzing things. I just wanted to be with him and cherish every second.

"So I was thinking we could take a drive today," he said.

"Where to?"

"Wherever the wind takes us as long as I'm with my favorite girl."

I felt on the verge of crying. It wasn't going to take much. I'd probably be losing it on and off throughout the day.

Something I'd forgotten about popped into my head.

"Katy wants to take you to dinner to thank you for all your help. I didn't give her an answer because I wasn't sure how you wanted to spend your last night."

"That's nice of her."

"Yeah. But we don't have to do that if you don't want to."

"As long as you're there, I'm good with it. Pretty much gonna be stuck to you like glue today."

That made me warm inside but sad, too. "Okay, I'll tell her it's a go. We don't have to stay long."

"We'll be out all day, so we can meet her somewhere on our way back. Is your mom going, too?"

"I have a feeling she's going to try. She keeps telling me how much she's gonna miss you."

My eyes suddenly filled with tears. The random crying had commenced.

Noah surprised me by placing his hand on my chin and bringing my mouth into his. *Well, that's one way to stop me from crying.* It was the first time he'd kissed me since the one night we'd spent together. Apparently, on his last day he had no fucks left to give. I was thankful, because his kiss was my oxygen right now. I'd forgotten how damn good it felt.

His warm lips covered mine, and I immediately went in search of his tongue. With his taste and smell flooding my senses, I felt my body go limp. With every push of his tongue against mine, my panties got wetter. If we'd been a smoldering fire the past several weeks, he'd just poured on the gasoline.

After forcing himself back, he cradled my face. "Fuck, I missed kissing you," he rasped before planting one more on my lips.

Smacking his chest playfully, I said, "That didn't make this any easier, you know. But by all means, keep making my day more difficult."

We ended up at a place I'd never considered.

Noah drove us to an amusement park about an hour away. We spent the car ride reminiscing about the summer as he held my hand. He introduced me to some of his favorite music, bands like Cake and Audioslave.

I'd never been more uncertain about the future, but I cared more about this man than I'd ever cared about anyone or anything. That was scary. No matter what happened after tomorrow, at the very least, I hoped to God I would see him again. I was crazy about him, and if he'd told me to hang everything up, run away to Vegas and marry him, I probably would have said yes.

That insane thinking was precisely why he'd say I needed to go away for a while, that I didn't know what I really wanted. I guess time would tell, but my money was on my feelings getting stronger with distance between us.

The afternoon at the park was a blast. We rode all of the big rides and ate some greasy food. Our time on the roller coaster reminded me of our very relationship, all of the ups and downs, twists and turns.

It was the first time since Noah's arrival in New Hampshire that we'd truly let loose away from home like this. It was a shame we didn't have time to visit more places together.

My favorite parts of the day, though, were the moments when we walked through the park holding hands. He must have known I needed his touch today.

Toward the end of the afternoon, we passed a little house where psychic readings were offered. I'd never been into visiting a fortune teller, but if there was ever a time in my life that I hoped for some answers about the future, it was now.

I nudged Noah's arm. "Will you do this with me?"

"You into that stuff?"

"Not normally, but I'm kind of curious."

He stared into the window for a bit, then shrugged. "Okay."

There was no one inside when we entered. Then, from behind a beaded curtain, a woman appeared.

"Hello. Reading for two?"

She had a nose ring and wore a head scarf.

I looked at Noah then back at her. "Can you do that? Read two people at once?"

"Yes, but the information I receive is very much out of my control, so it may not be balanced. The spirits decide whom they'd like to message."

"So...when you say spirits, are you a medium or a clairvoyant?"

"A little bit of both—depends on the day and what gifts I've been blessed with."

After we paid her, she sat us at a small circular table with a red tablecloth. She lit some tealight candles and stared at us for a moment.

"I am Iliana, by the way."

"Nice to meet you. I'm Heather, and he's Noah."

Noah remained quiet, with a skeptical look on his face. Suddenly, Iliana squinted in confusion.

"Okay. This is going to sound really strange. I don't even know why this question is coming to me. But I am going to ask it anyway. Who's the ass tickler?"

Ass tickler?

"Did you say ass tickler?" I asked. "What is that?"

"I have no idea," she said. "But that's what I'm getting."

I looked at Noah. I thought he'd be laughing, but instead he looked shocked. His eyes seemed frozen open.

"Do you know what she's talking about?" I asked.

He scratched his head. "Uhhh..."

"Noah?"

The color drained from his face. "Okay, I'm really freaked out right now," he finally said.

"Does that have meaning to you?" I laughed a little. "Ass tickler?"

Noah let out a long breath. "The night of your twenty-first birthday, you fell asleep on my bed. Do you remember that?"

"Yeah."

"I never told you, but you were talking in your sleep."

I covered my mouth. "Oh no."

"And you said the weirdest thing—that you wanted to tickle my ass, among other things."

"What?" I yelled. "I said that? And what *other* things?"

"We can talk about that later. Nothing bad, but the ass tickling was funny. I just don't understand how she'd know about that."

"I said I wanted to tickle your ass?"

"Yes."

"What the hell was I thinking?"

"I don't know, but I'm freaked out."

Iliana raised her brow. "Freaked out? Surely you didn't doubt my abilities?"

"I thought this was a bunch of bullshit. But you have my attention now."

"The introduction of that term is an indication to direct my attention toward Heather for the moment." Iliana closed her eyes for a while. "Okay. Wow."

"What?" I asked impatiently.

"You have some changes on the horizon. Is there a big move coming up?"

"Yes. I'm moving to Vermont for school."

"Okay. Yes. I'm sensing this looming transition. The next year will be life-changing for you in many ways."

"In good ways?"

"In *many* ways."

My stomach sank. "Does that mean something bad is going to happen?"

Why did I decide to do this?

"I can't tell you that. All I'm getting is that this year is going to change your entire life, and you should be ready for whatever comes."

I swallowed. "Okay."

Iliana closed her eyes again before turning her attention to Noah. "You're in love with her...am I right?"

Oh my God.

Time seemed to stand still as both of us looked at Noah.

"Don't answer that," I insisted. "It's not fair for you to be put on the spot. Please don't answer."

I couldn't bear to hear him say no. The longer he said nothing, the more excruciating this was. Noah just blinked.

Iliana placed both hands on her head. "Is everything okay with your head?"

"Depends on who you ask," he said. "As far as I know. Why?"

"I can't be sure. I'm feeling some pressure in my head, and I don't know what it means. It could be literal or figurative."

"What do you mean by that?"

"It could represent a lot on your mind or actual physical head pain. Just be cautious."

Noah seemed totally weirded out. "Okay."

Illiana concluded her reading, and we left her feeling more confused than when we'd walked in.

Noah grabbed my hand. "I suddenly have a headache."

"And I'm mortified because I'm apparently an ass tickler."

"I'm still freaked out that she knew that."

"What else did I say to you that night?"

"You really want to know?"

"Yes."

He stopped and leaned into my ear. "You begged me to fuck you."

What?

"You're lying!"

"I wouldn't lie about that. *Begged.*" He laughed. "That night was the beginning of the end of my resistance."

"I can't believe you never said anything." Pointing my finger at his chest, I said, "I need to be aware of these things. What if I do that shit at school? I'm going to have to get a roommate. What if I say something to them in my sleep?"

"You might want to warn them ahead of time, clarify that you can't be responsible for what you say. Tell them not to believe any of it—even if that shit *is* true half of the time."

On the way home, we stopped at a restaurant near our house that Katy had selected.

As predicted, my mother had forced herself out in honor of Noah. It was amazing how much she'd grown to like and trust him compared to the beginning of summer.

Katy pulled a piece of bread from the basket in the middle of the table. "So what will be first on the agenda when you get home, Noah?"

"I've booked some assignments starting in October, so I'll have a little time to get my studio in order again before I get back to work. My father has also been building a laundry list of things he needs me to do, stuff that needs to be fixed. He's in his early seventies, lives alone, and relies on me a lot."

She grinned. "He'll be happy to have you back."

"Yeah." Noah glanced over at me and offered a sympathetic smile.

He knew exactly what I was thinking: his father's gain would be my loss.

PENELOPE WARD

"Well, I hope the long break was just what you needed,"
my mother said. "Although you certainly didn't do much
relaxing while you were here. I can't thank you enough for
everything you did for us."

"You know it was my pleasure, Alice."

My mother reached for my hand across the table. "I
know you're sad about Noah leaving. But I have what I
hope is some news that will brighten your night."

"What?"

"Your father called me today while you were out. He's
changed his mind and has officially informed us that he
does not intend to take any money from the sale of the
house. Of course, it's not final until the paperwork is
signed, but he says he plans to relinquish those rights."

The breath rushed out of my lungs. "Wow, okay."

Noah squeezed my leg under the table. "That's great."

It was a weird feeling. I knew I should have been
happy, but the whole stress of my father threatening us
had been unnecessary in the first place.

Katy smiled. "I'm glad you won't have to deal with that
complication."

This dinner was nice, but I was antsy to have Noah to
myself again. It was only a matter of hours now before he'd
be gone. I knew he was feeling it, too, wishing we could
stop time. I'd felt his eyes on me all throughout dinner and
could feel an unspoken intensity in the air.

When my mother went to the bathroom, Katy busied
herself with handling the check. She'd refused to let Noah
give her money.

Without an audience for a moment, Noah turned to
me and mouthed, "You're so beautiful." It was as if he'd
been dying to say it.

243

"I want you," I whispered. So badly it hurt.

I couldn't let him go back to Pennsylvania without having him one more time. Even if I had to beg for it.

CHAPTER
TWENTY-FOUR

Noah

My insides twisted as we drove home from the restaurant.

I wasn't ready. I wasn't ready to say goodbye to this place, to say goodbye to Heather.

Earlier when that psychic had put me on the spot about my feelings, I'd wanted to tell her the truth: that she'd guessed correctly—that I *was* in love with Heather. In my heart, I knew she was right. It wasn't something I wanted to admit now, not with Heather's future on the line. But that woman was fucking *good*.

I drove past the exit we normally took to get to the new house. Heather didn't question where we were going. A few minutes later, we pulled into a desolate parking area that overlooked Lake Winnipesaukee.

I turned the car off and leaned my head back against the headrest before turning to her. "I wanted to look at the stars with you one last time."

Her voice was breathy. "Is that all you want?"

Fuck no, it isn't. I rubbed my hand over her thigh, feeling my erection growing by the second.

"I need you one more time before you go, Noah. Please."

No way could I stop this; I was feeling too weak. I'd been a Boy Scout these past several weeks, but I'd run out of whatever had kept me in control. I knew damn well why I'd taken her here. It wasn't *only* to look at the stars. I had to have her, too.

She reached over and placed her hand on my crotch, and I knew I was done. Her eyes brimmed with desire. I drew in a ragged breath as I leaned over to devour her lips, letting out weeks of pent-up frustration. She moaned into my mouth as our kiss grew frantic.

She climbed over to the driver's seat to straddle me.

Desperate to be inside of her, I unbuckled my belt and unzipped my jeans.

There was one major problem, though. I didn't have a condom.

I stopped the kiss long enough to say, "I don't have anything with me...no condoms."

"It's okay. I'm on the pill. I have been this whole time."

"Are you sure?"

"Yes, as long as you're—"

"I'm good. Got a clean bill of health before I left Pennsylvania, and I've always been safe."

She kissed me ravenously as she reached under her skirt and worked her panties down her legs.

I was rock hard as I took my dick out of my jeans and guided her body onto mine. Sinking into her warm pussy felt even more incredible than I'd remembered.

I'd only had unprotected sex when I was married; I'd never trusted any other woman enough to do it without a condom. I'd forgotten what it even felt like. But it had never felt *this* amazing. Nothing had.

"Fuck, Heather. You feel too damn good like this." I thrust into her harder.

Our eyes locked. She dug her fingernails into my hair.

The truck shook as we were completely lost in each other. It was terrifying to be inside of her with thoughts of tomorrow looming. She felt like mine in every way right now, and I didn't want that to change.

But I needed to let her go to know whether she really *was* mine.

It didn't take long for our starving bodies to lose control. We gasped for air as I quaked beneath her, emptying my cum as she squeezed her pussy around my cock. *That thing.* I was so freaking grateful to have felt it again, so freaking grateful for every second we had left.

The sound of birds chirping woke me. Heather was still asleep in my arms in the backseat of the truck.

I had only dozed off for a little bit. We'd been up most of the night.

Heather had fallen asleep before I did. In the middle of the night, I'd reached into my glove compartment for a notepad I kept there and had written her a letter. I would probably be too overwhelmed later to articulate my feelings, so I wanted to get them down while they were fresh. Being intimate with her again had brought out everything I'd been suppressing.

I'd lost count of the number of times we'd had sex last night. It seemed like enough to undo all those days of celibacy, though. And made what was set to happen today even harder.

Heather stirred before she looked up at me.

"What time is it?" she asked.

"I'm not sure. But it doesn't matter. I'm in no rush."

"I didn't think I'd be able to fall asleep." She yawned. "Figured we'd just stay up all night."

"Well, we definitely used a lot of energy. It's no wonder you crashed."

She curled into me. I kissed the top of her head as we stared out at the morning sun over the lake, a virtual clock ticking in my brain.

There were no words.

The rest of that day was one big blur.

Suddenly, I was standing in front of my packed truck with nothing left to do but say goodbye to Heather. I wished for something to delay me—a mishap or flat tire, maybe. But everything was in place, even Bonnie and Clyde, loaded up with tons of hay and situated in their carriers in the backseat.

I felt sick.

When I took her in my arms, Heather's cry was so intense it was silent. She buried her face in my chest. "This doesn't feel right."

I felt my own tears close to the surface. I fought them with all my might. I couldn't let her see my sadness right now. I needed to be strong for both of us.

"Heather, look at me." I swiped my finger beneath her eye. "Look at me, baby."

There was so much I wanted to tell her, but I needed to be careful. If I admitted I was in love with her, she might take that as a sign she shouldn't go away. I still felt she needed the experience that lay ahead of her more than anything.

Holding on to her face and looking into her eyes, I said, "This isn't goodbye."

Her voice trembled. "Why does it feel so much like it, then?"

"We'll take it day by day, okay?"

She sniffled and played with the buttons of my shirt. "I know you say you came here to help me, to set me on a good path. You did so much more than that. You're the first man in my life to make me feel safe, who truly believed in me enough to make a difference. I'll always be grateful for you and for this summer, even though I'm nowhere ready to let you go."

Tell her you love her.

I just didn't know if that was the right thing to do. So I kept it in, even though I felt those words so strongly in my heart they were practically bursting from my chest.

She wiped her nose with her sleeve and sort of laughed. "Is it weird that I'm jealous of Bonnie and Clyde because they get to be with you?"

I forced myself to crack a smile. "Spoiled rodents…"

Reaching into my pocket, I took out the letter. "I wrote you something while you were sleeping last night. I was wired because of all of the thoughts in my head. Read it after I leave, sometime tonight when you're feeling lonely and sad."

The paper crinkled as she clutched it to her chest. "Thank you. I will."

I looked around one last time. "I'd better go. If I don't force myself, I'll never leave."

Her eyes filled with tears again, but she nodded.

It killed me to see her this broken up, but she looked the way I felt inside. There was no easy way to do this.

She gripped my shirt as if to keep me from leaving. When she finally let go, I forced myself into the truck. If I waited for the moment when leaving felt right, it would never happen.

Heather hugged herself and backed up a couple of feet to watch me drive away.

I managed to start the truck but couldn't put it into drive yet.

After I mustered the courage to shift into gear, I pressed down on the gas and started to drive away. From the rearview mirror, I could see her bury her head in her hands. That broke my heart. I couldn't do it. I couldn't drive off and leave her crying in the driveway.

Rather than put the truck in reverse, I parked it on the side of the street and ran back toward her. She looked up in surprise as I lifted her into my arms and held her tightly.

This was what I'd been holding back in an attempt to avoid losing it. But escaping into my truck the way I had wasn't right. I'd been trying to avoid this pain, but she needed this. *I needed this.* We needed to hold each other—for as long as necessary—one last time before I disappeared.

CHAPTER
TWENTY-FIVE

Heather - Seven Months Later

Heather,

As I write this, I'm watching you sleep. You look so peaceful, and that's very ironic because I know there's a lot of confusion swirling around in that beautiful head of yours—mainly confusion about us, where things stand, what the future holds.

You're probably wondering how I could possibly let you go after last night, how I could walk away from something that feels so incredibly right.

Please don't mistake my leaving for uncertainty about you.

When I first came out here, it was to help you in any way I could. Because of my guilt, I felt I needed to atone for my past mistakes. But you have helped me more than I could ever help you. You helped me to see the good in myself, to see myself the way YOU see me. You brought me joy I wasn't expecting. My life is happier with you in it.

At the same time, I recognize that I'm flawed. I made a lot of mistakes when it came to my marriage, and while I feel like I learned from them, I still can't be one-hundred percent sure I would make the best long-term partner for you, that I wouldn't fuck up again. Despite those fears, I want to try to be the type of man you deserve.

I want to give it a year.

You know how I feel about you getting to be on your own, with nothing holding you back. It's a rite of passage and one I think you need to experience.

One year, Heather.

Go to Vermont. Conquer the fuck out of it. Enjoy your freedom. Focus on school. If after a year's time, you still want to be with me and still feel the way you do today, I'll be here. We'll figure out a way to make it work—whatever it takes— whether long-distance or otherwise.

I don't want you to feel you have to choose between me and the freedom you've damn well earned. This letter is me telling you if you want me to wait for you, I will.

"What are you reading?"

I jumped.

My roommate, Ming, startled me. I hadn't even noticed her standing in the doorway.

I carefully folded the piece of paper and placed it back in the drawer.

"Nothing."

I'd pulled out the letter Noah had written me the night before he left New Hampshire because I was really missing him tonight. Occasionally, I liked to reread it and think back to the summer, to that time in his truck when we'd made love all night long. I would have given anything for just one night back at the lake, sitting on the porch and chatting with him under the moonlight like we used to.

I'd tried to call him tonight but got no answer. It was earlier than the time we normally spoke on the phone, so it didn't surprise me that he hadn't picked up. I'd had a long day and just wanted to hear his voice. His voice was everything now, since I hadn't seen him in so long.

"What's on that paper?" Ming asked. "You can tell me."

"It's personal...just something Noah wrote me a long time ago. Well, what feels like a long time ago."

Seven months had felt like an eternity.

Ming's friendship had made the passage of that time a little easier. I was grateful for her.

On my very first day of apartment hunting in Vermont, tired and really homesick, I'd stopped at a Chinese restaurant in the late afternoon. It was a cold, raw day. The place had been totally empty, but so warm inside, and the most enchanting Chinese meditation music had played on the overhead. It felt like I'd walked into a dream.

Ming had appeared and walked me to a table where she later waited on me. Absolutely starving, I'd ordered a huge pu pu platter. She'd gotten a kick out of the fact that I'd ordered all that food just for myself. I'd explained that I'd had a very long, stressful day and planned to eat the entire thing.

Since the place was empty, Ming had sat across from me and watched with great interest while I devoured everything in front of me. She and I got to talking, and I learned her father owned the restaurant as well as some apartments upstairs in the building. It happened to be just around the corner from campus. Ming lived in one of the apartments and was also a student at the university. When I'd told her I'd been searching for apartments all day, she mentioned she had an extra bedroom. The rest was history. I'd snagged a place to live on day one, along with an instant friend—one with quite the sense of humor.

It was no surprise that my fortune cookie that afternoon had read: *You just ate cat.* Ming was in charge of ordering the fortune cookies and made it her mission to put the funniest stuff inside.

She sat on the edge of my bed. "How *is* Mountain Man doing?"

I'd shown her a photo of Noah—unshaven and wearing one of his flannel shirts while working outside the lakehouse—and she'd instantly given him a nickname.

"I haven't spoken to him today. I think he might have a late shoot." I sighed. "It always gives me anxiety when I can't reach him. I really needed to hear his voice. Today sucked."

"Nothing tea and dumplings won't solve." She winked. "My dad just made some fresh ones."

"That sounds awesome."

Ming and I retreated to the kitchen and devoured the dumplings she'd brought upstairs. I'd probably gained five pounds since moving in with her.

Ming blew on her hot green tea. "So, what happened today that was so bad?"

"I think I screwed up my microbiology exam—like really badly. Then at work, I spilled an entire tray of food on a customer."

"Ouch."

I'd taken a job at a restaurant right off campus that was always crowded with college students. It was far more hectic than my old gig at Jack Foley's.

I sighed. "How was *your* day?"

"I think I stooped to my lowest point today. I sniffed a baby diaper while babysitting."

I bent my head back in laughter. "Oh man. I think you did."

Shortly after I moved in, I'd caught Ming in the bathroom sniffing a white powdery substance. I'd nearly had a heart attack thinking I'd moved in with a drug addict. *Sweet little Ming is a cokehead?* Well, it turned out to be baby powder. She'd sat me down and told me all about this strange addiction she'd had since she was a kid. She liked to sniff baby powder and sometimes eat it. She'd even been featured in a documentary about strange addictions. She'd played it for me on YouTube as I sat there flabbergasted.

Between my sleep talking and her obsession with baby powder, we made quite the team. We didn't judge each other, though, and we appreciated our strange habits as things that made us unique. Aside from Chrissy and Marlene, whom I spoke to only occasionally now, I didn't have too many close girlfriends, so I valued Ming's friendship.

"You know I love you, right?" she said. "Like, more than Johnson & Johnson?"

That cracked me up. "Yes, oddly, I do know that, even though we haven't known each other very long."

"Well, as your friend who loves you, I'm going to ask you a serious question."

"Okay."

"Are you happy here in Burlington?"

I took some time to think before I answered. "It feels really liberating to be away from home, without any responsibilities except taking care of myself, but it's also lonely. I even miss my dog, and I don't mean that as an insult to you, because you're the best thing about this place. But I can't shake how much I miss Noah."

"You try not to show him you miss him. I notice that when I'm eavesdropping on your calls."

I rolled my eyes. "I try to sound upbeat, yeah. He believes this time away from home is important, something I *need* to experience. I think that's because his college life was a lot different than mine. I'm pretty sure Noah was a party animal back then, likely had girls throwing themselves at him. He thinks there's all this stuff I need to get out of my system, when in reality, I don't do much more than go to school, work, and come home."

Ming pointed to her fuzzy slipper. "I don't know...it's pretty wild up in here."

"It's so not." I chuckled. "I'm older than most of these freshmen, you know? The party ship has sailed. I feel like I'm focusing on my studies to avoid how much I miss him." Shaking my head, I looked down into my teacup. "The funny thing is...guys here have been hitting on me, especially at the restaurant. So I can see what my options would be if I wasn't so infatuated with Noah. And you know what? I'm not missing much."

256

"Can you pass those guys over to me, then?" She winked.

"Gladly. You should hang out there more often."

"Seriously, though, not that I want to lose you—because I really don't—but why not transfer after this semester?"

"I want to stick it out so Noah doesn't think I'm doing anything hastily. He told me to give it a year from the time we separated, and that works out to two semesters, since I can't just leave in the middle. So, it's really longer than a year."

"Are you supposed to see him at all this summer?"

"I feel like I'm going to burst if I don't." I sighed. "You know how some people call their parents when they're lonely at school? I don't think to call my mom or dad. I mean, I call my mother to check on *her*. And my relationship with my dad is not very good anymore. So, when I need to hear a familiar voice, when I need support for *me*, I call Noah. He's my only real comfort and my home. That's pretty scary to realize sometimes."

Noah finally got back to me an hour after our usual time.

"I'm sorry you had a bad day," he said.

"I wasn't sure if I'd hear from you tonight."

"My shoot ran super late."

"I figured it was something like that." Lying back on the bed, finally able to relax somewhat, I asked, "What was the shoot for?"

"It was a modeling portfolio."

"Anyone hot?" I asked.

"You'd like him."

Irrationally, I was relieved to hear he hadn't been working late with some beautiful woman.

"Talk to me, Heather. Everything okay? You still sound down."

"I'm okay...just an overall crappy day. I talked it out with Ming, though, over dinner. I'm feeling a lot better now."

"I'm glad you have her. She seems really nice. Remind me to send her some baby powder to thank her for looking out for you."

Laughing, I lowered my voice. "She doesn't know I told you about that."

He changed the subject. "So, tell me what happened today."

"I don't want to burden you if you had a long day, too."

"You're never a burden to me. You know that. Tell me what happened."

"I flubbed up on one of my tests and had a crappy day at work. That's all. It's no big deal."

Thinking back to my conversation with Ming, I wondered if I was doing the wrong thing in always trying to make things seem better than they were.

"Can I confess something?" I asked.

"Yeah, of course."

"Sometimes I don't want you to know I'm struggling, so I downplay things. I want to make you proud and do this semester justice, give it my all. But it's hard. If it weren't for Ming, I'm not sure I would want to be here at all."

"What did I tell you about holding things in? You should never feel like you can't tell me you're unhappy."

He let out a breath. "I am so proud of you—even if you're struggling. Struggle means you're persevering even if it's tough. That's a sign of strength."

"Thanks for always lifting me up."

After a bit of silence, he said, "So, there's something I need to tell you."

My heart started to pound. "What?"

"I'm gonna be a grandfather."

"What are you talking about?" I nearly shrieked.

"Remember you said your friend at the pet store told you Clyde was neutered?"

"Yeah?"

"Well, she lied. Bonnie's pregnant."

"Oh my God. What? How did you figure it out?"

"She was getting really fat, eating all of Clyde's food. I took her to the vet, and he confirmed it."

"Have you ever seen them have sex?"

"No. Sneaky fuckers must do it when I'm not home."

I laughed so hard I almost dropped the phone.

"You think it's funny, huh? What the hell am I gonna do with more guinea pigs?"

"You're considering keeping the babies?"

"I can't separate Bonnie and Clyde from their damn kids! I don't want that on my fucking conscience. It's gonna be a zoo up in here."

My amusement over this knew no bounds. I had to wipe my eyes.

"You're a good man, Noah. And to think I thought you were a hardass when I met you."

"Now I'm a pussy. Look what's happened to me."

"You old softie."

"Seriously, it's a good thing I'm taken, because imagine meeting a thirty-five-year-old dude and finding out he's breeding guinea pigs. I mean...would you trust that guy? I sure as hell wouldn't."

He was *taken*. While his actions had given me every impression that he was committed, he'd never *said* anything like that before. It was exactly the reassurance I needed tonight.

"You're taken, huh?"

Noah paused. "Yeah. I really am."

I shut my eyes. "Well, she's a very lucky girl, whoever she is."

"Nah, I'm the lucky one."

"What's she like?"

"She's really pretty—blond, blue eyes, killer body. But what drew me to her was her personality, how self-deprecating she is, honest, funny. And she's not afraid to ask for what she wants. That's a big turn-on."

"Like...she threw herself at you kind of thing?"

"At times. But I sort of needed it." He sighed. "Yeah, she's pretty amazing. Horrible taste in music, though. I can overlook that because she likes old men."

My cheeks hurt from smiling. "I have to say, whatever I was bummed out about today just went out the window. In fact, I don't remember much before this conversation."

"Well, I'm glad I could help you forget your worries. I wish I could do that in other ways right now."

"Me, too." I blew out a breath and closed my eyes again, imagining the weight of his body over me. "You know, when I was talking to Ming tonight, it occurred to me that while other people call their parents when they're homesick, I call *you*. I feel like home is wherever you are."

"Well, I have a confession to make," he said.

"Okay..."

"This isn't as easy for me as I might make it seem, either. I never want you to worry about me while you're trying to focus on school. So I downplay how much I miss you, too."

I clutched the phone to my chest for a moment. "Well, aren't we just perfect together?"

That night, I slept more soundly than I had in a long time.

CHAPTER
TWENTY-SIX

Noah

I kept meaning to pay Olivia a visit, to congratulate her and her husband on the birth of their daughter. But I never quite knew if Kirk appreciated my presence. No man is going to be completely comfortable around his wife's ex-husband. So I figured I would give it time, give them a little space before going over there.

One morning, though, Olivia called to tell me she was in the neighborhood for a pediatrician visit. She wanted to know if I was around to meet the baby. I told her to stop by.

It took my breath away for a moment to see her standing in the doorway with a little human strapped to her chest.

"This is Sam." She smiled.

Sam had thick dark hair and looked just like her mother. Olivia and I had been through so much together—seeing this lifelong dream of hers come to fruition made me a little emotional.

"Hey, cutie pie." Sam looked up at me and immediately started crying.

"Uh-oh. I swear, I'm none of the things your mom said about me on the way over here."

Olivia chuckled. "She's just cranky because she got some shots."

"Ah." Peeking in at her some more, I rubbed the back of my finger along her head. "She's really precious, Liv."

"Thank you."

After the baby calmed down, she asked, "Would you like to hold her?"

"Sure. Yeah," I said, rolling up my sleeves. The only babies I'd ever held were my niece and nephews. It had been a while.

My heart felt full as she placed the infant in my arms. It was surreal to be holding Liv's child. I really was so damn happy for her. She'd always wanted to be a mother. A sort of relief came over me—that I hadn't wasted any more of her time, that she was able to build a new life after our marriage and have a child before it was too late. What I wasn't expecting to feel, though, was a bit of envy—not because I wished to be the father of this baby, but because I longed for one of my own. I'd never wanted a child while I was married to Olivia. In fact, that lack of desire was one of the factors that ultimately led to our divorce.

But right now, as I held this precious, red-faced little angel, I realized maybe I did want to be a parent. And I knew the reason for my change of heart had everything to do with meeting the person I wanted to share that with.

It wouldn't be anytime soon—not even close. Heather wasn't ready. But maybe someday.

Holy shit.

Listen to yourself, Noah.

"You're a natural," Olivia said. "I never thought I'd think that, but you totally are."

"She's making it easy for me. And she's beautiful like her mother."

"Thank you." Olivia rubbed her hands together and looked around my living room. "So, how are you? I haven't had a chance to talk to you much with everything that's been going on since Sam was born."

After I returned from New Hampshire, I'd been reluctant to tell Olivia about Heather and me; I didn't think she'd understand. I hadn't felt like listening to her judgmental comments. She had advised me against going to New Hampshire in the first place, so to admit I'd gotten involved with Opal's sister romantically? Olivia would shit a brick. I didn't want to lie to her, though, so I'd ended up admitting what happened soon after I'd returned. She remained very skeptical.

"Things have been really good, actually," I told her.

Little Sam had fallen asleep in my arms.

Olivia walked to the corner of the room and lifted a frame off my desk. "This is her?"

I'd framed one of the shots I'd taken of Heather the night she'd worn the red dress—the night I'd first lost my shit and kissed her.

"Yes. That's Heather," I said, continuing to rock the baby as I walked over to Olivia.

She held the frame in her hands. "She's gorgeous."

I cringed, because I knew exactly what Olivia was thinking—that I'd become smitten because of Heather's looks and there wasn't any substance to our relationship. I could never make her understand the connection we had, and any effort to convince her she was wrong would likely be futile. Plain and simple, she didn't know Heather.

Olivia placed the photo back on the desk. "I hope you know what you're doing. I just don't want to see you get hurt."

"You don't need to worry about that," I said.

"I just think back to myself at twenty. I didn't know my ass from my elbow."

"She's twenty-one—twenty-two in a few months." I laughed under my breath because I knew that didn't make a lick of difference in her eyes.

"Oh, excuse me," she mocked. "Well, you know what I mean."

"Look, I might have agreed with you before I got to know her. In fact, I believed for a very long time that there was no chance for us because of her age. But people— they're not one size fits all."

Olivia nodded. "I'm sorry. I didn't mean to offend you. I just wonder if you might be better off with someone closer to our age at this point in your—"

"I'm not in love with someone closer to our age. I'm in love with *her*. So..."

"Love?" Olivia repeated.

Shit. I was shocked that it had come out so easily, but it had.

"Yes. I didn't plan on this. It just happened."

I could have gone on and on, but I didn't want to insult Olivia by admitting I hadn't *ever* experienced what I felt for Heather before.

I needed to nip this conversation in the bud.

"I was a shitty husband to you," I told her. "I still live with a lot of guilt over that. I really did think there wasn't any hope for me. But Heather awakened something. The future seems brighter. She could kick my ass to the curb tomorrow, and I'd still be a changed man—not that I want that to happen. I want to be with her, and I want to be the type of man she deserves. I feel like I can admit this to you now, because you've found the person you were meant to be with. I hope we can both be happy, Liv."

She searched my eyes. "Just because I'm happy with Kirk doesn't mean it's easy for me to see you in love with someone else, you know. I've *never* seen you like this— certainly not with me—and that stings a little. But I'll have to get over that, because ultimately, Noah, I want you to be happy, too. I mean that. I hope this isn't infatuation on her part, because you deserve the real thing."

"Thank you."

She looked down at the baby, still asleep in my arms. "Well, we'd better get going. I'm gonna need to feed her soon."

I carefully handed Sam back to her mother. "Thank you for coming by."

"I'm glad you got to meet her. I'll call you soon."

She'd started to walk away when I called after her. "You're doing a great job, Liv. Sam is really lucky you're her mom. I'm proud of you."

Olivia turned and gave me a wobbly smile. "Thanks."

"You're welcome."

After she left, I thought about what she'd said. A part of me had expected things to change when Heather went away to school. In fact, I'd been bracing for it. But after nearly eight months apart, we'd grown closer. The best part of every day was our nightly phone call. I had tried to give her space, but the more I pulled back, the more she sought me out. Physical absence had somehow made our relationship even more solid. Our conversations were deeper, more intimate. I wanted her more each day and was bursting at the thought of seeing her again. I knew it had to be soon, or I was going to lose my mind. During Christmas, I'd gone to visit my mother and brother in Minnesota. Then, during her spring break, she'd gone home to visit Alice, and I'd stayed here. She'd been begging me to come to Vermont. I could have gone to visit her but had specifically stopped myself in an effort to give her the space I'd thought she needed. But I had started to think my efforts were in vain. I missed the hell out of her. It was time.

Jesus. I'd just admitted my love for Heather to my ex-wife but never to Heather herself. I'd held that in long enough. Telling her I loved her was long overdue.

It was the middle of the day, and I was pretty sure she was in class. Still, I wondered if she'd pick up if I called. The need to get this off of my chest felt urgent.

To my disappointment, the phone just kept ringing. When her voicemail picked up, I left a message.

"Hey, baby. It's me." Scratching my head, I said, "I, uh, guess you're in class. Figured that would be the case but thought I'd give it a try. Anyway, I have something important I need to say to you. So when you get home, give me a call. It can't wait till the regular time. Hope you're having a good day. Talk to you later."

I reached over to the framed photo of Heather.

I'm a damn lucky man.

Feeling antsy, I decided to do some much-needed food shopping since I didn't have any work scheduled. Bonnie was due to have her babies anytime now, and in the meantime, she was eating double. I needed to replenish my supplies.

The supermarket was pretty crowded for the middle of the day. I laughed when "Young Girl" by Gary Puckett and The Union Gap came on as I rolled down the frozen aisle. The guy in the song is warning the girl to stay away from his old ass. That was ironic as hell—especially since my father used to tease my mother with that very same song. Instead of letting the song freak me out, I decided to take it as a blessing from the universe.

The checkout line was long, and I felt a headache begin to pound. It had been lurking all day, but finally moved to the forefront.

The old man in front of me started a conversation about how vegetables give him gas. He must have thought I could relate given all of the roughage I was purchasing for the guinea pigs. Rubbing my temples, I admitted that all the greens were actually for my pets. Undeterred, he asked me some questions about that.

I tried to answer, but it became difficult to make sense of what he was saying. Finally, I just drew a blank.

A rush of dizziness washed over me, and everything went black.

CHAPTER
TWENTY-SEVEN

Heather

There was no answer when I called Noah back. His message had me curious. Had he thought better of where things were going with us? Was he having doubts? What on Earth did he need to talk to me about that couldn't wait until our evening phone call?

When the phone rang a little while later and I saw it was him, my heart sped up a bit.

With a smile on my face, I answered. "Hey!"

My stomach dropped at the sound of a baritone voice I didn't recognize.

"Is this Heather?"

"Yes. Who's this?"

"This is Neil Cavallari, Noah's father."

Noah's...father?

"Oh. Hi. Where's Noah? Is everything okay?"

His voice was shaky. "I'm afraid not. Noah collapsed while out shopping today. The doctors think he has a ruptured aneurysm."

It took a few seconds for his words to compute. "Excuse me? What?"

"They just took him into surgery. We don't know—"

"He's alive?"

"Yes."

My heart started beating again.

His words were all jumbled. "They don't know how much damage was done to his brain. We won't know anything until he's out of surgery. I wish I could tell you more, but there's no news yet. I know how much you mean to him. They gave me his phone, and I found your number."

I felt frozen. I couldn't speak.

"Are you there?" he asked.

"Yes..."

"They expect the surgery to last about five hours. He just went in. They can't tell me anything until it's over."

Five hours. I have five hours to get there.

"Will you text me the address? I need to get on the next plane."

"Yes, of course."

Somehow I got off the phone with him, though I wasn't sure I even said goodbye. Ming walked in and saw the frozen look on my face.

"Are you okay?"

I silently shook my head.

"What happened?"

Barely able to get a word out, I muttered, "Noah..."

"Oh my God. What's wrong?"

Everything came out in fragments. "He...I...need to get on a plane. I need a ticket. He's in surgery. Aneurysm. I can't—"

"Okay. Calm down. It's okay. Just tell me which airport?"

I rubbed my temples. "Uh...Philadelphia."

"I'm calling right now. Grab your stuff."

I ran to my chest of drawers and threw clothes into a tote.

Ming rushed me downstairs where her father was waiting in the car normally used for food delivery. It smelled like crab rangoon and egg rolls.

She kept ordering him to drive faster. "Hurry!"

That was the only thing I understood because everything else was spoken in Chinese.

"When does the flight leave?" I finally managed to ask.

"An hour from now."

I felt her hand on my back, rubbing. What would I be faced with when I got to Pennsylvania? I couldn't accept anything less than Noah being absolutely okay. He was my strength, my rock—my entire world.

I couldn't let my mind go to the dark side. I needed to be there. I needed to be strong for him.

After Ming's father parked the car at the drop-off area, I expected her to say goodbye. Instead she grabbed my hand and prompted me to run with her. "Come on."

"You don't have to come with me. I can board myself."

"Are you kidding? I'm not letting you go to Pennsylvania alone."

She's coming with me?

"You don't even have a bag."

"I don't need one. Come on."

"Thank you," I breathed, overwhelmed by her gesture.

"Of course."

We managed to board the plane in the nick of time. When the engines roared, it was the first moment I could breathe. I was on my way to him. Ming grabbed my hand as we took off, and once again I thanked my lucky stars that I didn't have to go through this by myself.

As I stared out at the night sky from thousands of feet in the air, I tried not to think the worst. I tried not to focus on the fact that I knew damn well that aneurysms were bad news. In high school, I'd lost my beloved music teacher to one. But that wasn't going to happen to Noah. No. No. It couldn't. I couldn't bear to think about that.

Focus on the raindrops on the window. Focus on the sound of the juice cart being wheeled down the aisle. Focus on the feel of Ming's hand.

The hospital was about a thirty-minute drive from the airport. I'd done a good job of not focusing on the negative while on the plane, but things felt different now that I was on land again. I wanted to be better prepared for whatever I might find, so I made the mistake of Googling *aneurysms* on my phone in the car.

Fifteen percent of patients die before ever reaching the hospital.

Four out of seven people will have disabilities.

Even if people survive a rupture, there's a chance of re-bleeding. Approximately seventy percent of those people die.

My phone fell out of my hands, and I felt myself hyperventilate.

Ming held on to me. "You're okay. I've got you."

"Nothing can happen to him," I cried.

I kept wanting Ming to tell me everything was going to be okay, but she never did. I knew she didn't want to promise something she couldn't guarantee.

When we got to the hospital, Ming did all of the talking to find out where we needed to go. As we entered the surgical waiting area, I realized I didn't even know what Noah's dad looked like. Just when I was about to text Noah's phone, someone called my name.

"Heather?"

I turned around to find an older man with Noah's big brown eyes staring back at me—eyes that looked red from crying.

"Yes!" I cried. "Hi."

"No news yet. He's still in surgery," he said as he pulled me in for a hug.

His warmth was comforting. So relieved to finally be here, I expelled a breath. At least nothing had changed for the worse. There was still hope.

"Are you alone?" I asked him.

"Yes. Noah's mother and brother are flying in from Minneapolis, but they won't get here for another few hours."

It broke my heart that he'd been waiting here by himself.

"Oh, um...this is my friend Ming. She accompanied me here."

"Hi," he said.

Ming smiled. "Pleasure to meet you." She turned to me. "I'm gonna find a bathroom. I'll be right back."

After she left, I faced Mr. Cavallari again. The look of fear in his eyes was enough to shatter whatever protective mechanisms I'd been using thus far. I could feel my tears creeping in.

Judge Judy was playing on the television mounted on the wall. Her abrasive tone was particularly agitating, given my state.

"We have to stay positive." Noah's dad took my hands in his. "Do you believe in prayer?"

"In all honesty, I grew up without religion and never prayed much. But I've prayed non-stop since leaving Vermont. It's almost instinctual, just desperate wishes for anyone up there who will listen."

"Good." He nodded. "Keep it up."

"I will." I paused, my emotions bubbling over. "Mr. Cavallari, Noah is everything to me."

Still holding my hands, he said, "You mean so much to him. When he talks about you, his entire being lights up, like I've never seen before."

"He has to be okay. He just *has* to."

From the corner of my eye, I saw a woman with long, dark hair. I realized she was Olivia, Noah's ex-wife.

She looked right at me. With tears in her eyes, she said, "You must be Heather."

"Yes."

"I'm—"

"Olivia. I know. It's good to meet you."

"Good to meet you, too."

It was amazing how feelings like jealousy could take a backseat in times of crisis. In a strange way, I wanted her here. Noah needed the support and good vibes of everyone who cared about him right now.

Olivia embraced Mr. Cavallari.

"What's happening, Neil?" she asked him.

"They told me to expect the surgery to last about five hours. We've got another hour to go. No one has come out since he went in." He let her go. "I'm gonna go see if I can find anything out. I'll be right back."

Neil walked away, leaving Olivia and me alone in the waiting area.

"You got here fast," she said.

"Fast as I could."

Ming suddenly appeared. "Hey."

"Ming, this is Olivia, Noah's ex-wife."

After they shook hands, Ming gave me a look that said, *holy shit.*

Ming must have felt awkward, because she excused herself again. "I'm gonna sit down over there. Just holler if you need me."

"Okay."

"You know, I saw him today," Olivia told me.

"You did?"

"Yes. He seemed fine. Perfectly healthy."

"Around what time did you see him?"

"About noon. I stopped by his house for, like, fifteen minutes so he could meet my daughter. She had a doctor's appointment in the area."

I thought back to the phone message Noah had left me. That was sometime before one in the afternoon. It must have been right after she left.

"So he didn't seem off at all?" I asked.

"No. He didn't."

Olivia looked just as worried as I felt.

"You know what the last thing he said to me was?" she asked.

"What?"

"That I'm a good mother and he's proud of me." She burst into tears. "We've been through a lot, so that really meant the world to hear."

I reached out to hug her. We embraced as two people who needed each other's support. This wasn't the time for bitterness or ego. All that mattered was Noah pulling through. He needed us—all of us.

As I let her go, I said, "He's always spoken so highly of you."

Olivia sniffled. "It was hard for me to hear him admit he'd fallen in love with you."

What?

My heartbeat accelerated. "He told you that?"

"He did. Is that a surprise?"

"Well, he hasn't said it in those exact words, but..."

Could that be what he was calling to tell me?

"Well, he most definitely said it in those words today, Heather. He told me he loves you. I'd been questioning his intentions when it came to your relationship, and he shot that down. He's very protective of his feelings for you. I'd never seen that side of Noah. I thought you might need to hear that right now."

"You're right. I do. Thank you." We hugged again, and I laughed a little. "This is weird, right?"

"Totally weird." She smiled.

Such a strange mix of emotions swirled through me: joy from knowing that Noah loved me and excruciating fear that I would never get to hear that directly from him.

Neil Cavallari reappeared, looking defeated. "The nurse didn't have any new information. She promised to let me know if she hears anything from the doctors."

He took a seat across from us and placed his head in his hands. I went to sit down, and Ming moved from her seat in the corner to be next to me.

We all sat in silence, the sadness and fear in the air so overwhelming you could practically see it. I returned to saying prayers in a loop. It felt like my entire life was on the line. The fate of my future was down that mysterious hallway leading into the operating room.

Olivia suddenly stood. "My husband just texted. He's driving around with the baby, and she's hungry. I'm going to go feed her and come back. Please text me if the doctor comes out."

"Okay, sweetheart," Neil said.

A few minutes later, someone in blue scrubs came rushing toward us. Neil and I stood in unison.

He addressed Noah's father. "The surgery was successful. We won't know until he wakes up how much neurological damage there was. He was very lucky that the people in the supermarket acted fast and the hospital was nearby. We were able to get in as quickly as possible to stop the bleeding. But the fact is, if damage did occur, treating the aneurysm won't reverse it. Rest assured that we did everything we could, and his vitals right now are good."

"Can we see him?" Neil asked.

"I'm going to ask you to give us a little bit. Someone will come out and bring you into recovery soon. He's going to be in the ICU for at least two to three weeks while we monitor him for complications."

"How many people fully recover after something like this?" I asked.

"About fifteen to thirty percent of people escape major difficulties, so that outcome is the exception rather than the rule."

Oh my God.

My fear paralyzed me.

"What about the other seventy-five percent?" Neil asked.

"Anywhere from mild to severe brain damage. Once blood enters the brain, it damages the tissue. Brain function is impacted, causing, in many cases, memory loss and cognitive disability. It's why we acted as quickly as possible." He must have noticed how distraught we looked because he added, "Some people do go on to live perfectly normal lives without any long-term damage despite rupture. Don't give up hope. We'll know more very soon as he wakes up."

He placed his hand on Neil's shoulder. "Someone will be out shortly to escort you back."

"Thank you, doctor," he said.

We held each other, and I whispered, "He's alive. We're so lucky."

So many thoughts flooded my mind. No matter what happened, I was in this for the long haul. I would never leave Noah's side. I didn't care if he couldn't remember me or couldn't speak. I was here to stay.

A nurse appeared. "Both of you can come back, provided she's family."

"This is my daughter, his sister," Neil said without hesitation.

"Follow me," she said as she led us down the hallway.

"Thank you," I mouthed to him.

My heart felt like it started beating again at the sight of him. Noah was still asleep, hooked up to an IV. It was a relief to see that he looked pretty normal, albeit unconscious. His chest rose and fell, and I was never so happy to see someone breathing in my entire life.

Tears stung my eyes as I asked the nurse, "How long until he wakes up?"

"It varies. It's taking him a while, but that's not uncommon."

She wrote something down in her chart as if this was business as usual. I wondered if she realized this moment was the hardest I'd ever experienced, that for me, the world had stopped moving every second he wasn't awake. I didn't know whether the love of my life was going to be okay, whether he would even remember me. I didn't know what I would do if Noah couldn't speak. No matter what, I would be here. I needed to be strong for him.

Neil reached for my hand as we sat and waited for Noah to wake up.

An indeterminable amount of time went by before Noah finally opened his eyes. His dad and I leapt from our seats when his lids fluttered.

His father spoke first. "Son...it's Dad. I'm here. Heather's here, too."

"Hi, baby," I added. "I'm here, and I'm never leaving."

Noah blinked.

I knew it would take a while for him to fully come to, but the longer he wasn't saying anything, the more fearful I became.

I rubbed his shoulder. "It's okay. Take your time. There's no rush."

"You're going to be okay, son. I just know it."

I lay my head next to his and began to pray silently. The sound of his breathing grew louder.

When I looked up again, his eyes were almost fully open, and he stared blankly back at me.

Oh my God.

Say something. Please. Anything.

"Hi...hi," I whispered. "You have no idea how happy I am to see those beautiful eyes of yours. I love you, Noah. I love you so much."

He didn't respond, but a lone teardrop fell from his eye. He could hear me. But could he understand? Did he want to speak but couldn't?

I hadn't wanted him to see me upset, but I couldn't help it as my own tears fell.

"It's okay, son. Everything is going to be okay."

I reached for Noah's hand and held it. "We'll be here with you every step of the way. Your mom is coming, too... and your brother. And Olivia is out there. Oh my God—she and I actually hugged. That's how much we both love you."

Please say something.

Please.

I kept talking to him. "I'll make a deal with you. When you get better, I'm going to let you listen to every embarrassing song on my phone. You know I vowed never to let that happen. But you know what? It will be worth it. And I can't wait to hear you make fun of me."

For the next half-hour, Neil and I stayed at Noah's bedside, offering words of encouragement in a desperate attempt to get him to say something—anything.

Then everything went silent for a while. I turned away for a moment, stepped over to the window to clear my head.

"Hea…"

I whipped back toward him.

Noah pushed the words out. "Hea…Heather…"

"Yes!" I rejoiced. "Yes. It's me! I'm here with you."

Neil let his tears fall for the first time since I'd arrived. "Dad is here, too," he said.

Noah's voice was groggy. "Where am I?"

"You're in the hospital. You had surgery on your brain," Neil answered.

Noah turned to me and asked, "Wha…what are you doing here?"

"Where else would I be?"

For several seconds, I waited with bated breath for his response.

He swallowed. "Vermont?"

Neil and I looked at each other. *Vermont* was such a simple answer, but it meant so much. It meant his cognition was there. *It meant everything.* It meant Noah was probably going to be okay.

"Do you remember anything that happened?" I asked.

It took him a while, but he finally said, "I remember I love you."

CHAPTER
TWENTY-EIGHT

Noah

In a strange way, Bonnie and Clyde saved my life.

If I hadn't gone to the supermarket that day to buy their food, I might not be alive. The store near my house never seemed to keep the kale they liked in stock. So I'd gone out of my way to the market across town. It happened to be right around the corner from the hospital. My surgeon was convinced if more time had elapsed before the operation, I might not have made it, or at the very least I would have had brain damage.

Thank God I wasn't driving when it happened. And if I'd been home alone? I probably would have died. It was never easy to think about that. But I refused to dwell on what might have happened. It would have been easy to let all of the "what ifs" flood my mind, but I had too much to live for.

It had been three weeks since they'd admitted me, and I was finally set to be discharged today. I was more than ready to go home. Keeping me here was standard protocol, though, because of the high risk of complications after surgery.

I remembered very little about the moments before my aneurysm ruptured—aside from the urgent need to talk to Heather to tell her I loved her, and a headache. Other than that, I didn't remember anything until I woke up and found Heather and my dad hovering over me. It had taken a while to realize I wasn't dreaming.

It was better that I hadn't been aware of what was in store for me that day. If I'd known my head was going to be sliced open, and that fifty percent of people don't survive a ruptured aneurysm, I probably would have had a heart attack—especially since at the time, I hadn't had the chance to tell Heather how I feel.

The first week after my recovery was the toughest. People visited, but I still felt really out of it. Heather was my rock through it all. She'd left everything behind in Vermont to stay by my side. I couldn't even argue with her decision because I didn't know how I could get through this time stuck in the hospital without her.

There were no words for how grateful I felt to be alive. My memory was unaffected. My speech and motor skills were intact. Basically, I was a living miracle. I hadn't lost function, and in fact I'd gained something: a new perspective.

I could no longer waste my life in any way, couldn't get stuck because of indecision or fear. Every day, every moment needed to matter.

Heather had been sleeping at my house and spending each day at the hospital. My mother and brother had also been staying at my place. They'd just left to go back to Minnesota yesterday, so Heather had gotten to know them really well. I no longer had to wonder how my family was going to react to her. They'd fallen in love, just as I had.

My beautiful girlfriend beamed as she walked into my hospital room. "I just got word from the final professor I'd been waiting to hear from that I can complete my last few assignments from here. I won't have to go back to school to get full credit for this semester. I won't lose anything."

Sitting up on the bed, I leaned in to kiss her. "That's the best news. We can drive out there and get the rest of your stuff in a few weeks."

"Whenever you feel up to it. It's no rush. Ming says she's not going to get another roommate until the fall. So my stuff will just be sitting there until we get it."

"I owe that girl an entire *case* of baby powder."

Walking into my house after being gone for nearly a month felt freaking awesome. And it seemed more like home than ever, because Heather had put her touches on it. There were fresh flowers on the table and some candles scattered around.

It felt like I'd missed so much, like I'd come back from the dead.

I got emotional when I looked over at the cage—a new and much bigger cage—and saw it filled with four guinea pigs—Clyde and three babies. Bonnie had died giving birth. Evidently that was typical with older females. I'd barely cried over my near-death experience, but when I found out Bonnie hadn't survived her labor, I'd lost it. Heather had been the one to break the news. She'd gone to my house for the first time shortly after my surgery to feed them and realized the babies had been born. Soon thereafter, she'd discovered Bonnie wasn't breathing.

"Hey, little guys."

"We still have to name the babies." Heather was suddenly in tears.

She'd been pretty good about not losing it lately. I think she was just happy to have me home.

She rubbed my back. "Feels good to be home, huh?"

"It does, but mostly because you're with me. I couldn't imagine walking in here alone after all this."

We lay together on the couch for a while. I had a lot on my mind that I needed to let out. I hoped she didn't think I was crazy after what I was about to propose.

I took a deep breath. "Everything I thought I knew about how life is supposed to work has gone out the window," I told her. "I never realized how fast things can change. I pushed you away because I thought that's what was right for you. But if I'd died on that operating table, I would have thrown away the only time we'd ever have together—those months you were in Vermont."

She moved to straddle me. "Don't think about the what-ifs right now."

"I have to, only because it's related to what I'm about to say."

She kissed my nose. "Okay."

"I didn't go with my gut when I left you back in New Hampshire. If something doesn't feel right, it probably isn't. Leaving you *never* felt right. I thought the way for you to live your best life was to experience it apart from me, but maybe it should have been *with* me. Maybe things don't always have to be by the book. Maybe we need to go by what *feels* right."

"I never had any doubt that I belong where you are."

285

"I know you didn't." I caressed her cheek. "I've had a lot of time to think while stuck in that hospital. I asked myself, what would I want if I knew my time was limited? Because it very well could be. Aneurysm or not, none of us knows for sure if we're guaranteed a lot of time on this Earth. I decided what I want more than anything is to travel the world with you. I want to show you some of the places I've been, experience them again with you, and then discover new places together. Maybe it's not college in Vermont you need. Maybe traveling with me is how you can sow your oats."

"Wha—" Heather began.

But I forged ahead. "When I was lying there, recovering in that bed, I realized I haven't done nearly all of the things I want to do. And I've lived a pretty good life. In the end, all we have are memories. I don't have nearly enough memories *with you*. I want to make some. What do you say? Will you go on an adventure with me?"

"Really? Are you sure? I mean...how can we afford it?"

"I made some smart investments in my twenties. I have a lot saved up—probably at least fifty grand to play with before I'd even feel a dent. We can set a financial limit and stop when we've reached it. Then we'll come back, and you can enroll in school here, if that's what you want." I tried to read her expression. "If you think it's too reckless, we don't have to—"

"This sounds like a dream. I just can't believe it's an option."

"It's very much an option. And I hope you'll say yes."

After several seconds of silence, she said, "I would love to travel with you. The answer is yes!"

It felt like my heart was doing cartwheels. "Yeah?"

"Yeah." She wrapped her arms around my neck. "Let's make some memories."

Despite our excitement about our plans to travel the world, we had to be patient. Only after three months of follow-up visits did my doctor finally clear me for travel. Thanks to my father, who agreed to let us move the guinea pigs into his house for the months we would be away, we didn't have to worry about them.

The wait was worth it as I found myself looking out at the Grand Canyon from our rented van, parked at the spot we'd booked on the south rim side.

We were spending a week here before flying to Australia. We figured since we'd be flying toward the West Coast anyway, why not spend some time out here? Heather considered this another good exposure exercise for her fear of heights, too. Living out of the converted van allowed us to save funds for some of the more expensive parts of our journey to come.

This week our days had started early. Heather and I woke before the sun came up, because that offered the best lighting for the photos I'd been taking. We were documenting this entire trip and had dubbed it *Heather and Noah Do the World*. Heather had actually started a blog for it, and she was having a blast creating the posts. She'd brought along the Merry Wanderer Hummel I'd bought her for her twenty-first birthday, and she took photos of it in all different locations. I'd never imagined how prophetic that figurine would be.

After our morning photos, we'd cook some breakfast on a small grill before deciding what we wanted to explore that day.

Right now, we watched the reddish-orange sunset over the canyon as we lay in the van after a post-hike, late-afternoon nap. This was definitely the life.

I curled into her body. "Is it wrong that all I've wanted to do this week is look out at this view, eat, and fuck you? And then eat *you*?"

She rubbed her hand across my chest. "Do you see me complaining?"

I'd always been hot for Heather, but since my health crisis, I was completely insatiable. Having that brush with death made me want to feel everything all the time. And there was nothing I enjoyed *feeling* more than my gorgeous girlfriend. I couldn't get enough of her. I didn't remember when they said men reached their sexual peak, but mine was clearly thirty-five.

As if the day couldn't get any better, Heather slid down and pulled my cargo shorts along with her. My rock-hard dick bobbed as she took me into her mouth and did one of my favorite things. She began to rub her clit while sucking me off hands-free.

"Shit," I hissed. "You give the best head."

She really did, and she seemed to enjoy it as much as I did, which got me off even more.

Balls-deep down her throat, I threaded my fingers through her hair and enjoyed every second. My cock was lathered in precum as she went to town on me while continuing to massage herself. It didn't take long for me to lose it.

I held onto the back of her head and fucked her mouth harder as I came down her throat while she orgasmed.

Several minutes passed as we lay there, sated, a dry breeze blowing into the open van.

"How did I get so lucky that my girlfriend loves to go down on me?" I asked, pulling her up for a kiss.

She smiled.

"I tried," I told her. "I really tried. I just couldn't live without you—your fucking weird taste in music and all. I love you so much."

"I love you, too. And shit, you just reminded me of something."

"What?"

She sighed. "When you weren't fully conscious after the surgery, I promised that if you got better, I would let you listen to every song on my phone."

That cracked me up. "Are you serious? You vowed never to do that."

"I know. But now I feel like I have to. If I don't honor it, it's like an insult to the universe that granted me my wish. You don't have to take me up on it, though."

"Are you kidding?" I bolted up and held out my palm. "Hand that fucking thing over. Pretty sure it's the true reason for my incredible will to live."

I laughed. "You're gonna make fun of me."

"That's the point!"

She reached into her backpack and pulled it out. She braced herself as I took the phone from her hand.

She was already embarrassed, and I hadn't even pressed play yet. "I promise I'll be good."

"Give me one side of the headphones," she said. "I need to hear what you're listening to."

Handing her the left earbud, I put the right one in my ear and hit shuffle.

The first song was "Barbie Girl" by Aqua.

"Barbie Girl? Really?"

"Yes. And don't forget, you promised to be good."

After letting it play for about thirty seconds, I moved to the next song. As expected, many of the tunes in Heather's collection were one-hit wonders from well before her time in the late eighties and nineties.

A few songs in, I actually found one of my old favorites: "Sign Your Name" by Terence Trent D'Arby.

"Hey, I like this one. Good choice. Great song!"

The next two in a row seemed to match. "Livin' La Vida Loca" by Ricky Martin and Gerardo's "Rico Suave."

"You have a thing for Latin men?" I teased.

She rolled her eyes, probably just wanting this to be over, and remained quiet as I continued to plow through her library.

Next up was the theme song from *Friends,* "I'll Be There For You" by The Rembrandts. That one was tolerable enough to sit through.

I got all excited when I heard the beginning of "Smells Like Teen Spirit." *Fuck yeah!* But my hope was squelched when I realized it wasn't Nirvana at all. It was Weird Al Yankovic: "Smells Like Nirvana."

"Oh, hell no." I laughed.

Heather started laughing.

"I'm crying uncle." I handed her back the phone and tickled her. "You're lucky I love you."

CHAPTER
TWENTY-NINE

Heather - Five Months Later

H *eather and Noah Do the World* had been the time of my life. I doubted anything could ever top these past months. The experiences Noah had gifted me I would take to the grave.

In Australia, we'd visited the Great Barrier Reef and the Sydney Opera House. From there, we'd traveled to Hong Kong, where we walked along the Tsim Sha Tsui Promenade and visited their version of Disneyland.

After Asia, we traveled to Africa and saw the Sahara dunes of Morocco and the pyramids of Egypt.

Europe was our second-to-last stop but where we spent the majority of our time. We spent several weeks living in a rented apartment in Paris. We visited the Eiffel Tower and the Louvre and ate our way through the city.

After leaving France, we took a train to Italy and toured Rome and Venice before heading to London.

No amount of college education could have possibly made up for what I'd learned about the different cultures I experienced firsthand.

And now we'd come to the final stop on our trip, a place near and dear to Noah's heart: Havana, Cuba.

I'd fallen in love with his photos from here when I'd stalked his website. So when he'd asked me where I wanted to end our journey, this is what I chose.

Turns out Noah had been made an honorary family member the last time he'd visited this country. He called Ana "Abuelita," which affectionately means *grandma* in Spanish. She'd insisted we stay in her home instead of getting a hotel. Every night she cooked us authentic Cuban food like pork, rice and beans, and fried plantains. Then she'd whip up a delicious mango milkshake for dessert.

Noah agreed that we would stay with her, provided she let him do some work around her house. That physical labor turned out to be more extensive than we'd bargained for, so our Cuba trip stretched longer than we'd planned as we worked together out in the sun, much like we had during our summer on the lake. We knew this was the last leg of our trip, so we weren't really in any rush to get back.

We were having the time of our lives, yet anytime Noah got even a little tired or—God forbid—complained of a headache, it put me on edge. But I knew I couldn't live in fear of him having another rupture, so I tried to put those scary thoughts out of my mind.

When Noah and I weren't working together on Abuelita's house, we took in Havana's historic sites. We visited the Gran Teatro with its amazing architecture and toured Old Havana, which was a mix of baroque and neoclassical monuments and narrow streets lined with homes. Havana was the perfect place for people watching and taking lots of photos of urban life. My travel blog had accumulated a ton of followers, and they seemed to love the images we captured here.

On the afternoon of our second-to-last day in Cuba, Noah took me to the area where he'd done the feature on the orphanage six years ago. We were just turning toward Abuelita's car to drive back when he froze, his eyes fixed on a kid in a wheelchair across the street.

"Come on." He took my hand and led us toward the boy, who was with a woman.

He stopped a few feet away and said, "It's him."

I knew instantly what he meant. "The boy from the orphanage..."

"Daniel. I would recognize his face anywhere. My God, Heather, it's him. He looks so grown up now."

We approached them, and Noah began speaking in Spanish. I hadn't realized until we got to Cuba that he was pretty fluent. He knelt down to be eye-level with Daniel.

The boy reached out and touched Noah's face. At least on some level, he seemed to remember him. Though he didn't speak, Daniel typed something on a device that looked like an iPad. He flipped the screen around and showed us what he'd written.

Naranja.

A huge smile engulfed Noah's face. "That's right! *Naranja.* Orange. You remember! I used to bring you little oranges, *clementinas.*"

My heart turned to mush as Noah embraced him.

Noah continued talking to the woman and then entered some of her information into his phone.

"*Bueno. Adios. Hasta mañana,*" he said.

"Tell me what you were saying," I said as they departed.

"She said they had to leave to get him to a doctor's appointment. Her name is Rosita Jimenez. She adopted

Daniel about three years ago, so that would be a couple of years after I visited. All this time, they've lived right down the street from where the orphanage used to be. He was placed in foster care and ended up with her. He's been doing great and making a lot of progress. Since he can't speak very well, he uses that device to communicate. Even though he was in a wheelchair today, he's able to walk some now. I got her information so we can go visit them before we leave tomorrow. I want to bring him a whole bunch of clementines."

"Oh my God, yes. That's a great idea. It's so wonderful he remembered that."

Noah looped my fingers in with his as we continued walking. "Back when I told you the story of my Cuba trip, I didn't mention that it came very soon after the letter from Opal, during the height of my depression. Meeting Daniel really helped me to stop feeling sorry for myself—seeing how strong he was and how he persevered despite the odds against him. Everything feels more connected than it ever has right now—the way you and I met, being here with you, and running into him on the last full day of our trip. It feels like everything has come full circle."

He stopped walking and faced me. "When we were in Paris, you were napping at the apartment and I took a walk. I passed a jewelry store. I had no intention of buying anything that day, but then I happened to see a ring in the window. I couldn't believe how perfect it was for you. I knew I had to at least inquire about it. To be honest, I didn't really care how much it cost—I knew I wasn't walking out of there without it."

My heart raced as he continued.

"I told myself I wasn't going to give it to you for a very long time, that I was going to wait until you were done with school. But every single day since I bought it, I've had to stop myself from getting down on one knee. This morning I asked the universe to give me a sign that my gut was right—that I should keep the ring in my pocket and do it before this trip was over. I'm pretty sure running into Daniel was the sign I was waiting for."

"Oh my God."

"Traveling the world with you showed me even more clearly what I already knew, that you and I make the best team, that you're my partner. There's no one else I would rather continue the journey of life with. It doesn't matter where we are as long as I have you by my side. I believe everything that has happened to me thus far—the good and the bad— happened to get me to this moment. *Heather and Noah Do the World* might be ending when we get back to Pennsylvania, but I'm wondering if you'd start another kind of adventure with me—one that's forever. I know this isn't my first rodeo. I may not be perfect, and I may fuck up at times, but I have to put aside those fears and take the risk. I love you too much not to, and I just can't wait any longer to ask."

My big man got down on one knee and looked up at me with his beautiful brown eyes, the color of Cuban coffee. He reached into his pocket and pulled out a velvet pouch. When he opened it, I knew instantly why he'd had to buy this ring.

"Heather Louise Chadwick, will you do me the honor of being my wife? Will you marry me?"

The sparkling round diamond was adorned on each side by a beautiful opal—my sister, the fallen angel who'd brought us together. I normally shunned thoughts of her, but in this moment, I let myself feel her presence. It warmed me as the sunlight illuminated the stones. My sister was here with me now, shining through their brightness. I knew she was looking down and blessing this.

With my hand on my chest, I did my best to form words. "From the moment you walked into my life, nothing else seemed to matter. That feeling has only grown. I've wanted to marry you for a very long time, longer than I should probably admit. Heck, I would have said yes if you'd asked me in New Hampshire. I am crazy about you. So, yes—the answer is yes! I will take this adventure with you today, tomorrow, and forever."

EPILOGUE

Noah - Three-and-a-Half Years Later

Today we were ringing in Heather's twenty-fifth birthday. I won't mention the fact that I was now pushing thirty-nine and flirting with forty. It seemed like just yesterday we'd celebrated her twenty-first. We still had the *Poltergeist* cake top in our freezer, right next to the ice trays. It had traveled from New Hampshire to Pennsylvania in a cooler. Pretty sure that thing would outlast all of us.

Heather was a little over halfway finished with her nursing degree. She'd enrolled at West Chester University near our house shortly after we returned from our travels. When she wasn't studying, she was either bartending at a restaurant down the road or helping me with admin stuff at my studio.

The biggest recent change was that Heather's mother had come to live with us in Pennsylvania. After a few years of watching over Alice, Katy had had enough of living with her sister. She'd said she really missed Boston and wanted to move back to the city. Just before Katy left, Heather and her mother sold the New Hampshire house. While

Alice had been doing better mentally than in years past, Heather still worried about her living alone. I knew she didn't want to ask me if Alice could move in with us. So I saved her the trouble and suggested it first, making it seem like it was my idea.

That meant Fathead now lived with us, too. Between the dog, the almost-mother-in-law, and the guinea pigs, it was a full house. But I knew Heather felt more complete with her mom here. She no longer had to worry about her from afar. So that made Alice's occasional meddling worth it. The long-term plan was to buy a bigger house with an in-law apartment.

I should probably get on that soon.

Still engaged, Heather and I hadn't yet tied the knot. We wanted to plan a wedding after she finished her undergraduate degree. Right now she worked hard to balance school and work.

I wanted to make her twenty-fifth a special birthday, so I'd surprised her with a trip up to Burlington, Vermont, to visit her best friend, Ming. Heather hadn't had many chances to spend quality time with her over the past few years. Ming lived with a boyfriend now, and the four of us had a blast just chilling at their house and barbecuing. It made me happy to watch Heather and Ming reminisce about the short time they'd lived together. Ming was a forever friend. Don't think I didn't arrive at her place without a case of baby powder, either. Luckily, she has a great sense of humor.

After leaving Ming's, we hit the road pretty early on Sunday morning. Heather assumed we were heading back to Pennsylvania, but we had a stop to make on the way home.

"We're going to the lake?" she asked when we turned toward New Hampshire.

I winked. "Maybe."

When we pulled onto Heather's old property, she got a bit emotional. It looked exactly the same as I remembered it.

I parked over by the boathouse, and we got out.

She looked around. "I didn't realize how much I missed this place, but being here again brings everything back. It feels like just yesterday."

"Let's take a walk down by the lake."

We held hands as we enjoyed the tranquility of the water.

When we returned to the truck, I asked, "Wanna take a peek inside the boathouse for old time's sake?"

"Can we do that? Wouldn't that be trespassing?"

"Nah. It'll be fine."

I reached into my pocket for the key, then opened the door.

"What's going on? Why do you have a key?" Heather froze as she entered the room. Nearly everything was the same as it had been when I'd stayed here.

"Welcome home," I said, opening my arms wide.

Her eyes nearly bugged out of her head. "Home?"

"Well, not our permanent home, but our summer home—or our place to escape to whenever we damn well please."

"What?"

"I bought the boathouse from the owners."

Seeing her expression go from shock to pure joy made all of this worth it.

"Oh my God. This…is ours? The boathouse is ours?"

"All ours, baby."

She walked slowly around the space. "How? When?"

I took her hand. "This lake means everything to me. It's where I met you. It's where some of our most special memories were made. It represents your childhood and your sister, and it always broke my heart a little that you had to sell the houses. Then you moved to Pennsylvania to be with me, and that was a sacrifice. I wanted to give you a little piece of your history back."

She turned toward the corner of the room. "You even brought the old loveseat. When did you do all this?"

"Well, remember a couple of weeks ago when I had that out-of-state shoot? I was here setting everything up. I'd been working on the deal with the owners for almost a year. They had to split the land a bit as part of the sale, so it wasn't that simple. Back when I first contacted them, I figured it was a long shot, but it turned out they didn't like having to deal with renting it. They just wanted to be rid of it."

"I can't believe it. This is the most special thing anyone has ever done for me. I thought my life felt complete before, but man, now? Even better. Thank you."

I took her into my arms and kissed her head. "I know we'd planned to wait a while longer, but I was thinking maybe we could get married here next summer. What do you say?"

I wasn't expecting her to start crying. "What's wrong?"

"A wedding here would be perfect, but—"

"But what?"

"Not sure we can get married next summer. It might be…busy."

"Why?"

"I was waiting till we got home to tell you. But I don't think there's a better time than right now."

"What's going on?"

"I messed up recently."

My heart sped up. "Okay..."

"Remember that stomach bug I had? When I thought I was dying?"

"Yeah, of course. How could I forget?"

"Well, I didn't know that when you...*eliminate* like that, it can rid your system of things you need—like birth control."

It took me a few seconds to figure out what she meant. And once I did, I couldn't speak.

"I took a test this morning in Ming's bathroom. It was positive. I don't even know how it happened, I—"

All that would come out of me was, "What?"

"I'm pregnant. Only a few weeks along, but I was late, so I had a feeling. I looked up all the reasons birth control can fail, and sure enough, there it was: excessive vomiting. I should've known about that. I should've used a back-up—"

"You're pregnant?" My eyelids fluttered as I processed it.

She bit her lip and nodded. "Yes."

"Wow. I wasn't...this is...the last thing I ever—"

"I know. Me, too," she said. "This isn't the ideal time. I—"

I cut her off with the longest kiss to her lips. I held her so tightly. I'd held Heather like this many times, but it felt different, knowing she was carrying my child. It felt surreal.

Holy shit.

I'm gonna be a dad?

I'm gonna be a dad.

I'm gonna be a dad!

"So that sofa is going to have to go to make room for a crib," she said.

"I'll gladly get rid of it—burn that shit if I have to." I lifted her up and kissed her again.

I still woke up many days wondering if it might be my last on Earth. The chance of another aneurysm would always loom over me. I'd tried not to pressure Heather, but there's nothing I've wanted more than to experience having a child with this woman. As each year passed, the desire felt more urgent. But I thought it was too soon for her.

She wouldn't even be done with school when our baby arrived. But for me? The day I looked our baby in the eyes couldn't come soon enough.

"Are you happy?" I asked her.

"I'm growing a part of you inside of me. How could I not be? I'm shocked—but yes, so happy. Truly."

"Good, because this could be the happiest day of my life, and I would hate it if you didn't feel happy, too."

"The happiest day of *my* life was also the scariest—the day you woke up after your surgery and said my name, then told me you loved me. I'm not sure anything can top that."

"I love you even more today." I rubbed her stomach. "How about the three of us take a swim in the lake, for old time's sake? I was thinking we could spend tonight here before we go back home. Maybe I'll even go to the market and buy a big old loaf of garlic bread. I know you have class on Tuesday. We'll get you back in time."

After we changed into our swimsuits, we walked back down to the lake.

As we stood knee deep in the water, I said, "Originally my plan was to have a cigar out on the porch tonight. You know I haven't smoked one in years. But there's no way I'm smoking anywhere near my baby."

I knelt down, ignoring the rocks scraping my knees, until my face was eye-level with her stomach. "Hello in there. It's your daddy. I can't wait to meet you." I looked up at Heather, who seemed amused. "This is so wild," I whispered, then continued talking into her stomach. "I want you to know I love you already. And even though you're the size of a little seed, you're the best thing to ever happen to your mother and me. I can't wait to bring you here and show you where your mommy grew up and show you where Daddy robbed the cradle and started the process of you coming to be. Best thing I ever did, if you ask me."

Heather's stomach moved against my mouth as she laughed. She spoke down to it. "You have the best daddy in the whole world, little one."

"And you have the best mom, even though you're gonna come out with a warped sense of what good music is. We'll fix that soon enough."

"Hey! He might like my music."

"Or she might come out blocking her ears." I spoke against her belly again. "Some day I'll tell you the story of how I almost saved your mother's life on this lake. You're gonna laugh."

"Your daddy never did succeed in his botched attempts to save my life."

"It wasn't meant to work that way. I was never meant to save *your* life." I stood up and cradled her face. "In the end, you saved mine."

OTHER BOOKS BY PENELOPE WARD

Love Online
Gentleman Nine
Drunk Dial
Mack Daddy
RoomHate
Stepbrother Dearest
Neighbor Dearest
Jaded and Tyed (A novelette)
Sins of Sevin
Jake Undone (Jake #1)
Jake Understood (Jake #2)
My Skylar
Gemini

BOOKS BY PENELOPE WARD & VI KEELAND

Hate Notes
Rebel Heir
Rebel Heart
British Bedmate
Mister Moneybags
Playboy Pilot
Stuck-Up Suit
Cocky Bastard

ACKNOWLEDGEMENTS

I always say that the acknowledgements are the hardest part of the book to write and that still stands! It's hard to put into words how thankful I am for every single reader who continues to support and promote my books. Your enthusiasm and hunger for my stories is what motivates me every day. And to all of the book bloggers who support me, I simply wouldn't be here without you.

To Vi – I say this every time, and I am saying it again because it holds even truer as time goes on. You're the best friend and partner in crime that I could ask for. I couldn't do any of this without you. Our co-written books are a gift, but the biggest blessing has always been our friendship, which came before the stories and will continue after them. On to the next!

To Julie – Thank you for your friendship and for always inspiring me with your amazing writing, attitude, and strength. This year is going to kick ass!

To Luna –Thank you for your love and support, day in and day out and for always being just a message away. Here's to many more Florida visits with wine and mofongo!

To Erika – It will always be an E thing. I am so thankful for your love and friendship and support and to our special hang time in July. Thank you for always brightening my days with your positive outlook.

To my Facebook fan group, Penelope's Peeps – I love you all. Your excitement motivates me every day. And to

Queen Peep Amy – Thank you for starting the group way back when.

To Mia – Thank you, my friend, for always making me laugh. I know you're going to bring us some phenomenal words this year.

To my assistant Mindy Guerreiros – Thank you for being so awesome and handling so much of Vi's and my day-to day stuff. We appreciate you so much!

To my editor Jessica Royer Ocken – It's always a pleasure working with you. I look forward to many more experiences to come.

To Elaine of Allusion Book Formatting and Publishing – Thank you for being the best proofreader, formatter, and friend a girl could ask for.

To Letitia of RBA Designs – The best cover designer ever! Thank you for always working with me until the cover is exactly how I want it.

To my agent extraordinaire, Kimberly Brower –Thank you for all of your hard work in getting my books into the international market and for believing in me long before you were my agent, back when you were a blogger and I was a first-time author.

To my husband – Thank you for always taking on so much more than you should have to so that I am able to write. I love you so much.

To the best parents in the world – I'm so lucky to have you! Thank you for everything you have ever done for me and for always being there.

To my besties: Allison, Angela, Tarah and Sonia – Thank you for putting up with that friend who suddenly became a nutty writer.

Last but not least, to my daughter and son – Mommy loves you. You are my motivation and inspiration!

ABOUT THE AUTHOR

Penelope Ward is a *New York Times, USA Today* and *#1 Wall Street Journal* bestselling author.

She grew up in Boston with five older brothers and spent most of her twenties as a television news anchor. Penelope resides in Rhode Island with her husband, son and beautiful daughter with autism.

With over 1.5 million books sold, she is a twenty-time *New York Times* bestseller and the author of over twenty novels.

Penelope's books have been translated into over a dozen languages and can be found in bookstores around the world.

Subscribe to Penelope's newsletter here:
http://bit.ly/1X725rj

Made in the USA
Middletown, DE
28 February 2019